EMIGRANT DREAMS

MARY ROSE CALLAGHAN

POOLBEG

This book is for Kathleen Danaher

Published in 1996
by Poolbeg Press Ltd
123 Baldoyle Industrial Estate
Dublin 13, Ireland

© Mary Rose Callaghan 1996

The moral right of the author has been asserted.

The Publishers gratefully acknowledge the support of The Arts Council.

A catalogue record for this book is available from the British Library.

ISBN 1 85371 620 0

Cover photograph by Barry Lewis/Network
Cover design by Poolbeg Group Services Ltd
Set by Poolbeg Group Services Ltd in Garamond 10/13
Printed by The Guernsey Press Ltd,
Vale, Guernsey, Channel Islands.

Acknowledgements

I would like to thank my friends for advice and support
and all at Poolbeg Press.

"In dreams begin responsibilities."
WB Yeats.

CHAPTER ONE

* * *

I FIRST SAW THE OLD MAN ON THE PLANE. HE WAS SITTING ACROSS the aisle as we landed at Kennedy. It was August a few years back, and election year – Bush was on the way out, Clinton on the way in, and I was *en route* to Sweetmount College in Pennsylvania.

I hated flying. We'd been circling for a good half hour, but now the sea hurtled upward and skyscrapers leaned crookedly. My ears popped as we descended. On my Walkman headphones, John McCormack sang, *"Somewhere a voice is calling . . . "*

It was illegal to play your own tapes, but that sweet voice was haunting.

I concentrated on the old man. I had, of course, only a side view, but the details are exact, like those of a dream. He wore a rumpled white suit from another era with a red rose in his buttonhole. His headphones were on the wrong way – the band hanging under his chin. It seems strange now, but I didn't yet know who he was, or how he would hound me. I just had a *deja-vu* feeling.

"Somewhere a voice is calling . . . calling to me . . ."

Then the plane started whining.

God, were we crashing?

Everyone else was calm, but I clutched the armrests. I

unplugged John McCormack and whispered my relaxation exercises: "My right arm is heavy . . . my heart is calm and regular."

I repeated them three times, thinking we'd never make it.

But the plane thudded down safely.

As it taxied to a stop, some passengers clapped. Others shifted restlessly, gathering their belongings. It was 16.30 Mid Atlantic time, and a long cramped way from Dublin.

"Welcome to Kennedy International Airport. Please remain seated until the aircraft has come to a complete stop."

"I guess we're home." The young man beside me struggled into a blue denim jacket. He had an Irish complexion, black curly hair and a lithe body. He grinned stupidly. "You were scared, huh? Gee . . . never occurs to me."

I just looked at him. The world is divided, I'm convinced, between those who worry and those who don't. I think those who don't are insane.

This boy was one of our young exiles. He was from Cork and now worked as a barman in Philadelphia. Obviously he'd done well, as he flashed an expensive camcorder. He couldn't make enough money in Ireland for that. There were no jobs.

Now he shook his head ruefully. "I thought you were prayin'."

He meant my exercises, of course, which I continued silently. It was a German technique I'd just learnt. I'd met an old friend at the bus stop who was holding exercise classes at home. She looked sort of down-at-heel, so I signed up on the spot. Expecting something in the aerobic line, I'd worn a tracksuit and runners. But the whole class had been spent sitting in a chair, *thinking heavy*. You spoke in a certain sequence to different parts of your body: "My arms and legs are heavy and warm . . . my heart is calm and regular . . . my solar plexus is warm." You could will yourself to be warm. Not that I needed to now. I was sticky and needed a shower.

"Say, you should fly more."

I frowned. "What?"

"Fly more – statistically, it's the safest transport."

The safest way to die. "I know."

"You know what it means?"

"What?"

"Fear of flying?"

"No."

He giggled.

Well, I had read Erica Jong. Why didn't he shut up? Oh, he'd entertained me all the way over with chat about Irish literature. He was very well read for his age, for any age really. But now I was bored. Besides, I wanted to calm myself down.

"Ladies and gentlemen, there seems to be a back-up here at Kennedy. Please remain seated with your seat belts fastened until we are able to unboard."

There was a general groan.

"Shit!" came from the young man. His Cork-American accent sounded weird.

The old man across the aisle turned his head. He'd put on a straw hat – from the thirties, I decided. And there was a walking stick resting between the wide-trousered legs of his yellowing white linen suit. There was something not-quite-right about him I thought, even then. What? The hat? The red rose? Did I know him? And where had he come from? I was sure the seat had been empty all the way over.

Outside there were airport buildings and a hot sky. The

plane was stuffy too. I wiped my face with tissues from the loo. It wasn't stealing – you paid enough for the flight. I always flew Aer Lingus, because their hostesses were nice and bishops blessed the planes. They charged for drinks, of course, but I brought my own – six baby bottles filled with vodka. Then I simply asked for orange juice. This always brought hooting laughs from my husband, Fergal. "You're a bestselling author and you bring your own drink!" But I only drank two of them. Even I couldn't drink six vodkas.

It was my fifteenth flight with Aer Lingus. The first was in '69 to meet Ogie, my cousin and girlhood pen-pal. We were to make our fortunes as waitresses in Las Vegas. It was to be an adventure. I'd been reared on America, the land of dreams and Oonagh's youth – Oonagh was my mother. Ogie was called after her, Oonagh Og, young Oonagh, hence the nickname Ogie.

She was to be at Arrivals. What would she be like now? Las Vegas was over twenty years ago. Where had life gone?

The young man beside me stretched. "Great to be home."

I nodded. He had certainly acclimatised. But where was home for me? I'd been married to Fergal for seventeen years, but the last thing he had said was, "If you go to America, I won't be here when you get back." He hated me leaving for four months, and this time had kicked up stink. I had a half-yearly teaching job at Sweetmount. We didn't need the money, but I liked teaching. It got me away from writing. And cooking. Besides, I had to land in the US every year to keep my Green Card. I always expected to be dropped because of cutbacks, but they always renewed my contract. There was a demand for Irish women abroad. At home they stoned you. Although I don't know why they bothered with me. I'm a down-market hack, who writes historical sagas for money.

"First thing, I'm having a decent hamburger," my companion tried again. "At McDonalds."

Were there no decent hamburgers in Cork? I wanted a martini. Irish bars always palmed you off with Vermouth. America spoilt you. They had so many pleasant habits: the cocktail hour, Sunday brunch, cheap wine. Fergal accused me of thinking that the streets there were paved with gold. I wanted to emigrate completely, but he hated the place. Maybe he was right, but nothing's perfect. There are many Americas, after all. But the thought of Fergal was making me miserable. I felt such a failure. Lately, things had gone so wrong between us. That girl was always ringing up.

Blast him, anyway. The more I thought, the more angry I got.

And his latest hare-brained scheme was to start a free university in Dublin. The lectures were to be transmitted by computer eventually, on some new-fangled super communications highway. But for the moment he'd rented hours on a radio station and was paying lecturers – with *my* money.

Men just messed you about. Last week I had read the bank statement in shock. "There's two thousand pounds missing. I'd better ring them."

Fergal had looked up casually. He's a big Irishman who reads philosophy for pleasure. "Oh, forgot to mention it. I took it out last month."

I was puzzled, but said nothing for a minute. "You had a bill?"

He went back to his book.

"What did you need it for?" I persisted.

He didn't look up. "Oh, expenses. The radio station – lecturers' fees."

"But isn't there some way of charging the students?"

He got up. "No. That's the whole idea. It's free."

Talk about Don Quixote. Oh, it was a joint account, but I still had the right to be consulted. I had earned the damn money by sitting for hours, risking blindness, in front of the word processor. I have a practical bent, but God knows what he wasted.

"Does it take long to write a novel?" came from my flight companion.

"Eh – it depends." I stretched under the seat for my duty free Bailey's Irish Cream.

Perhaps I should've brought whiskey for Ogie's husband, Hans? I was staying the night with them, but didn't know if he drank. Ogie did a bit, beer and wine – at least she did twenty years ago. No, Bailey's was safer. Americans raved over it. That and smoked salmon. I had other bread and butter offerings, a fish in the overhead bin and chocolates for the children. Ogie'd always desperately wanted children, and I was dying to meet them. Having none is another of my failures.

"I sure enjoyed talkin' to you." The boy was trying again.

"Same here."

I smiled firmly – a smile perfected by years of teaching, a front to stop people arguing about their grades. I don't remember how long we sat there, only that it was hot and he kept nattering on about writing. It's a mistake to tell anyone what you do. But what if they ask? The truth is, I hated talking about my books. Maybe I'm ashamed of being such a hack. So to look busy, I studied the newspaper Xeroxes about our grandfather, Marcus Quilligan O'Neill, which Ogie had sent. She was always badgering me to write his biography. He'd emigrated in the 1860s, after the Famine. He was a poor boy who'd made good, got himself through law school, then become a "Deserving Democrat," and was appointed to a diplomatic post in the Caribbean by Woodrow Wilson. But he didn't interest me. I wasn't into ancestors, and my mother hadn't liked him.

Still, I flicked through the Xeroxes. The top copy was dated 23 July, 1913:

MARCUS QUILLIGAN O'NEILL TO SANTO DOMINGO.
WASHINGTON, July 22.
– It was said in Administration circles tonight that Marcus Quilligan O'Neill of New York had been selected for appointment as Minister to Santo Domingo. Mr. Quilligan O'Neill is a lawyer with offices in Park Row and was counsel for Bald Jack Rose in the Becker-Rosenthal case. In the Presidential Campaign last year he was a Democratic club organizer . . .

Funny, I always thought he'd gone to Haiti. The campaign was Woodrow Wilson's. But who was Bald Jack Rose? And what was the Becker-Rosenthal case? My mother always said our grandfather was a good speaker. But how had he become a Minister? It had taken a month to vet him. But he depressed me – the whole topic did. So I perused other articles, finding one about telephone charges in 1913 – a public phone call cost ten cents then. Expensive enough, really, compared to today. And Macys was advertising summer suits at $18, half their regular price. The next story had Marcus arriving at Havana and taking a steamer to Santo Domingo. And underneath there was a piece about William Jennings Bryan's appearance on the vaudeville stage with yodellers, jugglers, and magicians. Imagine Clinton's Secretary of State doing that? What was his name? Christopher Warren? It sounded like Christopher Robin.

But on that hot day in Kennedy, I knew nothing about Bryan, the Great Commoner. How he had united the Democratic party, served grape juice in the White House, and befriended our maverick grandfather. On our trip twenty years ago Ogie had talked non-stop about Marcus. Like most Irish-Americans, she lived in the past. I stuffed the Xeroxes in my bag, planning to return them to her along with other genealogical stuff.

Would Ogie be older looking? I could never forget that bus journey from New York with the Chinese man beside me reading a pornographic magazine – I don't know why he scared me, maybe too many Fu Manchu movies?

Then running for the connection in Chicago.

Then days and days of travel. Nebraska's endless plains of wheat and thinking all the towns were named Exxon. How could anyone be so green?

The boy leaned over. "Let's split a taxi to Penn Station."

"Sorry, my cousin's meeting me."

"Oh . . . Guess I won't see you again, then?"

"Guess not."

Was he serious? I wasn't a boynapper. I was forty-seven years old and going white, for God's sake. White, not even grey. He was probably underage. He'd drunk Harp all the way over.

"Well, enjoy school," the boy pestered.

I nodded brusquely. He'd even picked up the quaint American habit of calling university "school," but we were unboarding at last.

"Please check the overhead racks before leaving the plane . . . Thank you for flying with us."

I gathered my stuff and moved slowly up the aisle.

At the exit my hostess friend smiled. "I'll look out for your next book, Anne."

She'd be looking in vain, as I hadn't written anything in months. But the woman had given me a free drink and meant well, so I thanked her, hoping my facial tic wasn't noticeable. Lately my upper lip trembles at the oddest times. But I couldn't stop it.

I followed the other passengers through long white corridors and past signs saying, WELCOME TO NEW YORK.

"Can I carry your bag?"

The boy again, breathless.

"No, I'm OK!" My keep-fit classes hadn't been wasted.

"Aer Lingus, this way!" An officious Hispanic woman waved us into a line for Baggage Reclaim and Customs. Luckily, our passports had been vetted at Shannon. The straw-hatted old man was now ambling ahead. He turned, fixing me with curious pale eyes behind thick-lensed wire glasses. Why was he so familiar? He had a large moustache, yellow at the edges to match his faded suit. And he mopped his forehead with a big red handkerchief.

"I'll call Sweetmount!" the boy insisted.

Christ, why didn't he vamoose? "Look, piss off! Will you?"

He grinned cheekily. "Sorry, Ma'am – "

"Another word and I'll report you for harassment!"

He fled.

Was I drunk? Normally I'd have laughed, or been flattered instead of over-reacting. I mean, it *was* funny. He must be a rather naive boy. Perhaps he was lonely? Or wanted a mother figure? But at least my explosion had shut him up. And no one seemed to have heard.

Kennedy is Hell's kitchen. It must be the most crowded airport on earth. People with walkie-talkies vetted us now. Officials make me queasy. At Shannon the US immigration officer had checked a directory for the kid before me and sent him to a supervisor. What were they looking for?

Members of the IRA? "Illegals" – young unemployed Irish who flocked over on Visitors' Visas and then stayed to work? Over three hundred thousand had emigrated in ten years. They were part of the diaspora that our President, Mary Robinson, was always talking about.

Yet was it so bad? America had opened up my life. But I had a choice, unlike the young who worked illegally on building sites and in Irish pubs. Like my flight companion. But, despite the camcorders, it must be difficult. Some of them were without papers. The US officials were never friendly, but now they dragged people off planes as if they were secret police. With a Green Card, I'd nothing to fear, yet was always nervous – an imaginary Jew.

Was fear passed in the genes? Was it some racial memory? Had our ancestors felt this, landing on Ellis Island with a one-way ticket, tired and probably sick? The hungry Irish, having to face doctors, afraid of being sent back to starvation and certain death. But the sweat shops of New York and Boston were as bad a fate. Worse.

I was the fourth generation to ferry back and forth between two continents: my great-grandparents had carried my grandfather over, my mother had been born in Ireland and brought back to America by him. They lived in New York, but when the depression hit, drove to Florida. At eighteen she came to Ireland, and got stranded there by the war.

What if you could meet your ancestors? Maybe I was too hard on mine. At least I'd got stuff for Ogie. I'd bought her a copy of McLysaght's *Irish Family Names* and seen a genealogist in the National Library.

This was to be a reunion. Our last meeting was in the Gotham Book Mart when she visited New York from the West coast. We lunched in the Russian Tearoom. I ordered yogurt, the most non-fattening item on the menu, and got a basinful. Ogie'd had a plateful of duck livers. I had watched in horror as she ate the innards. She was putting on weight then and had got religion badly. Claimed that she could feel God through the vacuum cleaner. She had just remarried, was into motherhood, and complained of being poor. But Hans was a California lawyer. Was she poor now?

The luggage carousel revolved emptily. Where were our cases? Tiredness was getting to me. The straw-hatted old man was in the distance again. He tapped the floor restlessly with his walking stick, staring not at the carousel but at me. I ducked behind a pillar. Bags of all shapes were now being disgorged. At last mine emerged through the flaps. When it came alongside, I grabbed it and made for the customs line.

"When did you leave the United States?" The official perused my passport and return ticket.

"Last December. I come every year. I'm visiting Professor at Sweetmount College."

"Sweetmount College?" He looked amused. "You have any sausages, bacon or blood pudding?"

Was he joking? I shook my head, afraid to mention the fish.

He glanced at my duty free bag. "Whatja have in the line of alcohol?"

"Just a bottle of Baileys."

Wearily he stamped my white form. "Welcome to the United States, Ms O'Brien."

The Arrivals lobby was crowded with people meeting planes. I was elated to be through. Did anyone welcome the Irish coming off the coffin ships? Once, passing Ellis Island on the Staten Island Ferry, I got goose pimples. How many millions had passed through it? They must have had a feeling of freedom too – even if short-lived.

Give me your tired, your poor,

Your huddled masses, yearning to breathe free . . .

How did it go? Oonagh used to recite it. Also "Abu Ben Adam" and "Barbara Fritchie." Relics from her southern childhood.

Shoot if you must this old grey head. . . .
But spare your country's flag, she said.

I looked for Ogie. All nationalities milled about. Some held up signs with names written in foreign languages. There were tearful reunions – shrieks, hugs. A boy kissed his girlfriend passionately, oblivious of all else. I remembered her from the plane. She was dumpy, but loved. Fergal never did that, not any more. "If you go to America, I won't be here when you get back." Did he mean it?

I dragged my gaze from the lovers, searching the faces near me. The old man was now ahead. His old stained suit hung loosely on his big frame, as if he'd recently lost weight. He met my stare through his thick glasses, one eye slightly askew. Then took something from his pocket and stared at it in the palm of his hand. As if he was counting pennies. How had he got past me? He was last seen waiting for a bag. Would I never lose him? He was like a dog who followed you home. Funny, he had no luggage. And his trousers looked peculiar, too baggy. Also the red rose. What was he staring at?

He's waiting for someone, I told myself. Everyone's waiting for someone. Could Ogie be in the loo? Last time we met, she was wearing a kilt and navy blazer. But there was no one remotely like her here. Perhaps something had come up? Traffic. The children. Or she couldn't get off work. She worked in a children's bookshop somewhere in New York. Had she left a message?

An Aer Lingus official shook his head. "Sorry, Miss."

I stepped back into the crowd, wondering if I should

take a cab. It was crazy. I loved America. I wanted to come. Yet I dreaded leaving the airport on my own. Cities frightened me. And what if no one was home at Ogie's? Should I go straight down to Oldcastle?

"Excuse me, Miss." A girl in Islamic dress waylaid me. Her brown eyes were fanatical, the rest of her face covered by a veil. She waved a clipboard in my face. "Can you spare a minute?"

"I've no change."

"Just a signature. In America they cut the babies from their bodies. Against Allah's will . . . "

As I moved away, she went on raving. You had the same sort of fundamentalists in Ireland. Years in America had changed me. Also my friends, Molly and Theodora. They were Quakers who never judged anyone, and one of my reasons for coming.

The lobby smelt of sweat. Damn, I should never have agreed to be met. Things always went wrong between Ogie and me. Fergal could never understand the relationship. Yet something bound us. Girlhood letters? Or common ancestors?

I was an eejit that summer long ago, retarded. But Ogie was hyper, and Dallas was the end. People remembered it for Daley Plaza and President Kennedy, but for me it meant something else – a terrible row with Ogie. But twenty years changed you. For one thing Ogie had two children now by Hans. It seemed OK. Hans was German-Jewish. Happiness should mellow Ogie.

The cocktail bar was gone – the Gulf War, someone explained. Pity, Fergal and I had had good times there. But that was all over now. I needed more control over my life. He never consulted me about anything. Another thing he had done was cut down a tree. It was a Sumach, the nicest tree in the garden, but he said it was dead and killing all the shrubs.

I went for a cab.

Outside the wall of heat took my breath away. As I dragged my case to the queue, a battered old boat of a car braked beside me. A sign in the windscreen said, LIVERY.

"Cab, Miss?" the old black driver asked. He was right out of *Driving Miss Daisy*. His red baseball cap was pulled over frizzy white hair.

"Can you take me to 428 Riverside Drive?"

"Sure can, Miss."

I got in, hauling my case after me. His cab wasn't yellow, but there was a line for regular cabs.

A redfaced man in a smart business suit banged the window. "Hey, this is fucking America!"

Was he drunk? "I – ."

His nose dilated like an angry dragon, as he pulled at the door. "You didn't stand in fucking line!"

"Dis is a private engagement!" My driver skidded forward, leaving the protester in the dusty rear. He turned his head, eyes rolled in exasperation. "Some folks!"

I breathed deeply. You usually didn't see such old taxi drivers. Was he competent? As the car nudged slowly into the airport traffic, I closed my eyes. I hadn't slept properly in a week. On the flight over it was impossible to avoid being awakened for meals. And that idiotic boy hadn't stopped nattering. But I had to forget about tiredness now. I was in New York City and had to feel the buzz. Maybe I'd stay for an opera. Singing always filled me with hope. Ogie might like to go. She was an expert on Broadway musical minutiae. In New York ten years ago she'd waved wildly at a woman who turned out to be Jane Powell, from *Seven Brides for Seven Brothers*. And on the trip twenty years ago she'd sung Stephen Foster in a sweet clear voice on long drives through the hot night. *"Skeetas are a hummin' in the honeysuckle vine . . ."* Ogie was a southern girl.

"Hey, asshole!" someone shouted at my driver. We'd back-ended a car in front. Immediately an oily-looking man jumped out. "Whatja tink yer doin'?"

God, would we ever get out of the airport?

"I thought you asked for a push," my old man pleaded.

The white man raised his fist. "Do that again, asshole, and you're in deep shit!"

"Sorry sir, sorry! I thought you asked!" My driver turned frantically. "Didn't you think so, Miss?"

"Yes." I nodded obediently.

Would there be a fight?

"Aw, fuggit! Fuggit!" He stormed back to his own car and revved the engine again, but he was well and truly stuck. Served him right. He was typical New York. Why was everyone so aggressive here? It was disgusting to shout at an old man. My driver had got deferential, like a character out of *Gone with the Wind.*

The sky was aflame. There was a smell of pollution. Horns blared and brakes screeched as we merged onto the Van Wyck Expressway. The three lanes on each side were choc-a-bloc. But I had to think of something else. As we narrowly missed a car in the next lane, I took out my genealogy folder from the National Library. It contained lists of emigrant ships and a map of Ireland with family names. It was good to have something concrete for Ogie. Maybe now she'd write the biography herself. I didn't want to write about a real person – certainly not a man. Or a relative. You never knew what you'd find out. And people would say I was letting the family down.

There was one skeleton I couldn't exhume. My suspicions would die with me. It was a secret that could never be shared. Not even with Fergal. My mother's voice haunted me. "I'm telling you this to help with your writing . . . Promise not to tell anyone – "

"Some folks . . . Didja see that, Miss?" my driver called back.

He was some driver. It was like the bumpers, and his car rattled in strange places as we careered down the expressway. Now he was changing lanes, waving calmly out the window. Everyone must be doing over seventy. What if we hit something at this speed? Why hadn't I waited for a regular taxi? I hated cars. Lately I'd given up driving and couldn't get into one without fear. It really puzzled Fergal.

The traffic had stopped but my heart still pounded. There was a smell of burning rubber. Was something wrong? Distract yourself, I told myself, think about something else. Anything . . .

We pulled off the expressway.

I put on my glasses, searching for overhead signs. The sun was in my eyes. Where on earth were we? Some grey suburb, with tattered yellow ribbons hanging from a scrubby tree. Apartment blocks were scrawled with graffiti. And there was rubble everywhere. I'd read *Bonfire of the Vanities*, and knew what happened to people who drove down the wrong street in New York.

Then I noticed there was no meter.

"Hey," I tried to say.

But my voice was gone.

In the back of a passing car, the old man from the airport lifted his straw hat. Smiling cryptically now. How had he got there? He was definitely following me. Well, there were laws against that.

Why had I got into this jalopy? You were warned on the Aer Lingus video only to take official taxis. But the cab had pulled out of nowhere. It was a trick – the two old men were in league. The roof began to close in. I couldn't breathe.

Oh, God, let me out.

Let me out!

No, "My right arm is heavy."

What was happening? This wasn't real. I was paralysed and sweating. It had happened before – always when travelling. Twice during the summer when Fergal was driving, I'd screamed at him to stop, imagining the car was going over the mountain. He'd bought me a drink.

A group of young blacks huddled at the edge of a basketball court. As one of them looked up, my thoughts ran riot. I had a sort of flashforward, crazily imagining they were the driver's accomplices – waiting for me. Then I was in a ditch, battered, beaten, and robbed of every penny. Next thing I was in a hospital bed with two hideously black eyes. Fergal looked grimly down at me, raspberry faced, as usual, his steel-wool hair wild, his thick scarf tucked into his shabby jacket. "Well, another fine mess!"

"I have to get out!" I heard myself sob.

My driver looked worriedly back. "What is it?"

I dug my nails into my palms, fighting for control. "Please, stop the car!"

He pulled onto the shoulder.

I felt blindly for the door handle. "Let me out! Please!"

"Ya mean, here?"

"I'll pay you anything!" I fumbled in my bag, then struggled again with the door. Panic took my breath away. Vomit rose. I could hardly see. "I have to get out."

"Butcha can't get out here!"

It was true. We could be on the moon. Cars whizzed past on the desolate suburban highway.

He was still staring. "But what is it?"

I got my breath at last. "You're not a *real* taxi!"

He dug into his breast pocket. "I sure am. Here's my ID, Miss."

I scanned it quickly – he was legal. "But you have a partner?"

"A pardner?" He shook his head slowly. "No, Miss."

"An old man in a white suit?"

"An old man? In a white suit?" Nervously he ran his tongue over his tobacco-stained teeth. "No, Miss, dis my own car. I moonlight weekends."

Was I paranoid?

"I *promise* to getcha safely to yer destination, OK?"

"But you left the expressway."

"The traffic was *terrible!*" He was exasperated now. "Dis a short cut to the Triboro Bridge."

The Triboro Bridge? Where was that? I didn't know any of the bridges in New York. I usually flew straight on to Philadelphia and was met by friends. But it was true about the traffic. "Is that the best way to Riverside Drive?"

"It is, Miss." He sighed patiently. "Especially in dis traffic. We'll go through East Harlem."

"Will that cost more?"

"It'll be thirty-five dollars, Miss." He spoke slowly. "Now, if dat's too much, you gimme thirty."

"No, thirty-five is fine. I'm sorry. Please, go on."

The old man looked back kindly. "Someone's been beatin' on you?"

"No, I'm just tired – sorry."

As he pulled out, horns blared again. But he weaved on blithely, picking up speed. Hot wind from his open window blew in my face.

"If I'd a daughter, I hope she'd ask for IDs too," he shouted back over the roar of traffic. "Yes, siree. Dere's strange folks dese days, Miss. *Strange folks!*"

And some were mad Irish women. Ahead was a sign for the bridge. And one for Flushing where my mother had lived as a child. What was wrong? Was it just tiredness? Fergal? "I won't be here when you get back!" he bellowed again in my head.

I blocked my ears.

CHAPTER TWO

* * *

EAST HARLEM HAD A THIRD WORLD LOOK, BUT THE UPPER WEST Side was familiar. Yellow cabs tore recklessly ahead, honking hysterically. As we rattled down Riverside Drive, I felt foolish. I was a basket case – Fergal was right. The panic attack was bad, but it's cracked to imagine you're being followed. My mental state came from isolation, the monastic, chilblained trade of writing. I had to get out more.

As the driver pulled into the curb, I groped for money.

Ogie must be well off – 428 was what a Dublin real estate agent would call "a well appointed" brownstone. It was typical New York with a high old-fashioned stoop to the front door. Other steps down from the street led to a basement entrance.

The driver turned his head, "Now, Miss. Ain't we OK?"

"Yes. Thank you." Avoiding eye-contact, I gave him forty dollars.

He handed me change.

"That's fine."

He jumped out and hauled the case from the car. The sleeves of his skimpy shirt were half-mast on his bony wrists. "I goddit."

I grabbed the handle. "Thanks, I can manage."

"Well, you take care, Miss."

I met his kind brown eyes. He must've been eightyish.

He pulled his cap down on his forehead, got back in the car and was soon elbowing into the blaring traffic. I dragged the leaden case up the steps, cursing myself. I always swore to carry less. Fergal managed with hand luggage. But the semester was four months. At the top, I pushed a bell for Hans and Oonagh Max.

No answer.

Where was Ogie? Had we missed each other at Kennedy?

I tried again.

Then there were noises from the basement.

"Yeah?" a young voice shouted up.

I looked over the stoop wall. A dark child – about ten – in shorts and a T-shirt stood with arms akimbo. It looked female, but you couldn't be sure it wasn't a long-haired boy. The child had thick bangs and a pudding-bowl haircut. Like an angel from a Renaissance painting. It was one of Ogie's two – I knew by the dark colouring. Every year I stuck their Christmas card snap on the fridge.

"Whatcha want?" the child barked.

I cleared my throat. "I'm Anne O'Brien, your Irish cousin."

"Sorry, wrong bell!"

The door slammed shut. Some angel.

I checked – it was the right bell.

I buzzed again.

This time two children stared up. The first, I decided, was a boyish girl. The second, a chunky little brother with a baseball bat in tow. He had the same thick black hair, but short with only one bang.

"Ya hit the wrong bell," repeated the girl.

"Eh – I – I'm your Irish cousin – "

"No, you're not! You're a bag lady!"

The boy brandished the bat. "GO WAY!"

They weren't the friendliest. But they were my cousins. Jessica Sinn Fein and Jason Ira – called after the IRA, Ogie had written gleefully. I had tactfully answered that nowadays these movements were associated with violence. The IRA were criminals. But it was no good. Ogie was typically Irish-American – the sort of person who worshipped ancestors and liked my books.

"Listen," I reasoned, "your mother's expecting me."

"Get lost!" The boy batted the railings.

The door slammed again.

I stood there, startled. Did I look like a bag lady? My denim coat was shapeless and always reminded Fergal of a Beckett character – Estragon waiting for Godot knows what.

"Hey, come on down! Dis de way in."

A big black woman appeared beneath the stoop. She wore a white towel dressing-gown with another white towel wrapped turban-like around her head. She looked like a black ghost, but was a housekeeper perhaps. I staggered back down to the street. Then down more steps to a basement door.

"Hi, I'm Anabelle. I was in de shower," the woman said jovially. "Dose damn kids are too ornery to open de front door. Dis de bell."

There was another bell. The children were right.

Anabelle reached for my case. "Here, lemme help."

"I can manage." My case toppled on its wheels.

"Mrs Max expectin' you. She be back soon."

"Did she go out to the airport?"

The woman shook her head. "Naw. She workin'."

Anabelle double-locked the door from the inside. Then led me along a dark basement corridor with paintings and old family photographs on the walls. We passed a stairway and the open bathroom door before coming to the family room which had an iron-barred door, opening onto a courtyard. Ivy covered the side of the neighbouring building, curling around high gothic windows. It was like a movie set for Dracula's basement.

"You be sleepin' on dat couch, so leave your stuff dere," Anabelle said. "And dere's de bathroom."

Did the family sleep upstairs? The children were now watching a giant colour TV. The girl was sprawled, bottom up, on the couch, while two exotic cats crawled all over her. The boy lay on the floor a few inches from the screen, his chin in the heels of his hands. One chunky leg wagged back and forth, banging the floor with his Nikes. Both chewed gum.

The girl screamed. "She can't sleep here!"

"You hush, Jessica! And Jason! Switch off dat TV!" The housekeeper hurried back to the bathroom. "You know whatcha daddy say!"

The children ignored her. Jessica Sinn Fein hugged a cat. And Jason Ira wriggled even closer to the set, flicking the remote control.

"Asshole! Stop it!" shouted Jessica. "Anabelle, Jason's messin' up the TV!"

"I'll finish my shower, Miss!" The housekeeper turned to me. "You help youself. Dere's soda in de icebox." And she banged the bathroom door.

I hung my jacket on the hall rack. When the bathroom was free, I'd have a shower. My nerves were ragged from the flight and taxi ride. To avoid the noisy TV, I studied the faded sepia photographs in the darkened hallway. There was one of my grandfather, Marcus, as a young man, looking rakish in a pince-nez and boater – I'd seen it somewhere before. And one of his wife, Nora, in a long brocade dress. She wore a pince-nez too. It must be a studio portrait because my mother'd had a copy. There was another of their wedding day, I'd never seen. They looked so happy. Marcus in a long frock coat, holding a top hat. Large, blustery and fair with a gash of a moustache. My bespectacled grandmother was dark and almost Jewish-looking, in a Limerick lace veil. I was told the veil had been made for the Queen when the King had visited Kilkenny. At the time, the story went, my Healy great-grandfather had refused to meet the King so the lace couldn't be presented. But he'd felt sorry for the workers, so bought up all the lace himself. He'd also refused a knighthood, being a Nationalist, a Home Ruler and Parnellite. It was a tradition for the Healy women to wear the veil when they got married. I didn't want a white wedding because Fergal was an ex-priest.

"Whatcha doin'?" Jessica stood brattishly behind me.

"Looking at your great-grandparents."

The child grimaced. "They're gross!"

"I don't think so."

"You're weird!"

I said nothing.

"You talk weird too!" She stamped off. "Mom doesn't like stuff touched."

Anabelle came out of the bathroom. She was now fully dressed. She charged to turn off the TV.

The boy zapped the remote control.

Angrily she flicked it off again. "Jason! Move yuh butt! Ya got readin'!" Then to me, "I gotta go now, Miss, but Mrs Max be back soon."

"That's OK." I was to be left with the terrible two.

The old woman put on her quaint old ladies' black hat and coat and fussily gathered plastic bags from the hall closet. "Do ya homework now, kids!"

They ignored her.

"Bye now, Miss."

"Bye, Anabelle."

As the door slammed, Jason zapped on the TV.

"What about your homework?" I suggested tactfully.

"Aw, shut your face!" came from the girl.

"But it'd be done – over with . . . "

"No way!" the boy chimed.

Defeated, I went back to the hall. I was out of touch. But the kids I'd met in Pennsylvania were polite. Maybe these would be when the parents came back.

I was uneasy about being in the shower when Ogie came in, so I studied my grandfather's rakish photograph. What was he really like? It was a kind and humorous face. He looked a bit of a card, actually. Overweight . . . Oonagh said he'd got thin at the end. "I never remember my father as anything but an old man." He was in his heyday here, the days of his legal and diplomatic career. He'd always been a hero. Like the rest of the family, I took a vicarious pride in his fame. But my mother had ruined my illusions.

It was shortly before her death. We were having a cup of tea in the kitchen. She was a faded beauty, old before her time, with thick white hair and lopsided hornrims. But her eyes were still blue, still her most striking feature. We must have been talking about her childhood because suddenly her shoulders heaved.

I was alarmed. "What is it?"

"I'm telling you this to help you with your writing."

"What?"

"I never liked my father. I wasn't sorry when he died."

"But that's no reason to feel guilty."

My mother fiddled nervously. "Don't tell anyone, but he wasn't a proper father."

Next she was in tears. I was too diffident to pursue the matter, and then she had died. It wasn't a deathbed confession. Yet it was one of the last conversations we had. She always took my writing so seriously. But what was I not to tell? And what did she mean by "a proper father?" Had she been an abused child or what? Had he beaten her? Why didn't I find out exactly what happened?

Whatever it was, I'd picked up the tab. I'd looked after Oonagh when she was drinking. Once I followed her onto a bus with only a nightgown under my coat. She took off and disappeared, sometimes for days. I could still see her lined face. She was a cured alcoholic. She finally licked it. So her death was a terrible shock . . . a week after, I ran into her house, calling her name. Only last year I followed an old woman down Pembroke Street, imagining it was her. Crazy.

As I sat on the couch, Jessica plonked rudely onto the floor. The cats jumped onto my lap, clawing my clothes. I batted them away, but they kept coming back, loathsome, short-haired, rat-like. There was a smell of cat spray. I recognised it, because a horrible Tom always picked my window in Dalkey. It was my imagination, Fergal said, but the smell came through double glazing. I'd tried pepper and bits of glass. Then someone on the radio suggested lion dung from the Zoo. One sniff and the cat would flee. It was a joke, of course. Fergal had laughed at me, telling all he'd been sent up to the Zoo with a bucket.

I batted the cats again.

"Whatcha laughin' at?" the girl snapped.

"Nothing."

"You were laughin' at us!"

"No, it was something – private."

"I'm telling Mom."

Ignore her, I told myself, concentrate on the boy. He was now intently watching cartoons, his face magic.

"Jason, don't sit so near the screen."

No answer.

My sister's children often behaved badly too. An air of confidence was called for.

I cleared my throat. "Sit back, Jason. You'll do yourself an injury."

The boy looked up briefly. "Aw, shut up!"

"What'd you say?"

"He said shut up!" The girl didn't take her eyes from the TV. "It's a compound word."

A compound word? That had echoes of junior school, the age for definitions: *a noun is the name for any person, place or thing. A verb is a doing word.* So *shut up* was a compound word. Well, I'd learnt something today.

How had I got off on such a wrong footing with my young cousins? I couldn't relate to my sister's children either. I knew it was important to give them things – that they judged you by that. Perhaps I should've presented the chocolates immediately? But that might offend the parents. No, nothing to do but wait.

Would Ogie be a fussy parent? In Las Vegas she'd been typical sixties: a hippyish conservative in Levis who read Ayn Rand – a writer I'd never heard of. I'd never been anywhere before that neon city. After five days of no sleep and reheated greasy food, of clinging to a weedy English boy in seedy bus stations, my newly-met cousins had dragged me off to a topless night club: Ogie and Marcus O'Neill, junior – our Cousin Bud, a card dealer in the Desert Inn.

The place was like outer space.

The English boy got off with me. It was like stepping off the world. But Ogie ran to hug me. She'd been so warm in the beginning. So had Cousin Bud. Like Ogie, he had a nickname. His distinguished him from his father who was also a Marcus. Bud was a knockout in those days, dark and movie-star handsome. He had quizzed me about our grandfather. I gave him the usual spiel about the poor immigrant making good.

The summer was a nightmare. The Strip had topless waitresses, others dressed as bunnies, teenagers hanging on the arms of old men. And no one ever went to bed. Or turned out the lights. No regular meals or public transport. Being carless was like being legless. I went for a walk and was picked up by the police. People gaped if I spoke, so I clammed up. And you had to join a union to work. I didn't have the money, so spent most of the summer frying myself in cocoa butter by a pool. Or else sitting in a darkened apartment to avoid the desert heat. The American Moon landing was on TV.

Las Vegas was lunar too. I just sat there, running out of money. Finally they sent some from home. But even then I couldn't leave Ogie to her grief. Her own mother had died the previous spring, and her new boy-husband had been killed, training for Vietnam. He'd fallen out of a helicopter.

As Jason channel-surfed, George Bush flashed briefly onto the TV screen.

"Today the President addressed a meeting of . . . " an announcer droned.

The President stood with some businessmen.

I leant forward, freezing. "Jason, please – !"

The old man from the plane was on TV. He had removed his straw hat to reveal thick yellowish-white hair, but stared crookedly through the same wire glasses into the camera. How had he got there? Was the President in New York? What had the announcer said? A meeting of what?

Jessica kicked the floor. "Jason!"

The boy flicked back to his cartoons.

I was in a cold sweat. "Could we go back to the news?"

"Naw!"

"Please, for a second." I had to make sure of my sanity. "Please!"

Amazingly the little boy relinquished the remote control.

"Jason!" Jessica screamed. "Ja-son!"

I found George Bush again. His speech was over, and everyone was clapping. But there was now no sign of the old man. Where had he gone? Why did he frighten me? The news flashed to something else. Now I knew why he was familiar – he looked like Marcus.

Jessica was still kicking and screaming.

I gave the remote control to Jason and went out to the hall photographs, consoling myself with the dead.

No. Marcus merely resembled the old man on TV.

The marriage portrait was typically Victorian. No, Edwardian. It was 1910, Victoria was well dead. I'd been brought up on the love story. How Marcus had seen my grandmother riding to hounds outside their Kilkenny house and vowed to marry her. Then he'd brought her to New York which she'd hated. Then to the Caribbean, and finally back to Dublin. It was Happy Families until then. In 1919 his elder son, Daniel, died of flu. When told he was going to Heaven, the child had begged his mother to come with him. She agreed and died herself three weeks later. Her last meal was a boiled egg. "It was tempting fate," Oonagh had told me. "Never tempt your fate." Marcus, who had been in America, heard at Cobh that his son was dead and his wife dying. Although older, he'd survived her by years. "Don't mourn for me," he told Oonagh when he was dying. "I've waited sixteen years for this day."

Was it myth or fact?

Still, handy to marry an heiress. Marcus was an adventurer. We knew nothing about our grandmother, except that she smoked in public. Nora must've been her own woman. A bit of a suffragette. She looked out from old sepia photographs with those quizzical, short-sighted eyes. Eyes that had always haunted me. I couldn't forget her dying words to the Healys, "I'll leave my money to my husband, and he will look after my children."

Everything I knew about her came from Oonagh, who had been told it by someone else – probably Marcus. Were they just stories? She was always losing her glasses, so Marcus ordered her a dozen pairs, which were delivered after her death. But he was in America when she got sick? It'd make a great weepy novel, but I wasn't writing it. I didn't know enough. How did you find out about the past? And what were these people like? Nora had trusted him. Lucky you couldn't see ahead. Her death had overshadowed three generations.

I had often walked past her Pembroke Road house, imagining it in 1918, full of flowers. What if she walked out? A big chestnut tree still grew in the garden. Cut flowers were meant to be unlucky. I studied my grandmother's photograph now. It was a good face. Not especially pretty, slightly buck teeth.

"I tried to look after Oonagh," I whispered.

Nora stared silently back.

But where did the dead go? Could they possibly be watching? Listening? Sort of behind a curtain? Or at your shoulder, motivating your whole life? In a sense you were their immortality.

I went to the kitchen cupboard. Maybe there'd be something to drink – a drink would steady my jitters. But there was only some Aunt Jemima Corn Muffin mix and a tin of Chock Full O' Nuts coffee. Ogie didn't seem to shop much – unusual for an American. The fridge had some low fat milk and an opened bottle of Diet Coke. I poured a glass then, remembering my vodka, spiked it.

I went back to the couch.

"Ya didn't get us some," the girl whined.

"Sorry!" I jumped up again.

This was a peace gesture, so I fixed two more cokes.

The boy took his without comment, but the girl screamed, "Ya touched it! Ya touched it!"

What was wrong now? "I – I didn't."

"Ya did! Ya touched the glass!"

"But I had to!"

"Ya didn't wash yer hands!" The child kicked hysterically. "I don wandit! I don wandit!"

"But – I had to touch it."

"Dump it! Dump it!"

It was some cleanliness phobia. Best not make too much of it. "It's a pity to waste it! Coke costs money."

"Ya didn't pay for it, did ya?" The boy's beautiful dark eyes glinted defiantly. Oddly, it was a look of my mother's.

I handed the coke to the girl. "Don't be silly, Jessica."

She was red with temper. "DUMP IT! DUMP IT!"

CHAPTER THREE

✳ ✳ ✳

ABOUT EIGHT O'CLOCK THERE WERE VOICES, AND THE SOUND OF A key in the basement door. Then it was unlocked again and Ogie came up the hall, carrying brown paper bags. Seeing me, she dropped them and bounded over.

I was rooted to the spot. "Hi, Ogie."

She smothered me in a bear hug. "Annie!"

My cousin had always been big, but now was huge. She wore a flowing purple tent dress, and a wide-brimmed summer hat over purple eyeglasses. As she took them off, I saw lines etched in her face. Cats and kids immediately clustered round her, squalling.

"Mom, Jason wouldn't let me watch my programme!"

"She hogs the TV!"

Ogie took off her hat to reveal snowy hair in a scraggy ponytail. "Y'all hush up! I'm greeting ma cousin. Gee, I'm glad to see ma moon-faced Mo."

I giggled. It was her crazy, southern nickname for me as a child – my sister was tow-headed Mo. As we hugged again, Jessica Sinn Fein hovered sulkily.

Ogie gave her a bag. "Here, new slippers. Have yuh been looking after your Irish cousin?"

The child poked in the bag.

Ogie winked conspiratorially at me. "Jessica's the brains

of the family. She gets it from our side. She's mad 'cos I wouldn't buy new sneakers."

"I *need 'em*, Mom!" She stamped her foot.

"But I gotcha slippers!"

"I don't want slippers!"

"OK, I'll take 'em back!"

"OK!" The child flung the bag onto the couch and ran screaming from the room.

Completely unfazed, Ogie held me at arm's length, beaming. "You haven't changed at all!"

I shrugged. "I'm ten years older."

"And I'm fatter! Go on, say it!"

"You can . . . lose it." I tried not to stare. We'd once been the same size or nearly – twelve-ish.

"Oh, isn't this exciting?" Ogie crushed me in another hug. "How was the flight?"

"Fine! I didn't miss you at the airport?"

She frowned, hitting her forehead with the heel of her hand. "Was I meetin' yuh?"

"You wrote – but it doesn't matter. I got a cab."

She grimaced. "Damn! Sorry, I forgot! We had late opening."

"It's OK."

There was real affection in Ogie's blue, blue eyes – they were just like Oonagh's. Then she scowled again in mock irritation. "It ain't fair!"

"What?

"You look thirty-five!"

I laughed. "My hair's going white."

"Only up front. You'd pay a lot for that."

Ogie waddled to the kitchen area. Her behind was huge, her facial features almost lost in puff. Was she in good health? With the white hair she looked older than Oonagh even, of whom she'd once been a sort of clone. But she was still like her, eerily like her. Was that why I loved her? Even her voice was the same.

"I've tried dieting," Ogie went on, "but it never works. Food's my drug of choice! Ya can hold the crack, but give me my Tortilla chips!" She giggled chestily.

I went to my bag. "Well, hope you like smoked salmon."

The kids were back

"YUK!" Jessica shouted.

"Yuh have anything for us?" Jason whined.

Jessica pushed him out of the way. "I wanna present!"

I gave her the chocolates. "Here, share them out after dinner."

The girl examined the box sulkily. "But we're not allowed chocolate."

The younger one grabbed the box. "Lemme!"

Ogie thudded across the room and snatched it. "We can have salmon! We won't wait for Hans!"

I took out the Bailey's. "I got him this."

"Bailey's! My favourite! How'd ya know?" Ogie went to the kitchen area, hugging the trophies. She put them down and headed for the bathroom. "I'll go change, then I can start the meal."

I found a snack board by the sink and set out a quarter of the pre-sliced fish. The cats hovered, attracted by the smell.

Ogie came back, pulling on giant levis.

"Do you have any crackers? Or lemon?"

"There should be crackers." Shooing off the cats, she reached for a slice. "Yummy!"

The Saltines were in a tin box on the counter. I was dying for another drink, but didn't dare ask.

Ogie put more salmon on a cracker, doubling it over

deftly. But the cats still pestered, so she squirted them with a water pistol. "They hate water! Now, tell me about yourself. Are you happy?"

"Happy – ?"

"How's Fergal?"

I frowned. "Fergal is . . . well . . . Fergal."

Ogie perused my face. "Something's wrong?"

I looked away. "How'd you guess?"

She sighed. "It takes one to know one."

There was an awkward pause.

I broke it. "You mean things aren't going well?"

Ogie glanced warningly toward the children.

Catching her meaning, I went over to my case. "By the way, I got some genealogical information for you. And a book on Irish names – for your research on the Quilligans."

Ogie glanced at them, then disappeared into the bedroom. "I got somethin' for you too."

She brought back a box of stuff. "Xeroxes from the *New York Tribune*. Articles about our grandfather. And letters to Mom in boarding school."

I put on my glasses. Surely not more newspaper cuttings? I was sick of Marcus. And didn't want to think about him, now that I kept seeing his look-alike. "If they're the Farrell Investigation reports, you already sent them. I've brought them back – they're in my case."

"But they're to keep."

"But – ."

"And there's more here! Did you know Marcus put down a revolution? Have a browse while I get into my sneakers."

Tiredly I examined the stuff. Why would anyone care?

"Fascinating, aren't they?" Ogie was back, wriggling into sneakers.

"Ever heard of Bald Jack Rose?" I asked.

"Who was he?"

"Our grandfather acted for him once. He cropped up in the last lot of Xeroxes."

"Marcus was a famous lawyer."

Should I tell Ogie what Oonagh had hinted at? I'd never even told Fergal.

"I – I was hoping . . . " Ogie's voice trailed off, "but I suppose it'll never happen now?"

"What?" I knew what she was thinking.

She reached for more salmon. "You promised to write Marcus's life."

"Did I?"

"Yes, years ago."

I bit into the fish. "Why's he so interesting?"

Ogie finished her mouthful, beaming. "Because he's our ancestor!"

My tic started. Our ancestor, the child molester? My mother, the incest victim? Perhaps it wasn't true, but I didn't want to share my suspicions with Ogie. Not just because her children were listening. "Promise not to tell anyone," Oonagh's voice said in my head.

Ogie wolfed more salmon. "He was a great man. He just got mixed up with some crooked bankers here in New York."

I nibbled without appetite. "What'd your mother think of him?"

"She hero-worshipped him."

"But she was only eighteen when he died." I hesitated before going on. "Oonagh didn't like him."

Ogie took more salmon. "How d'ya know?"

"She told me."

"She was biased."

I said nothing.

"Is it true he founded the IRA?" Jessica piped, now somewhat cheered up.

I was alarmed. "No one in our family ever had *anything* to do with the IRA. They're criminals!"

"But Mom said – "

"What about Cousin Elizabeth?" Ogie broke in.

"Isn't she dead?"

"She's alive, living in Washington."

I frowned. "But she never answered my letters."

"That's because she *has* all our stuff."

"What stuff?"

"Our grandmother's china. Linen. A christening gown. Mother told me. And Marcus's journal. He was in the IRA. So was Elizabeth."

"A journal? But they weren't in the IRA, surely?"

Ogie was vehement. "They were!"

"In the IRA?"

"Yes, Elizabeth was a runner."

"A runner?" I was irritated. Where had that myth come from? "I never heard that. It must've been the old IRA. Our grandfather was arrested by accident once."

Ogie's eyes widened. "When?"

"In 1916. He was walking down Baggot Street. And ended up in Kilmainham Jail. Oonagh said he talked all his life about the bravery of the young insurgents. Tim Healy raised the matter in the House of Commons."

Ogie was intrigued. "He was that famous! But who was Tim Healy?"

I was about to explain that he was Parnell's great enemy, but she wouldn't have heard of Parnell. Anyway the children were fighting again.

"Mom! Jason took my pen!"

"Jason! Give that back!"

The boy tore across the room and up the stairs. This threw Jessica into another fit. She lay on the floor, kicking. "I WAN MY PEN! I WAN MY PEN!"

Ogie ran after Jason. "You come back here! Come back!" The cats ran after her.

I stood in the middle of the room. Americans didn't realise how sick of IRA violence the Irish were. Just before leaving, I'd bought a stamp for London in Dalkey Post Office. The official called me back worriedly. "I'd better give you another." He explained that it wasn't suitable for England. The stamp was of Chuchulain and commemorated the 1916 Rising. But the young man had looked so worried, I took the plain one.

Then another key turned in the basement door. There was the usual fuss with locks. Then a big, rumpled-suited man came in. Tiredly he dumped his umbrella and briefcase on the hall stand and shuffled into the living room with a newspaper.

It was Hans. He was dark and balding with worried brown eyes, and sallow skin as if deprived of sunlight.

"You must be Anne." He barrelled over, smiling and holding out his hand and completely ignoring the upstairs din. "Did Ogie get to the airport on time?"

"Eh, no. I got a cab."

He frowned. "Hmm . . . that's funny, she had the car."

At that Ogie charged down the stairs. "Jason's taking time-out. Hans, speak to him. He's gettin' out of hand."

Hans looked pained. "Huh?"

Ogie paled. Her upper lip thinned in anger. I knew that look and it made me queasy now.

"I want ya to speak to yuh son!" When excited, she spoke more southern.

"I get this after a day's work?" he bellowed, stamping up the stairs.

Ogie looked angry. "That's swell! Act like Prince Charming when my relatives come!"

I took refuge in the bathroom.

37

The shouting receded into the distance. Ogie's anger reminded me of our trip. In '69 the Vietnam protest was hotting up; Edward Kennedy had the accident with Mary Jo; Sharon Tate was murdered – a few miles from the Los Angeles boatyard where I was staying. Hiding-out, with a draft-dodging cousin and his family of cats. One day the FBI questioned me. Then all my cousins had been long-haired hippies; now they were shorn conservatives. I was twenty-four and on leave from a typing job. Ogie was twenty-five and a widow.

Then there was Dallas. I played that row over in my mind. Ogie's Texas boyfriend had been another stop on our cross-country trip. After dinner he brought us out for beer and ballads in downtown Dallas. I got happier and happier, so Ogie thought I was flirting with him. Later, back in the apartment he refused to sleep with her, so she drove off in a rage. I was stranded in the middle of America with no money and a madman. A madman with an erection.

I stared into Ogie's bathroom mirror. Was I getting a drinker's nose? There were black circles round my eyes. He wouldn't be so interested now.

He'd chased me around the room, his penis erect, bobbing under a skimpy dressing-gown. But I only wanted to sleep. I'd never had sex, and wasn't interested in any one-night stand. In the end he followed me to bed, lying beside me, but never touching me. Ogie came back and saw us together in the big double fourposter. But I didn't care. I just watched her flounce out again with her bundle of dresses on coathangers.

What was the guy's name? Tom? Dick? Irving? In the morning I showed him my worldly goods – $7, so he offered to fly me to New York. But then Ogie collected me, having spent the night in a parking lot. We drove off and never even talked about it. It had been too awful.

Still, I'd seen everything that summer: the Mojave desert,

Death Valley, the Grand Canyon, all that red earth. At the end, we drove back cross-continent to Florida where both our mothers were brought up. Where my dead aunt's lipsticked cigarette butts were still in the ashtrays of her St Petersburg house – it had seemed like a mansion to me. But it was an average American middle-class home.

We'd stopped in Mississippi to help another cousin, a Red Cross staff member, organise victims of Hurricane Camille – mostly poor blacks. I spent hours brushing and braiding the children's hair. "Do y'all like this kind o' work?" a National Guard had asked me. It was my first taste of prejudice. Later we were turned out of a cafe for being with a black social worker. "God bless you and your company," the other diners had chanted as we left. It was an ordinary Friday night, and we went into Hattiesburg for an ordinary hamburger.

The whole summer was bizarre. We slept in the car, locking ourselves in. One night we lay under the stars. That was a high. But Ogie scared me about snakes. I put a piece of string around my sleeping bag to ward them off. Where was that? Aspen. Yes, Aspen, Colorado. Then Ogie ridiculed my fears. She'd ridiculed a lot of things – my appearance, clothes . . .

"She's not like us," I heard her whisper to her sister on the phone. "No make-up. Homely."

I was a country cousin, bookish, without Ogie's interest in make-up. One night she fitted me with false eyelashes and we went on the town. Everyone was gambling madly. Terrible. The evening ended with me bursting into tears at the slot machines in Caesar's Palace. Ogie'd hustled me into a bar-booth and ordered a drink.

Travel was always stressful.

So was visiting relatives.

All was quiet, so I came out of the bathroom.

Ogie was in the kitchen, and Hans was thudding back

downstairs, having changed into jeans. He slumped heavily into the couch and, flinging off the cats, opened his newspaper. Immediately he found Jessica's new slippers. "What's this?"

Ogie grabbed them. "Did yuh speak to ya son?"

Hans got up again, folded his paper and, walking heavily from the room, muttered, "If you've been spending again!"

"Jessica needed slippers!" Ogie's face was contorted in anger.

Hans stamped up the stairs. "Well, bring 'em back! We can't afford 'em!"

"What do ya mean?"

"I mean we can't afford 'em!"

"I work! I'll pay for them!"

"That's a joke! It's $300 bucks a month to park your car! Anabelle's $250 a week!"

"I hate Anabelle," one of the children whined.

"Scrooge! Scrooge!" Ogie screamed, tearing into the kitchen area. She furiously unpacked the groceries, slamming them onto the counter.

I followed nervously. "Can I help?"

Ogie ripped open some hamburger meat. "Prince Charming! He always acts like this when my relatives come!"

Ignoring me, she banged a skillet on the stove. Then sloppily poured oil into a chip pan, spilling some on the floor. I wiped it with a paper towel, then stood around, wondering what to do. Ogie was savagely slapping the meat into patties.

Then Hans came downstairs again. This time he dumped a large Bloomingdales shopping bag on the floor. "What the hell is this?"

Ogie grabbed it. "I got a dressing-gown and slippers for Jason too!"

"Well bring 'em back!" he roared.

"Scrooge! Scrooge!"

I needed a drink.

CHAPTER FOUR

* * *

"FERGAL!" I HEARD MYSELF SHOUT.

Damn, where was I?

Have you ever awakened in the dark and wondered where you were? Or thought someone was in the room? I did my first night in Ogie's apartment. The barred door terrified me. Then slowly my surroundings became familiar – the bars led to Ogie's ivied yard. Moonlight from there flooded the basement room, casting eerie shadows. A crossbreeze ruffled the curtain. But what time was it? It wasn't new for me to wake in the small hours, but in my dream I was being chased.

By whom?

I couldn't remember.

Was someone here now?

No. My eyes were gradually adjusting.

The monstrous shapes were furniture. The giant TV was blind. In the kitchen the fridge throbbed mechanically. I couldn't see my watch so had no idea of the time. It was jet-lag. My circadian rhythm was zonked, and would be for days.

Then something soft touched my leg.

What was it? I daren't look under the blankets.

It brushed me again.

God . . . was someone in the bed?

It was furry.

I flicked on the light.

The blanket moved and a cat peeped out, its eyes an angry yellow. As it ducked back, I breathed more easily.

"Go away!" I got up and shook the blanket.

It appeared again, so I slapped it with a pillow. Then it leapt from the bed and tore into a corner where it was joined by its mate. Both hissed malevolently.

I armed myself with Ogie's water pistol and left the light on. The light always consoled me, a hangover from childhood.

Ogie and Hans's tiff had been curious. Afterwards they laughed and chatted through dinner, as if nothing had happened. But that was Ogie – an emotional yo-yo. Later that evening, while she put the children to bed, I struggled through a conversation about Ireland's economic state with Hans. We talked about Mad Cow Disease. How Fianna Fail were crooks but better for business than Fine Gael. How I was tempted to vote for them, because they supported the arts. Hans had been intrigued that artists in Ireland were tax free. I'd kept going, blue streak, until suddenly, overwhelmed with sleep, I had almost nodded off in mid-sentence. But luckily, having made up my couch, the parents followed the children.

Ogie didn't seem any saner. Or happily married. Perceptively she'd picked up on my row with Fergal. Hans must be mean. At least Fergal wasn't – the opposite, really. Fecklessness was his problem. Everyone liked him. No wonder, he tipped like a drunken sailor. But relationships ran their course. Ours certainly had. It was time for divorce.

I'd told him last thing that I didn't want to fund anymore of his mad schemes.

He'd looked exasperated. "Why's it mad?"

"Because it's wasting money."

"Well, if that's how you feel, I'll make other plans."

"For what?"

"For our lives."

I was stung. "You've been doing that already!"

He feigned surprise. "What do you mean?"

"You're fucking that girl!"

"What girl?"

"The one who hangs up the phone when I answer it."

He looked ready to hit me, but instead stormed from the room, a study in outrage. Men.

Damn Fergal and his bloody girlfriend. How could he wipe out seventeen years? I was becoming bitter, but couldn't help it. I didn't want to be alone. I'd tried to earn money so we wouldn't be poor. So that no one in the family would be poor again. And Fergal was throwing it all away.

I had to stop thinking of him. Now.

A drink would knock me out.

I got a vodka and filled it with orange juice from the fridge. The *New Yorker* was gone, and there were no other books about.

I'd finished my paperback on the plane, so opened McLysaght's *Irish Family Names*. The Quilligans were listed. The clan originally came from Thomond, which was medieval Clare. Culligan was another form of the name. I flicked back to O'Neill. They originated in the North, but a branch had also settled in Thomond. All the O'Neills were descended from Niall of the Nine Hostages, and were known as *Cleann de buidh* – fairhaired tribe, who'd given their name to the Northern town of Clandeboy. That should interest Ogie, I thought – descended from Irish royalty. Great. Pity it wasn't the High Kings.

The National Library had a letter which mentioned a Major General Quilligan of the Rebel Army being exchanged as a prisoner in the American Revolutionary War. Ogie'd love that too, though our grandfather hadn't emigrated until the eighteen sixties.

"Remember, our family emigrated from choice. We were never starving," Oonagh had said. But hadn't many of our relatives died of TB in their new-found-land? Wasn't there a story about our grandfather, Marcus Quilligan O'Neill, leaving school at thirteen to support his mother and sisters? His father had died early. But he'd got to Yale, somehow. And now the torch had passed to Ogie's ghastly kids.

I was always told my great-grandfather O'Neill had been a Kerry school teacher and made a living in America by correcting college maths papers. He was meant to be too clever for the ordinary high schools. That was probably a story to keep the side up. The National Library also said he could've been formally educated. In the nineteenth century, Catholic teachers were trained in a Dublin college. Also, there'd be a record in the Teachers' Salary Books in the National Archives as to why he'd emigrated. It could've been for political reasons. But first I had to find his christian name. That would be on my grandparents' marriage certificate in the General Registry Office, but I hadn't had time to follow up on the leads. Maybe our ancestor had built the railways like all the other Irish. But could a labourer produce a Marcus Quilligan O'Neill?

Marcus was meant to be wonderful company. Then I remembered his letters to my aunt:

Dear Eithne,

I put your dresses into the cleaners today, so you will get them the end of next week.

I am enclosing two dollars with which to buy a hat and if you can get it cheaper the balance will do for other little things that you might need.

Don't think that this is easy for it isn't by any means. And for several weeks to come, you may have to do with less spending money. However, we will both hope for the best. I was glad to hear of your good times on the golf links. And I am pleased to hear that you are meeting nice people. Remember, however, that the social end of your being up there is secondary and that the main business is school. I am sending you back your report card and note what you say about getting a better one next time. The report was good except in mathematics, and I accept your explanation about that. Remember that there are no school subjects that cannot be mastered by average attention. I need not say that you are travelling ground you cannot go over again, and this means that you cannot afford to have any failures. I rely on your determination to make something of yourself.

We are all happy and working hard. Mark today got 99 in psychology and is doing first class work in Junior College. Oonagh passed her first test with very fair marks. I am not anxious to work her too hard and I think she will get by all right.

Love from all, Daddy.

He didn't sound like an improper father. More of a penny-pincher, but it was during the Great Depression. My mother said Eithne had given him trouble, running wild with boys and crashing the car. The next letter was about money too and mentioned my mother.

Darling Eithne,

Your Uncle Tim was here and cleared up the hospital bill which was eating my heart out. He left 10 dollars for you: the same for Oonagh.

I am now certain to be able to take care of your graduation. I had terrible doubts on the subject and I ought to admit your writing about my illness to Ireland turned out for the best after all. Do not ask me to write about St Patrick. This letter has exhausted me.

Please acknowledge this ten and the last dollar by post. Oonagh will send your dresses tomorrow. Now Eithne, no foolishness with this money. Use your head. It will eat up the best part of 200 dollars to finish you off up there.

Love from both of us, Daddy.

Our grandfather had wanted to be an old Joe Kennedy, but hadn't made it. After meeting Presidents and speaking before the King, he'd died in Florida – poor, an utter failure, haggling over pennies.

Should I share my suspicions with Ogie? My mother'd been terribly angry, deep down. If only she'd had some sort of counselling. You thought incest was "out there," a problem for the poor in overcrowded conditions, but it was everywhere.

Freud discovered the extent of crime.

Why was it such a taboo? A cardinal sin? The subject of

great plays? Oedipus Rex had blinded himself. What sort of man abused a child? An orphan too. Funny, Marcus had always used his mother's name, Quilligan. "Always remember, my grandmother was Quilligan and not O'Quilligan," Oonagh had said. But that was rot. They'd just dropped the prefix. "We lived in a slate house and emigrated with two servants," Oonagh had also instructed me. Our family's big on side. And hopeless about money.

I still couldn't sleep. Lately drink kept me awake, but I don't take pills.

Ogie's newspaper Xeroxes were with the letters. Idly I read the top copy.

HURRIES TO SANTO DOMINGO
Minister Quilligan O'Neill Hopes to
Avert Prolonged Hostilities.

Washington Sept 8 – As a result of a long conference with Secretary Bryan to-day, Marcus Quilligan O'Neill of New York, the new Minister to the Dominican Republic will hurry to Santo Domingo to do what he can toward bringing the revolutionary outbreak to an end. News that government gun boats were bombarding Puerto Plata, which the revolutionists hold, brought the Washington Administration to the conclusion that Mr Quilligan O'Neill's presence in the republic was necessary . . .

Travelling with Mr. O'Neill was his niece, Miss Elizabeth O'Connor . . .

A cat hissed from the corner.

As I squirted, it arched its back spookily.

So Cousin Elizabeth had gone with him. The brilliant lawyer and ogre of Oonagh's childhood. Amazing she was still alive.

There was spicy stuff about the customs scandal. The story broke about a year after his appointment. William Jennings Bryan was accused of whitewashing Marcus.

MARCUS QUILLIGAN O'NEILL DENIES ALL CHARGES.

MINISTER O'NEILL DEMANDS FULL INQUIRY.

President Wilson eventually ordered one. I flicked through the boring reports, stopping at one:

QUILLIGAN O'NEILL OK'D BY BALD JACK ROSE
Jack Rose Now in "Movies"

Jack Rose, who gave his address as Norwalk, Conn., and said that he was President of the Humanology Motion Picture Film Company of Boston and author of its photoplays, one of which is called, "Are They Born or Made?" denied that Quilligan O'Neill had ever been his press agent when they both lived in Waterbury, Connecticut.

"He covered sports for the Waterbury paper, and the paper gave us publicity for which we paid by advertising in their amusement column," said the witness. "Mr Quilligan O'Neill was never my press agent nor were we associated with the promotion of prize fights. The only venture in which we were ever partners was one year when we owned the Danbury franchise in the Connecticut State League."

The witness denied knowledge of an alleged prize fight where Quilligan O'Neill was said to have decamped with the gate receipts. A letter was read into the record. In it Mr Quilligan O'Neill denied he had gone into the

*promotion of one boxing match with the idea of raising
funds to go to law school.*

*"Quilligan O'Neill was my lawyer in the Rosenthal
murder case," said Rose. "Because I sent for him and
asked him to help me as a friend. He knew I couldn't pay
any fee or retainer and he never got one dollar out of it.
His only fee was a thank you, and his only question
when he took up the case was whether I had done the
deed. I said I had not, but at first I was obedient to the
law of the so-called underworld and would tell him no
particulars . . .*

But what was the crime? It was the world of Damon Runyan.
Of guys and dolls, hoodlums and highrollers. The next story
was funny.

QUILLIGAN O'NEILL NOT A DRESSY DIPLOMAT

*. . . M Pemberton Parks said that he did not consider Mr
Quilligan O'Neill as an ideal diplomat, not on account
of any lack of mental fitness but because he was careless
in his personal appearance. "He used to sit about his
home in a negligee shirt and suspenders," said Mr Parks,
"with trousers larger than the New York tailors would
advise one to wear." "How are the Dominicans clad?"
asked Mr Farrell. "The officials," said Mr Parks, "wear
silk hats and Prince Albert coats on the hottest day. They
look as well as you or I." As to the story that Mr Quilligan
O'Neill received other diplomats in his undershirt, Mr
Parks expressed some doubt, but added, "That's a hot
country down there, and most people wear as little as
they can."*

The old man in the plane had wide trousers.

Then something moved in the corridor.

Was it the cats?

John McCormack was singing again, *"Just a song at twilight . . ."*

But my walkman was off.

"When the lights are low . . ."

Someone was coming up the passageway.

"Eh – who's, there . . . ?"

"And the evening shadows,
Softly come and go . . ."

Christ, who was it? Was my tape on?

A small red glow pierced the gloom – a cigarette or cigar tip. It came nearer . . . followed by a figure, trousered with a wide hat. God, was it a burglar? But how had he got in? The place was like a fortress. Maybe it was Hans, come downstairs for something?

"Is that you, Hans?"

No answer.

The figure kept coming, smoking a cigar like a depth charger.

Was I drunk? No . . . it was him . . . the old man from the plane. He was wearing the same old-fashioned straw hat and white suit with the red rose in the buttonhole. He was like a figure out of the early thirties.

I couldn't move. It wasn't happening.

But he hobbled on into the living-room, dragging a leg and thumping the floor with a stick.

I closed my eyes.

When I opened them, he was still there. It was definitely

Marcus – he'd been following me all day. I recognised him from his photographs.

"What do you want?" I heard myself say.

Silently he took off his hat. Then smiled eerily, staring cross-eyedly from behind the thick wire glasses. His ragged bushy moustache and ashen face gave an impression of faded yet dignified dishevelment. His hair was yellowish-white too and his baggy tropical suit wrinkled and stained. The wide trousers were held up by braces.

"Ah, so you've finally noticed me!" He spoke gruffly in broguish New York.

"What do you want?" I whispered.

The old man rested his stick by the armchair and sat heavily into it. He puffed on his cigar and, hooking one thumb into his braces, kept staring. At last he said, "You wanted to know about my life?"

"No! Go away!"

"All right." He mopped his brow with the red hankerchief, breathing chestily. "Let me rest first!"

I was in a cold sweat. It was an older version than the hall photo, but Marcus all the same. "I never remember my father as anything but an old man," Oonagh's voice said. This Marcus was a figment, I knew. Yet he seemed a real flesh and blood figure. He had Oonagh's thick white hair.

He raked it, saying gruffly, "Don't be afraid."

"You're Marcus?"

He bowed his head gravely.

"But why are you following me?" I was paralysed with fear.

51

He coughed chestily, then got his breath. "You may need help with my biography."

I hid the Xeroxes under the sheet. "But who said I was writing it?"

He sighed heavily. "You could offer me a drink then."

"There isn't any."

He threw up his hands in irritation. "No drink? That's a fine thing!"

"Oonagh said you never drank."

"That's right. It's a curse." He pulled reflectively on his cigar. "What about an ashtray then?"

"They don't smoke here."

"I don't believe it!" He raised his bushy eyebrows in disbelief, poking around for one.

"Look . . . please!" I closed my eyes tightly, willing the apparition away. But he still rummaged noisily and, when I looked again, was sitting calmly in the armchair, his cigar butt now resting in a plant saucer.

"I thought there was someone . . . then the cats – "

"I'll lock them away." He struggled up, limpingly shooing them ahead of him. They scuttled ahead into the bathroom. He shut the door, then came back to the armchair. "They won't bother you now."

I studied him, breathing deeply. "But you died."

"Unfortunately, yes."

"I don't understand."

"People today think they can understand everything."

I was feeling calmer now. "You're taller than I imagined."

"The O'Neills are big men. Women too. Look at Ogie." He rolled his eyes upward. "Her mother was worse. I didn't know what to do with her."

"Eithne gave you trouble?"

"Ah, she was just a kid." He spoke in sort of panting gasps, but seemed benign enough.

But I had to clear things up. "Were you on TV earlier?"

"Was I what?"

"On TV?" I pointed to the corner.

He peered at the TV suspiciously. "What is it?"

"It's like the movies."

"In your own parlour?"

I nodded. "You were on it, talking to George Bush."

"George Bush?"

"Yes, the President."

"Funny name for a president. Wilson was America's best president."

I knew nothing about Wilson.

He frowned. "Whatcha reading?"

"Newspaper reports of your diplomatic appointment."

"So you are interested."

"There's nothing else to read."

He puffed out his chest. "I was plenipotentiary, Minister Extraordinaire, and I want a biography."

"Who was Bald Jack Rose?"

He looked outraged. "How'd ya hear about him?"

"From the newspapers."

"Oh, them." He did an Oliver Hardy slow burn. "Jack was a sport. We used to go to Saratoga together. Play the horses." He paused. "They were the days. Jack walked into town like he owned it. Wore a seersucker suit and Panama hat. The place was full of big shots. Big shots and fakers."

"Did you run crooked boxing matches?"

"That was Jack's idea. They weren't crooked though." He wagged a finger. "Get that idea outa your head."

I picked up the Xeroxes. "I have proof, right here."

"What proof?"

"Newspaper reports!"

"Give me those!"

He came for me, waving his stick. So I threw the Xeroxes at him.

Then he was gone.

CHAPTER FIVE

* * *

I GOT MYSELF DOWN TO OLDCASTLE THE NEXT DAY, AND STUMBLED through the first week at Sweetmount, organising classes, seeing students, calling friends. I didn't tell anyone about Marcus – Ogie would think me bonkers and my Sweetmount friends insist on a psychiatrist. It'd look great, wouldn't it, a visiting professor being chased by a ghost?

D H Lawrence wrote that "the dead don't die. They look on and help." Ghosts are meant to be their spirits. But I don't believe in an afterlife. No one's ever come back from the dead. Everything's physical. We're molecules or atoms, coded to come together in a certain way. But the same man had stared at me in Kennedy airport. And passed in another car. Was Marcus a phantasm? An obsession which had walked out of my subconscious?

But he wasn't any ghoul in the cellar. He was practical and he'd got rid of the cats. The next morning they were still locked in the bathroom. I let them out, fearing Ogie's wrath. Then examined the plant plate – it was back in its original place. There was no ash, yet a definite smell of cigar smoke. Was that a delusion too? Arctic explorers see figures making love in the snow. And the stressed have disturbed visions. Mine were so real that I wrote them down in detail.

Was my mental state caused by unhappiness about

Fergal? My panic symptoms might be my age. Before my trip, I'd gone to the Well Woman Clinic for a check-up. At the desk they had asked if I were menopausal. I'd been taken aback. Me? I couldn't be. But perhaps that was the reason for my anxiety. There was a simple explanation. Everything boiled down to your physical health. And you could will yourself to be well.

But it could be a brain tumour. Or the first stages of Alzheimer's. I recited telephone numbers and generally tested my memory, but it seemed OK. I'd been drinking, so maybe I'd had incipient DTs? But dead relatives demanding biographies?

In Oldcastle I was sleeping better, but still awoke early. Perhaps I was run down? I cut down on alcohol, and took B vitamins – huge horse tablets, impossible to swallow but recommended by the Main Street drug store for nervous problems. They must have worked because Marcus hadn't appeared since my arrival. Maybe he was a New York ghost and would stay there. Or maybe he didn't appear because his real obituary was among Ogie's Xeroxes. It was dated August 17, 1935, and comforting:

MARCUS QUILLIGAN O'NEILL, EX-DIPLOMAT, DEAD
New York Lawyer Served Two Years as Minister
to Santo Domingo under Wilson

ONCE ARRESTED IN DUBLIN

Held on political charges in 1916
in connection with Uprising –
Counsel in Becker Case

It was a whole column, beginning with his death of heart

disease in St Petersburg, Florida. It mentioned his stormy career, and that he'd spoken before King George V when the monarch visited Ireland after his coronation. That he was born in 1873 and came to America as a boy. Oonagh said he lied about his age, taking it down by ten years. Did that mean he was born in 1863 and was really in his seventies when he died? I skipped to the bit about his legal career:

He grew up in Brooklyn and later went to Yale University where he studied law. After practising in Connecticut for a time he came to New York and as a cousin of "Big Tim" Sullivan took an active part in Tammany Hall politics. He was counsel for "Bald Jack" Rose, the informer against Police Captain Charles Becker in the trial for the murder of Herman Rosenthal, the gambler.

The Rosenthal case kept cropping up. And Bald Jack again? Was "Big Tim" Sullivan another cousin I'd never heard of?

The obit said that Marcus's diplomatic appointment was largely due to William Jennings Bryan. Also that he'd been investigated by the State Department but cleared of the charges against him. It mentioned that in later years he had lived in New Haven, Connecticut. That was untrue, surely? Oonagh had been brought up in Florida. There was no mention of her as a survivor, or of her sister and brother. Only his public life was deemed worthy of mention. Still there was a story there, if I could get back to writing.

In other years I had rented pleasant houses in downtown Oldcastle, but this time someone's sabbatical had fallen through, so I found myself in an apartment complex called Bella Vista, on the edge of town. It was American soul death – air-conditioned, with bland carpets and bland walls. There was a Mazda which I couldn't drive and a cat for companionship. It was a large, furry creature called BC – Beautiful Cat or Bad Cat, depending on how it behaved. But so far it had basically ignored me – unlike Ogie's horrors. But I had to exercise it on a lead after dark, because the neighbours disapproved of cats, especially roaming ones. Despite this, the apartment was comfortable with three bedrooms, two bathrooms and a balcony. But it was beside the Interstate with the usual cluster of gas stations – a truck-stop, really. And it was scary crossing the road. There was no place for a human to walk, you had to take your chances with the traffic. But there was a Roy Rogers and a Howard Johnson's, which would be handy for eating out.

I planned to stay out as much as possible, working in the library. In the mornings I took a small city bus to Sweetmount College or else walked, before it got too hot. I'd forgotten the heat. Although I liked to be warm, it often went up to the nineties.

Sometime during the first week, I met Chuck Matthews in the bowels of Memorial Hall.

"Hi, Anne!" he called.

I locked my office door, waiting as he was caught by a student. I knew him only slightly. He was the handsome tennis star of the department who'd just been appointed assistant chairperson.

"I'll be right there!" he called again.

"OK."

I was off to the Department for my mail. There was always something: ads for upcoming cultural events, notes from students, or memos about department affairs. My appointment was non-tenure track, so luckily I didn't have to attend the endless and boring meetings. I was a sort of permanent Visiting Professor. Still, I liked to know what was going on. America was an injection – the climate, or something, was energising. I went to everything possible on campus. It certainly beat staying at home. Thanks to the college, I now had an identity. I wasn't just a writing zombie, sitting all day in front of a word processor, hugging a heater to keep warm. Why did people want to be writers? There had to be easier ways of making money. Yet here I was, teaching it.

Chuck hurried over. He had the flirtatious grin of a young Jack Nicholson. His dark hair was even thinning in the same way, but he was small with a boyish muscular body. "Good to see you back."

We shook hands. His courtliness was typically American, also his short-sleeved Oxford shirt and tie.

"It's good to be back."

"How was the Emerald Isle?" He spoke nasal Boston.

"Fine when I left."

"No bombs?"

"Not in Dublin – we've only been bombed once."

Americans think all of Ireland's a war zone, something like Beirut.

We chatted through the labyrinthine basement corridors of Memorial Hall to the stairs. At the top Chuck opened the door to the front lobby which held a Remembrance book for the names of war dead and a large SMOKE-FREE ZONE sign.

As usual, sparsely-clad students swarmed everywhere.

"All set for tomorrow?" he asked at the next landing.

I nodded. "I'm giving my usual introductory spiel to the writing class – the importance of plot. And I'll talk about *Castle Rackrent* to the others."

"Must read it one of these years." Chuck was an American Studies scholar. "I see your classes are full again."

"Yes, we've disappointed a few."

He shook his head jocosely. "A popular woman."

My nervous tic started. "Oh, it's nothing to do with me."

"It's everything to do with you!" He grinned, even, white teeth showing up his tan. If Americans have a characteristic, it's their good teeth. That, and their suntans.

"No, people just want to be writers. I'm selling hope, that's all."

"Well, hope works. Remember Ken Harris?"

"Ken Harris?" I racked my brain. At the end of every semester, students' names were erased as if I'd pressed a button. It was always embarrassing to be hailed the next year in the street. I knew the face, but never the name. But other teachers complained of the same thing.

Chuck flexed his muscles. "He was big with red hair."

"Big . . . with red hair? Oh, yes . . . he was writing a murder mystery. It wasn't bad."

"St Martin's Press took it, with an advance of a thousand bucks."

"Gosh, that's very good news."

He chuckled. "You bet! And *something* to do with you."

"He was talented – "

"And had a good teacher."

We'd reached the English Department. The mail boxes were in the main office where Sarah, the secretary, sat in front of a word processor. She was a pretty, slim woman of about forty dressed in black pants and a white T-shirt. She looked up as we came in.

I hailed her. "Hello, Sarah."

"I was telling Anne about Ken Harris," Chuck said.

Flustered, I took mail from my box. There was nothing important, just the usual junk.

"He sure lucked-out." Sarah's voice penetrated my embarrassment. Why did praise always throw me? I grinned stupidly.

"I'm very happy for him."

"The Chairman's happy too. He's dancing a jig! You do a class job, Ma'am."

"Someone called about the writing class," Sarah said. "I told them you were full."

"Eh – thanks." I frowned at a circular advertising musical events. "The string quartet's doing Beethoven."

Chuck lit a cigarette. "How about lunch?"

His grin took me aback. Did he mean me or Sarah?

But he was looking at me. "Free for lunch?"

"Eh – no. I'm having it with a friend – Molly Springstein. We go to the gym first."

"Chuck!" Sarah pointed irately to a NO SMOKING sign.

"OK! OK!" Irritably, Chuck pulled some letters from his box. He glanced at them quickly, then put one in his pocket and wadded the rest before throwing them into the waste basket. "Molly's Dean Jackson's friend?"

"Yes."

He patted his sparse hair, uncomfortable. "The Dean's quite a character – certainly fights for you women."

"Yes, she's very committed."

"Chuck!" Sarah stood up. "Put *out* that cigarette!"

He ignored her, looking at me. "What about tonight, then?"

I was flustered. I mean, he was married. "Well . . . I'm busy tonight. I've reading to do – you know, classes."

"Saturday then?"

". . . OK."

"Good! I hear you're renting the Petersens' house?"

"Chuck!" Sarah wagged a finger.

I looked awkwardly at her. "No, it fell through. I'm out in Bella Vista apartments."

"Beside I-95? I'll pick you up at seven!"

And he was gone.

Waving grumpily at the cigarette smoke, Sarah popped letters into the different boxes. "Well . . . he's wasting no time!"

"What do you mean?"

"He's just walked out on his wife." Her voice was matter-of-fact.

I flicked through my mail – there was a flyer from a publisher, advertising a book on style; a memo about an upcoming department meeting.

Was Sarah warning me? Over the years, the secretary had become a friend. Perhaps she was trying to tell me something now. The department office was a den of feminism. Or maybe she just didn't like smokers. They're pariahs in America.

I broke the silence. "Why'd he leave her?"

"Mid-life crisis," Sarah said flatly. "He turned forty and got scared. They all do." She chuckled. "It's like musical chairs around here at the moment. The hottest new couple is Wanda and Peter."

I frowned. "I can't place them."

"She's a part-timer and he's an instructor in the writing centre. His wife, Penny, moved in with Jim Henderson."

"Who's he?"

"An assistant professor in the History Department."

"Oh . . . " Above all, Sarah mustn't think me fast. "I don't want to get into anything."

"Well, our Chuck's a smooth operator. But you're not getting into anything by having dinner. By the way, a few drop/ads were looking for you."

"They found me."

"Debbie'll do your hand-outs in the morning."

"Thanks. I'll collect them before class."

"They'll be in your box. Let me know if there's anything else."

Sarah returned to her work and I to my office. She'd been right to warn me. Feminism had come to me late, but now I had the zeal of a convert. Fergal's behaviour, especially, had made me distrust men – he was definitely having an affair. And he was jealous of my job in America. Why did men always want to control you? But what could Chuck have in mind? Surely he'd go for younger women. There were oodles of them around. The campus was like some human beauty farm. You couldn't help but stare after the sleek, well-nourished kids in the street. With such specimens, he couldn't be interested in me. But dinner didn't commit one. It's civilised, it'd pass an evening anyway. But was it a date? When had I last gone on a date? It had to be before Fergal. He hadn't taken me on any – he could hardly, he'd been a priest.

My office belonged to a woman professor on sabbatical in London. It was cosy with a chintzy armchair and a big poster of Virginia Woolf on the wall – the fey, youthful one with the wisp of hair. In a few hours it'd be time to go over to Molly for lunch. I'd use the time by filling students' names into my grade book. There were fifteen in the literature seminar, the same in the writing class. It shouldn't be too difficult to learn their names. Fergal, a gifted teacher, had a trick for remembering. He called a roll every morning and by the end of the first week knew everyone.

The classes would keep me busy, but I usually worked on a novel as well. Maybe I should work on Marcus's biography. Already I was getting sucked into his time. It was strange reading your family history in newspapers – and everything the opposite of what you'd been told. It was reality versus myth. Marcus was a chancer from the beginning. He'd come up the hard way and had trouble paying bills. As well as organising crooked boxing matches in Connecticut, he was once pursued by a tailor for the price of a coat. But he was never editor of the *Hartford Courant*. He'd simply won a prize from that newspaper for selling subscriptions. He persuaded households to cancel their original order and re-subscribe under another family name. Clever.

He'd made his name on the Rosenthal case. It was a gangland tale – a gambler was murdered at the request of a Police Czar. There were many walk-on parts, but three main characters: Charles Becker, the cop; Herman Rosenthal, the victim; and Jack Rose, who'd hired the murder car. Jack was a professional card player, completely bald from childhood typhoid. He'd been a friend of Marcus in Waterbury where, as young men, they ran a baseball team and organised the boxing matches. In 1912 Marcus was a New York Police Court lawyer, while Bald Jack had become a collector for Becker. Nowadays the only Becker listed in the big encyclopedias was Boris, but the policeman had made it to a dictionary of criminals:

BECKER, CHARLES, Murderer and Extortionist (1869-1915), was a corrupt New York police lieutenant who took protection money from illegal gambling casinos in the Tenderloin area of New York. When one gambler, Herman Rosenthal, refused to play ball, Becker ordered his murder. Becker was convicted and executed three years later, along with four young gunmen. He was convicted on the testimony of another gambler, Bald Jack Rose, who was also implicated in the murder but who received immunity for turning state's witness.

Becker was a big man with criminal looks and huge hands. The model for Stephen Crane's brutal policeman in Maggie, A Girl of the Streets, *he was born and brought up in New York and rose through the ranks to become head of Commissioner Rhinelander Waldo's "Strong Arm Squad." This squad had the task of cleaning up the gambling and prostitution then carried on openly in the city. Instead, Becker took bribes from the gamblers, hassling those who would not pay. When he placed a patrolman in Rosenthal's house, Rosenthal, a small-time gambler, swore an affidavit against Becker and the "System", claiming that Becker held a mortgage on his premises and earned seven to ten thousand dollars monthly from gamblers. But the night before he was to testify before the Grand Jury, Rosenthal was shot on Becker's orders by four gunmen outside the Hotel Metropole in New York. It was the first time an automobile was used in a crime.*

District Attorney Whitman, who later became Governor of New York, was determined to clean up the police force and took charge of the case from the start. Despite the first jury's decision, the case was appealed and Becker was re-tried. However, the result was the same. An appeal to Whitman, then Governor, did not bring about a reprieve. Becker was to learn that crime does not pay, as his execution in Sing Sing prison was the most botched in history. It took many jolts of electricity to kill his massive frame. His wife, who always believed in his innocence, put a plaque on the grafting cop's tombstone:

CHARLES BECKER,
*Murdered July 7, 1915
By Governor Whitman*

The execution sounded gruesome. But Bald Jack was

involved. How come he could testify? And what was the evidence against Becker?

A knock on my office door made me jump.

A ratty girl with prominent teeth and long black greasy hair was outside. She wore an eccentric battered straw hat with a Clinton/Gore button on the rim, thick hornrims and unattractive denim cut-offs. "I have to see you, Professor."

"Certainly." I stepped back inside. "Come in and take a seat."

But she stood at the door, gaping in horror.

"What is it?" I was taken aback.

"You're wearing silk!"

I looked down at my maroon shirt. "Eh – yes. It's a bit hot."

"It's hotter for the worms!" She spat the words at me. "They *boil* them to make it!"

"Do they?" Was I being cruel to silk worms?

Outraged, she came in, sat in the armchair and waved a paper at me. It was a drop/ad form. "I need your signature – to register for your Images of Irish Women seminar."

"But I'm afraid it's full. Eh, what's your name?"

"Teri Scales."

"Sorry, Teri, you'll have to find something else." I went to the door again, showing her out.

But she stayed put. "I wrote you a note, Professor."

"I didn't get it, Teri."

"But, Professor – " The girl was about to cry.

I stood my ground. "Fifteen have registered already. The book store hasn't ordered any extra books."

The girl reddened. "But I have all the books. I've read them all! Years ago."

I doubted this, but placated her. "Look, here's my list."

Pushing up her hornrims, she examined it shakily.

"You're a senior?" I asked.

"A graduate assistant, Professor O'Brien. I need your class for my MA."

I was losing patience. "But it's full."

She looked panicky. "Shit! You won't let me in then?"

"No, I'm sorry."

There was silence, then her mood shifted to anger. "You won't get away with this!"

I kept my voice level. "It's a question of space, Teri."

"But I *need* a seminar!"

I was taken aback. How was I to get rid of her? She was now sobbing, her hands on her face.

I stood up firmly. "Look, why don't you go somewhere and collect yourself?"

Her shoulders shook. "No! No!"

"But you can't stay here."

She wiped her eyes roughly. "I'm not leaving! Unless you admit me!"

God, what was I to do?

She sat on for a few minutes, eyeing me defiantly.

I fidgeted with papers on my desk then got a brainwave. "Why don't we both go see the chairperson?"

She looked suspicious. "Now?"

"Yes."

Her glasses glinted. "Shit! I don't believe this. You're blackmailing me!"

She was unbelievable. "I'm – "

"But you won't get away with it!"

Before I could reply, she was out the door.

I closed it and sat down, shaken. I did some breathing exercises. I had to keep calm. She was just some sort of nutter. Who ever heard of boiling silk worms? But did they really?

When I looked up, Marcus was climbing in my office window. He was still in the white suit with a red rose in his buttonhole. Christ, hadn't I enough real problems? I blinked, but he kept coming, pulling a black wooden cat on a string.

I waved the Xerox. "You're dead! Here's your obituary."

He heaved himself into the arm chair. "Don't believe everything you read!"

"But you died in 1935."

He blinked through thick glasses. "How're you getting on with my biography?"

Then I got a brainwave. "I'll have to dig up the dirt."

He looked outraged. "What dirt?"

"Crooked boxing matches. It's right here."

Now he stamped the floor with his stick. "There you go again! Believing everything you read!"

Was I dreaming? I didn't think so. God, this was getting funny. And what was he doing with a toy cat?

He held it up. "I brought you a present."

"Thanks."

"Whatcha laughing at?"

I composed my face. "I wasn't."

Now he pointed his stick at me. "You can criticise me, but it was hard to be Irish then."

"Please don't wave your stick!"

"Hmmph!" He slumped back into the armchair, peering at the Virginia Woolf poster. "Is that one of your suffragettes?"

"In a way, yes."

"She's too skinny."

"She was an abused child."

"A what?"

"Her step-brother raped her."

He peered again at the photograph, shaking his head. "That's too bad." Then he boomed, "Well, how far have you got?"

Christ, he was serious. Perhaps I should play along with him. I checked my notes. "Why did you want the diplomatic job?"

He looked at the ceiling. "To get even."

"You were accused of not paying your bills?" I leafed through the Xeroxes. "A hotel and a tailor."

He stood over me. "You don't have to concern yourself with my debts."

"Oonagh said our grandmother hated New York. That she married you and then refused to live in your country."

"Just a minute! Hold it right there!" He held up the walking stick threateningly. "I won't hear a word against my wife! I'll go right now!"

"Great!" I shouted.

He made for the door, turning at the last minute to see if I'd repented. But I kept reading.

He sat back down. After awhile he ambled over, dragging a foot, and looked over my shoulders. "Well, how far have you got?"

"You acted for Bald Jack Rose?"

He paled, shaken. "I was his lawyer."

"Wasn't he a murderer?"

Marcus stared cross-eyedly then made for the door again. "In this country a person's innocent until proved guilty."

"Tell me about the Rosenthal Case."

But this threw him. "That's not important."

"According to the papers, it was."

"I'm not listening to this!" He stamped his stick again. Then got up and clambered back out the window with all the dignity he could manage.

"Wait," I called.

But he was gone, along with his cat.

This was too much. If I was asleep, I had to wake up. I went out to the Women's Room at the end of the corridor, wet a paper towel there and dabbed my face. I stared in the mirror. I was awake, I knew I was. It was me, Anne O'Brien, a middle-aged woman with a white streak of hair. Why didn't I feel old?

With the towel to my face, I went back to my office. Marcus had been reluctant to talk about the Rosenthal Case. Why had Oonagh never mentioned it? She talked about the Thaw case and the film about Evelyn Nesbit, *The Girl on the Red Velvet Swing*. Perhaps she had mixed up Rosenthal with Thaw. The last two syllables sounded alike.

Why was I so fixated? All my grandparents were dead before my parents met, so maybe it was the lack. There were faded family portraits in our house, all right, but only one of Marcus.

In my teens, some relative had died and more photographs were sent. But my mother always talked of her Depression childhood – how you didn't need a coat in the South and went to the movies to keep cool. We had a book about famous Americans which had a photo of Mark Twain in a white suit. So somehow my imaginary Marcus had got mixed up with him.

Perhaps I was breaking down again? I'd spent a spell in a psychiatric hospital after my father's death. I couldn't feel anything, even parts of my own body. I'd been afraid to look down – I had this idea my feet weren't there. But the doctors just drugged me – there was no therapy. One of them told me it was an obsession, like not walking on pavement cracks. A nurse said I was schizophrenic with a symbiotic dependency on Oonagh. I consulted a dictionary – schizophrenic: a split between the emotions and the intellect. And symbiotic was something to do with two organisms living on each other. But was love a symbiotic relationship? Surely it was just grief – mixed up with adolescence? And Oonagh kept nagging me about college. I tried to live up to her ambitions, but only found peace when I worked. I typed all day in a solicitor's office, and later went to night writing classes where I'd met Fergal.

CHAPTER SIX

* * *

I GOT A LETTER FROM FERGAL:

> *Dear Anne,*
>
> *Hope all is well and that you arrived safely. I'm taking advantage of your absence to paint the upstairs rooms. I started out in your study and on the first day found that ESB bill you lost. And a slice of toast behind your desk. It must have slipped down there, during one of your marathon types last spring. Also I found your pearl brooch – enclosed. And a savings deposit book. You have five hundred pounds stashed there. I take it this is for the rainy day. There were also three of my odd socks under the armchair – the ones you told me the washing machine had digested. Apparently they'd been upchucked.*
>
> *Things are going well with FRU. We have fifty enrolments and the first module is being broadcast in two weeks.*
>
> *Take care of yourself and give my best to the girls,*
> *Love, Fergal.*
> *PS – Send me your phone number.*

He seemed calmer. He was probably glad to have time for his girlfriend. The "girls" were Molly Springstein and

Theodora Jackson. I'd certainly convey his message to them, but I had no intention of sending my number. I didn't want to be bellowed at. The money was just some deal the bank offered last year – if you saved five hundred you got a reduced flight. I'd forgotten about it. Still, it was good he'd found the pearl brooch. It was my mother's only inheritance and lucky. It had survived all our poor years, unlike other heirlooms which were sold or lost. Now it had even escaped our recent burglary, by being behind my desk. The thieves took everything else.

Later that week Molly knocked on my office door. For the last two years we've exercised twice weekly at noon. Sometimes we'd swim afterwards, which was marvellous for my mood and Molly's weight. She was a buxom fifty-five-year-old, an Amazonian, with wild white hair, a big nose and a brown weatherbeaten face made beautiful by integrity.

"Hi! Got everything straightened out?" There was a Bronx twang to her accent.

"In a tick." I gathered my stuff, while she read a noticeboard in the passage.

Molly was curious about everything. Now she was on a high about Clinton's promise of success in the upcoming election. Everyone was, except for the Republicans and Ross Perots. Clinton promised so much after the selfish Reagan and Bush years. Molly had gone up to Philadelphia to hear him, and he'd picked her out in the crowd, admiring her earrings. She said he had Kennedy's Irish eyes and would make a great president. Molly was all for the underdog. People like her are our conscience. So long as they're standing guard, we can relax. She was a New York Jew – in this PC time, I probably shouldn't even have mentioned that.

In America, nobody was anything any more. A porridge

of politeness had oozed over the land and seemed to be spreading world-wide. Except for Somalia, Bosnia etc. – where they had bodies lying in the streets, and people dying like rats in the cellars of cities we'd never heard of.

Everyone should be nicer, and maybe PC would make us. But Molly disagreed. She said it was a puritan smokescreen, that the liberal conscience was being duped, so it could ignore real things like poverty, homelessness and Aids. So long as people were pro-feminist and didn't call blacks, black, but African-American, they weren't being racist or sexist.

Molly was tough and old-fashioned, a potter who converted to the Quakers. A Jewish Quaker is, she said, a contradiction in terms, but she believed passionately in peace and often hums a little ditty:

Roses are reddish.
Violets are bluish,
If it wasn't for Christmas
We'd all be Jewish.

She regularly helped out in a shelter for abused women. That day she wore a T-shirt with YOU CAN'T BEAT WOMEN printed on the front, and HONEY, I'M NOT YOUR VICTIM on the back. What did Theodora think? I wouldn't be caught dead in such a garment, but Molly bounced along, breasts flopping unselfconsciously.

Halfway down the corridor, she asked, "How's the apartment?"

"Grand."

"The cat's not bothering you?"

"No. It ignores me."

As we turned a corner, Teri Scales almost bumped into me. I froze, remembering her silk worms.

She was still wearing the hat with the Clinton/Gore

button and a baggy T-shirt over the hideous cut-offs. But this time she was beaming. "Hi, Professor O'Brien!"

"Hello." I nodded coldly and went on.

But she barred my way, pushing her hornrims up on her nose. "I'm on the way to your office."

"Come back this afternoon."

"I have to see you now."

"Come back at two, Teri. I have office hours then."

"But someone has dropped out of your seminar." Triumphantly she waved a drop/ad form. "I need your signature."

"You're sure there's space?"

"Yeah. I checked at the office."

Did I want such a contentious person in my class? Her behaviour had been insane. But I couldn't prevent her signing on, as far as I knew. Still, I had to be firm. "I'll sign it at two."

"Thank you, Professor. I appreciate it, Professor."

I joined Molly, pulling a face.

"Looks like you're popular, Professor," she joked, looking after Teri.

I laughed nervously. The girl overdid the titles. In America everyone had a title – unlike Ireland where they still had lowly lecturers. But I was nervous of Teri Scales. Did she really need an undergraduate class for an MA?

The corridor was crowded. Everyone was off to lunch, both students and office workers. Sweetmount's administration was mostly carried out in Memorial Hall. It was a domed redbrick Federal-style building which faced one end of Main Street and had once been part of Sandford, a men's College. Sweetmount had joined it in the late sixties. A pity to take in men, but that's progress. Memorial's two wings contained lecture halls, seminar rooms, various departments, the Dean's and staff offices. It had been built by wealthy Sandford alumni to commemorate the dead of two wars. Nowadays co-eds swarmed everywhere. In winter they idled in the hall. But now it was a hot September day, so some played on the grass with frisbees, while others lay half-naked under the trees, reading or lazily entwined. The neighbouring colleges, Bryn Mawr and Swarthmore, probably got the brightest students, but we didn't do badly.

All the way down the steps and along the tree-lined Mall, I contemplated telling Molly about Marcus. Were delusions a result of panic attacks? In the college bookstore I had browsed through a book on Carl Jung, looking for some explanation. Amazingly, Jung believed in angels. These are the spirits of dead ancestors who guide you through life. He thought paranoia was a symptom of schizophrenia, and the paranoid personality was an aspect of oneself which surfaced from the unconscious. Did some aspect of myself see Marcus? It sounded as creepy as believing in angels. No, I couldn't explain Marcus to anyone. Besides, Molly already thought me a hypochondriac.

"You're very absorbed," she said now.

I looked up sharply. "Oh."

"Miles away."

"I was thinking about that girl. She got hysterics in my office because my class is full."

Molly shrugged. "The students are like that."

I felt better. You forgot the intensity of youth. "It's peaceful here – idyllic really."

"Yeah, except we've no water pressure now that the kids are back. In this weather everyone hits the showers together. And look at that guy across the street."

A boy was in army camouflage.

"Why's he dressed like that?"

"There's now an ROTC on campus. To which I object. The college was founded by Quakers."

We crossed Main Street to Sweetmount's original campus. Tall redbrick Federal-style dorms stood on either side of grassy lawns. Everything was picturesque. Only a low wall separated Sweetmount from Oldcastle's eighteenth century brick pavements. Anyone could wander off Main Street onto the leafy campus. This added to the quaintness of the town, which was a bit of ye olde Americana, stranded in the middle of the spaghetti highways of the busy east coast. In olden days it had been a river town, servicing big ships on their way to the Atlantic. Today it attracted Sunday tourists as well as visiting parents. In the evenings, lamps lit the uncurtained windows of the Georgian brick houses. There was an old spired church surrounded by graves going back to the Founding Fathers, half a dozen antique shops, a couple of gourmet restaurants, and an ice cream parlour which sold the best frozen yogurt in the USA. No one ever mentioned the nuclear power station across the river. Or the dioxin dumps on the edge of town.

"I had an awful morning," Molly said suddenly.

"Why?"

"Oh, Theodora got herself worked up. She lost the cheque book, so she thinks she's got Alzheimer's." She sighed wearily.

"Well, it's frustrating to lose things. Did you ring the bank?"

"Yeah, they're taking care of it. By the way, you got my message?"

"What message?"

"Fergal called last night. I left a message on your answering machine."

"What did he want?"

"You're to call him! Also, are you free for dinner Saturday?"

"Oh . . ." I'd made a date with Chuck.

"You can't make it?"

"I'm having dinner with Chuck Matthews, our assistant chairman."

"He's the tennis player?"

"Yes, but I can change it."

"Don't. We'll get you again. It's a movable feast."

But what if Chuck was dating me? What would my friends think then? They didn't know about my troubled marriage. "What did Fergal say?"

"Nothing much. Just checking you'd arrived safely. He hadn't heard from you."

Why had he rung my friends?

Molly searched my face. "You don't seem overjoyed?"

I felt myself redden. "It's just that we – well, he's having some sort of crisis."

"That's funny – he says *you* are." Molly gave me a curious look.

I walked on. What *had* Fergal said? That our marriage was breaking up? That I was having some sort of crack-up? I obviously was. But should I confide in Molly? Then how could I explain Marcus? No, I couldn't lay things on my friends – it was like vomiting all over them.

"I can assure you, *he's* having the crisis," I said calmly.

Molly didn't look convinced. "Well, then you should call him. What's up with him?"

I was flustered. I didn't want to confide my suspicions about Fergal either. I remembered Sarah's diagnosis of men. "He's fifty and getting scared. In Ireland they get scared ten years later than everywhere else."

Molly laughed. "The viropause?"

"I dunno – he's having an affair."

Molly didn't seem shocked. "Are you sure?"

"No, but he sees a girl. And we're not getting on."

Molly was thoughtful. "He's married to a successful woman."

I hid my irritation. "I'm not very highly regarded!"

"But you make money. That's hard on him."

"He wants to waste it all on his free university."

Molly had a habit of getting worked up and she was forceful now. "He told me about that. I admire Fergal. I admire his ideals. Women don't realise how hard it can be for men!"

We walked on in silence. Did she realize how hard it was to write my muck? Recently a critic in the *Sunday Tribune*, Patsy Digby, had attacked me for being "commercial." "Ms O'Brien has again assaulted the popular fiction market with an historical non-novel, *Cromwellian Castles*. Like *Derelict Dunes*, her opus of three years ago, it is pap for the mind. These books satisfy an expatriate American image of Ireland and fail to reflect reality . . ." The critic went on about true literature as an attempt "to imagine the other," and ended up by calling me an embarrassment to Ireland. But I *wasn't* reflecting reality. I was recreating history, entertaining people by providing them with an escape from the ever-rising mortgage interest rates and the electricity bill. If I made money, there was nothing wrong with that. The reviewer didn't deign to mention that *Derelict Dunes* was on the American best seller list for 1988, and had been the only Irish book on the British list of top-selling paperbacks for that year. It had sold nearly five hundred thousand copies and had had a gross yield of nearly one and a half million. Of course, I'd only got twelve per cent royalties. But it was enough to keep us for a few years.

Fergal joked about money and "what's yours is mine," etc, so I'd never thought of it as being hard on him. But why was Molly on his side? She sometimes sounded more like a conventional faculty wife than a feminist. Surely a feminist should take the woman's side? She and Theodora were outspoken, but it was just their style. They were sixties types, mellowed but basically unchanged by middle-age. They hadn't sacrificed their principles or their sweetness about life. They were the sort of people who joined student fasts for places like Ethiopia. Molly's unemployed ex-husband lived on and off in their attic. It was typical of their generosity. They were a mixture of sophistication and simplicity really – into the environment in a big way. They organised all the recycling in the community, collecting the lot in their old van – glass, plastic, beer cans and paper. They even re-used envelopes, which made me feel guilty. The computer was meant to save paper, but spewed it out in reams. How many trees had I gobbled up? Although that hadn't been a problem lately.

"Are you still recycling?" I turned cheerfully to her. Then I saw him.

Marcus – who else?

He was white-suited again and stared with that hang-dog expression from the other side of the street. Christ, he was carrying some empty wine bottles in a wire shopping basket. He lifted his straw hat gallantly.

Don't look, I told myself. Close your eyes and he'll go away.

"Yes, we're asking people to come to us," Molly was saying.

"Eh, what?" I kept my eyes on Molly.

"You were asking about recycling?"

"Ah!"

She gave me a funny look.

I'd lost my train of thought. "Eh – there are some bottles in the apartment."

"Good! Drop them over. And I'll need help Monday. We're painting the Shelter."

"Monday's out, sorry. I'm reading for class."

"You can't read on Sunday?"

I shook my head. "I'll be preparing then too."

As Molly chatted on about her plans for involving others in the Shelter, I glanced back across the street. Now Marcus was hiding behind a tree. He was pointing to his basket of bottles. This was getting worse.

"I'm trying to get people involved . . ." Molly was now staring. "You're very pale."

I couldn't speak.

"You OK?"

"I – just feel, eh, weak."

"Are you up to jumping around?"

I nodded. "I'll be OK in a minute."

I didn't dare look back across the street. I once saw a TV horror movie, where a woman was followed by a ghostly old man. Why was it happening to me?

"Is Fergal coming over?" Molly asked.

"Eh . . . what?"

"You're on another planet!" She was mildy irritated. "Is Fergal coming for Thanksgiving?"

"I'm not sure."

Molly walked on without comment.

Fergal usually came halfway through the semester. But this time, we hadn't discussed it.

At the gym door we showed ID's. I glanced back briefly through the glass doors. Marcus was gone. In future I'd ignore him. That would zap him out.

"What are you working on these days?" Molly asked as we walked down a long corridor with squash courts on one side.

I looked back again . . . still, no one.

"Are you writing anything new?" she repeated, puzzled.

"Writing? Oh, no."

"You're not working on another novel?"

"No."

She searched my face. "Well, that's a surprise."

The corridor was still empty. "I seem to have lost it."

"What do you mean?"

"Lost – whatever ability I had."

Molly gave me another funny look.

The fitness room was full of weights and the most complex machines for strengthening and stretching muscles. They looked like medieval torture devices, but we'd become adept at using them. We signed in and made for the warm-up bar at the end of the room.

Molly stretched her arms, then her legs. Although heavy, she moved lithely. "How can you lose your ability?"

I touched my toes. "It happens."

"But you lose things like a passport! Surely a talent is different?"

I kept my head down. "I haven't written a word in months."

"Fergal mentioned you weren't sleeping. And you're thinner. Are you eating properly?"

"Of course! I didn't sleep before the flight, but I'm fine now." What right had he to talk about me?

"You should get a check-up while you're here. The college pays for an annual."

I did some sit-ups. "I got some vitamins."

"Well, you could be rundown."

"No, it's burn-out."

Molly stretched her other leg on the bar. "Don't tell Theodora. She's fighting a case with a guy who's suing the college. Claims unfair dismissal. He's got several shrinks to certify this burn-out condition."

"It's a case of publish or perish?"

"No, laziness. The guy plays chess all the time."

I plonked onto the floor mat and began push-ups. Why couldn't Molly take my side? Why was she being so judgemental about the chess player? Theodora had been writing a book herself, for the last ten years – on eating disorders. "Well, burn-out can happen."

Molly picked up a small weight, flexing her wrist. "Theodora runs a tight ship. Has to."

"It can't be easy being a woman Dean."

She lifted another weight. "A woman's OK. A dyke's the tricky thing!"

I had to laugh. Americans are so open. You'd never hear an Irish person talking like that. We're all so repressed. But then so were most people at Sweetmount. Still, you couldn't generalise. Molly and Theodora were an incongruity in a college which was a hive of well-heeled conservatism. For years the administration didn't know the truth about their relationship. And, by the time they did, it was too late. Theodora had been a stuffy bluestocking until their meeting, Molly always said, and a sexual zombie; while Molly herself had been unhappily married. Now Theodora had come out of the closet, and Molly, who was bi-sexual, had chosen to live with her. "You think lesbianism's something different," she once told me. "But it's just another way of life."

We did our usual ten minutes on the exercise bike, then fifteen on the rowing machine.

"You've given up writing then?" Molly went on.

"I – I might try a biography."

"Well, that sells. Who'd you write about?"

"My grandfather," I heard myself say. "I've already started the research. He was Irish-American."

"There's a market in Irish-America. Was he well-known?"

"Not really. But my New York cousin's been nagging me."

I told her about Marcus, the Irish emigrant making good, etc. "Have you heard of the Rosenthal case?"

Molly looked interested. "The Rosenberg case?"

"No, Rosenthal. It was in 1912. A cop was executed. A man called Bald Jack Rose was involved."

"Wow, what a name! Is it anything to do with the Jack Rose cocktail?

"Is there a cocktail?"

"Yes, it's like a Manhattan."

"My grandfather was his lawyer – I don't know much else about Bald Jack Rose."

"Why not send an author's query to the New York Times book section? Anyone who knew Bald Jack Rose, please contact . . ."

"There'd be no one left alive."

"Might be!"

"Afterwards he was a diplomat in the Caribbean."

"Bald Jack?"

"No, my grandfather." I hesitated. "It was some sort of payoff. He may have compromised himself."

"He couldn't have done much for the Caribbean!"

I laughed. "He made a mess of it. He wasn't suitable – temperamentally."

Afterwards we had our swim. We changed in the women's locker room and went into the chlorine-reeking chamber. The college pool was competition size and marked out in swimming lanes. The water a cold blue. The other lunchtime swimmers had gathered as usual at one end, waiting for a class to finish, while at the other, students hauled themselves out of the water, hovering round the instructor.

Molly looked statuesque in her togs. She chatted to another woman while I dipped my toe cautiously. When the students were out, Molly, who didn't like lane swimming, jumped into the diving pool. The lunchtime swimmers now flopped and splashed into the different lanes of the bigger pool. As they raced ahead, I hugged the side-lane, swimming slowly under the nose of the girl lifeguard.

At the deep spot in the middle, I saw Marcus.

He came in through the men's door, hobbled to my side of the pool, and stared at me.

Jesus.

"Put your head down!" he roared.

I swam on.

He stamped his foot. "No! You have to put your head in the water!"

Then he was stepping into the pool.

I lost my breath, and was sucked under.

I came up, but sank again.

Then there was a splash, and I was pulled out by the guard.

As I sat by side of the pool, Molly hurried over. "What happened?"

The girl shrugged. "She went under."

"I lost my breath!" I gasped, coughing.

Molly was puzzled. "You OK?"

"Yes . . ."

"You're sure?"

I was shaken, but nodded vigorously – Marcus had gone.

She came with me to the locker room, where we showered and dressed. Then we made our way back through the town's paved streets to Molly's house.

All the way there, I kept looking back – no Marcus.

CHAPTER SEVEN

***

ALTHOUGH I WAS ALONE AND FREE OF COOKING, I HATED BELLA
Vista.

Maybe it was perversity. Oh, the apartment was
comfortable. And there were trees and flowers in the
grounds, but basically the place was a cemetery. Although
cars were parked outside, you hardly ever saw anyone, or
heard anything. I did hear screaming once, and another time
rock music, but that was about all in four months.
Sometimes people walked their dogs after dark. I nodded to
them while exercising the blasted cat. They nodded back
but, on the whole, I felt stranded. Molly invited me to dinner
and events on campus, but there was still time to get
through alone, especially at weekends.

At the beginning of the semester, I spent Friday and
Saturday afternoon by the pool. It was shaded by trees and
had a proper diving board. If you sat under the big
umbrellas, it was a good place for reading and class
preparation. And I could swim when it got too hot. You saw
people out there – the bronzed girl lifeguard; and some
Bella Vista inmates: single, yuppie types who lay on
recliners, covered in sun cream, and never gave you the
time of day. Also older, retired people, who entertained their
grandchildren in the pool. On the whole the retirees were

frosty, and one hatchet-faced woman kept nagging me about the proper identification button.

But there were exceptions: a raucous black family who splashed and ducked each other, while noisily hailing everyone. And Frances. She was a jaunty, older woman who always wore purple – shorts, baseball cap, even purple Nikes. And purple-red lipstick smeared on like Bette Davis. In fact, she looked like Bette Davis – she had the same pencilled eyebrows and rouged cheeks. She'd obviousy been treated for cancer, because, under the cap, which was always on back-to-front, she was completely bald. She sat by the pool all day with a baby stroller. At first I thought there was a real baby in it, then I discovered it was a *doll* – one of those rubber ones. I decided she was minding it for a grandchild who was probably splashing loudly in the pool. But none of them belonged to her. No, the doll was hers. She'd sit for hours, rocking it, or chatting to it, or occasionally changing its diaper, or carrying it over to the toddlers' pool for a dip.

I watched, intrigued. One day Frances beckoned me to share her umbrella.

I went over. "I'm Anne O'Brien."

"I'm Frances. And this is little Frances." She cradled the doll, cooing over it, "Sorry, sweetheart, is the sun in your eyes? It is?" Then carefully, lovingly, she laid the doll, also dressed in purple, on its back in the stroller. "Is that better?"

I was curious. "You're both wearing purple? For feminism?"

"Just my favourite colour, hon." She hugged her baby. "We go everywhere together. Down to Roy Rogers for breakfast. Then we take the bus into Philly and walk around where it's cool."

"It's cool here, under your umbrella."

"Yes, but I'm a a prisoner here."

"You don't like Bella Vista?"

She shook her head vigorously. Then went on, "I like shops and people. Life. There's no life here."

"No. You like Philadelphia?"

Her eyes lit up. "Yeah, sometimes we go to the Zoo. Little Frances loves the zoo. Don't you sweetheart?" Dotingly, she rocked the stroller.

It was quite a haul to Philadelphia, so Frances must have spent a while travelling. I had no children. Would I end up like her, lonely and living in fantasy? Already I had an imaginary grandfather. Was it so different from an imaginary baby?

On Labour Day, Frances invited me to a pool picnic. At first I thought it was some Bella Vista residents' affair and I'd have to get tickets, or bring something. But she said, "You don't need tickets, hon, just come eat!"

The only other guests were the two girl lifeguards. Hatchet-face sat apart with a pudgy, spoilt-looking grandson and glared at me as I sat down. There was no sign of Little Frances. The food was ham and cheese rolls, with coke to drink. And the conversation was jolly, the girls teased Frances about the cougars in the zoo. Hatchet-face came over at one point, saying her grandson wanted a sandwich.

"Of course, hon," Frances said happily, "help yourself."

The woman made a ham and cheese roll and took it to the boy. He took one bite and turned up his nose. So hatchet-face brought it back, half-eaten, saying he didn't want it. I had never seen anything quite like the rudeness. I wasn't hungry but I had another cheese roll for solidarity.

Over the weeks, Frances and I became more friendly and, as September progressed, were the only takers for the pool. I often came home in the afternoons to join her, as she sang lullabys to Little Frances. Gradually she told me about her life. Her parents had been German immigrants who had come over after the First World War and didn't speak a word of English. When young, she had worked in a band in New York. During her marriage, she had owned a Cadillac. She had a daughter who was a teacher, or "something like that," but didn't see her much now. She lived alone with Little Frances, and the two of them stayed up all night, watching TV, mainly cartoons. The doll had even been in hospital with her. It was a salutary lesson about how the old are treated.

Then I got another letter from Fergal.

Dear Anne,

As I haven't heard a squeak from you, I take it you're still pissed off. Forgive my outburst the day before you left. I didn't mean it. You know I love and miss your awful cooking. Over the years, I've developed a taste for charred sausages and burnt hamburgers. I'm sure some future research will prove the benefits of carbon. So we're ahead of the posse.

The first FRU lecture was broadcast – an introduction to Greek Philosophy. Believe it or not we got a write-up in The Irish Times.

Write to your bereft husband. Fergal.

Hmm. He was very conciliatory. But men were obsessed with food. It'd do him good to cook for himself. Was I such a bad wife? Fergal always twitted me about my awful housekeeping, but he seemed to have calmed down about America. Perhaps I was a bad cook? I'd tried to make marmalade last year which all went bad. I was always burning myself – which drove him crazy. My mind wanders.

I once brought *Pickwick Papers* to a launderette and absentmindedly put it in with the clothes. I still have the water-stained copy.

Fergal was a big Kerryman and loved nothing better than an evening in the local. Whereas I hated it – the smoke got to my chest. Was that the cause of our drift apart? Not doing enough together? What had happened to us? It was sixteen years since we met in one of his classes – "Writing for Pleasure" – in the Dublin Institute of Adult Education. Then I'd wanted to get into journalism, imagined myself on the staff of the *Times*. But it hadn't worked out like that.

Oh, I fell for Fergal, not his looks, particularly. He was already grey when we met. His hair stood up like wire, contrasting with his Irish, raspberry-red complexion. No, his humour attracted me – he had a wonderful laugh. And the way he handled the class. We were a mixed bunch – housewives, and young office workers like me who yearned for something else.

Something different from the daily grind. Once at the end of class, we got chatting.

"I'm only doing this because they're stuck," he said. "The Director's a pal. But if I don't get paid, they can't pressurise me to do it again."

Fergal was always wonderfully unmaterialistic.

Then he said, "Fancy a pint?"

I nearly fell over. He was a priest.

He laughed heartily. "Don't worry, I don't bite!"

We went to a little hotel – I forget the name – in that street leading into Mountjoy Square. He thought it'd be anonymous. But, of course, someone recognised him. They knew what you had for breakfast in Dublin.

After that we drove out to a Dun Laoghaire hotel. He wore a scarf over his collar as we sat over our beer – that's what I remember about Fergal, sitting over beer. But Vatican II was still in the air, and clerics were jumping ship in droves.

"I'll marry you in six months," he said one night.

No question of proposing, just a flat statement.

And he did. I was thirty-one and he was thirty-six.

The years of our early marriage were so happy. Fergal had various jobs in journalism and taught it in Rathmines Tech. We'd started out in a little terraced house in Portobello just down the road from the school. It had only two bedrooms but there was a lovely little patio where we ate *al fresco* in the summer evenings. Fergal joined the NUJ (National Union of Journalists) and found work in the *Herald*. I went to Trinity and got an MA. I had him to thank for that. Then I started writing at night. My first novel sold, so I got a big advance for the second. Writing seemed easier then. I typed all day, then every evening about five, went shopping for the dinner. Fergal came home about eight or nine and we shared a bottle of wine. Before that I'd never had much to drink. Because of Oonagh's bout with alcoholism, I'd been afraid of it. But wine was so pleasant. It helped me communicate with Fergal, shed my inhibitions. But that was another life now. Why did things have to change? I just couldn't put up with his drinking. And now his philandering.

Still, he'd have some sensible opinion about Marcus. It had really scared me seeing him in the street. What if he came to my class? I always went in armed with a large black coffee to keep me alert. Should I see someone? A few months back I'd tried a therapist for my writing block but quit, thinking it ludicrous, paying for psychobabble. But this therapist had suggested a workshop in the Graf Method – a breathing technique to get in touch with the subconscious. It was meant to help creativity. But I didn't go.

The workshop was in Grangegorman, Dublin's oldest psychiatric hospital, a fact which brought the usual cackles from Fergal.

I still hadn't returned his call. Why did he always jeer me? My whole bloody life was spent concealing things from him – self-help books, articles on cholesterol, Royal Jelly, fish oil tablets.

According to him, I was cracked. I sometimes imagined specks were bugs. Or that birds were rats. But the delusion was always gone when I looked again. My notion that birds were malevolent probably came from that Hitchcock movie. There were some movies I'd pay to have deleted from my brain – *Psycho* for starters.

Was Marcus an extension of the bird thing?

I decided to try another therapist. I was afraid to ask anyone at Sweetmount to recommend one, so looked up the Philadelphia Yellow Pages. There were several columns of experts offering counselling. I didn't know whom to pick. But then, the name Mike Kelly caught my attention.

EFFECTIVE TREATMENT FOR DEPRESSION, PANIC, STRESS, AND MOST SEXUAL PROBLEMS.

He must be Irish, or of Irish extraction, which might be a help. He was in the west Philadelphia area, near Pennsylvania University. Maybe I needed to talk to someone? So I rang for an appointment, explaining that I was having disturbing experiences, and was fitted in the next day. The fee was $90.

Mike Kelly turned out to be a burly, six-foot black man. His hair was cut in an Afro style and he wore a gold earring and trendy gold aviator glasses. Without ceremony, he pointed me to a couch in front of his desk. He sat in a swivel chair behind it.

I waited for him to say something, like what's bothering you? But he just gazed at me quizzically.

"Did the receptionist tell you about my experiences?" I began awkwardly.

Silently he shook his head.

"Well, that's why I'm here. I've started having these – sort of – hallucinations. I mean, I seem to be awake, but I'm dreaming. An old man appears constantly. I think he's my grandfather."

Mike Kelly swivelled his chair round and gazed dreamily out the window, his back almost to me.

"Have you ever heard of that?" I asked. "People from the past appearing?"

He continued to gaze outside.

I tried again. "It's not very normal, is it?"

No answer.

"Dr Kelly – ?"

At that he swivelled round, giving me a puzzled but benevolent look. "It's Mike, Anne."

"Eh – Mike. Could you tell me if these – eh, awake-dreams are normal?"

He had eyes like a kind horse. "What's *normal*, Anne?"

My tic started, dammit. "I don't know. I'd just like to know if they're common . . . if anyone else has them?"

He kept staring.

"In your experience?"

"What do *you* think, Anne?"

"Eh, I know people have vivid dreams, but – "

"Why don't you describe one of yours."

So I told him about that terrifying night at Ogie's. Then about the time in the office. "He keeps asking me to write his biography."

Mike Kelly just nodded concernedly. Then looked back outside.

There was another silence.

God, it was like communicating with a blank wall. My words seemed to bounce back.

I tried again. "Why should he pick on me?"

He remained placid. "What do *you* think, Anne?"

"I don't know."

"You've no idea?"

"No."

Again, silence. Dammit, I was paying for an opinion. Was he going to say nothing. For $90?

Then I started babbling, "I think it might be something to do with my mother. I really loved my mother. Then I found out about her childhood. I think she was abused. I'm not sure. Anyway, she was unhappy."

He looked out at the street.

I felt desperate. "Could it be something to do with that?"

There was another long silence.

I broke it. "Do you think I'm obsessed?"

"I don't know, Anne."

"You've no opinion?"

"No. What do *you* think?"

The back of my neck was sweaty. I hated talking about myself, especially to a stranger. It was like confession, except a priest would say something. And for free. This man was offering nothing.

"Look, I want to know if I'm crazy?"

He frowned. "Did I say that?"

"No, that's just it, you've said *nothing*."

He sighed wearily. "But I don't offer opinions."

"Never?"

He shook his head.

"You won't advise me at all?"

"I can't do that, Anne."

Then the time was up. He stood up and opened the door, saying, "Make another appointment at the desk, Anne."

Ha!

CHAPTER EIGHT

* * *

As I was going up the stair,
I met a man who wasn't there.
He wasn't there again today.
I wish, I wish, he'd stay away.

As children we prayed for "the communion of saints, the forgiveness of sins, the resurrection of the body and life everlasting. Amen." So ghosts weren't that strange. No stranger than living for eternity.

But why was Marcus haunting me?

I'd got no answers from Mike Kelly. But he was a Freudian. A Jungian might have had more sympathy. But I didn't want a repeat experience, so I went back to the books.

Jungians believe that the past, even the distant past, lives on in our dreams. My experiences were dreamlike. On a few occasions I'd had them before sleep. No one knew how long a dream lasted. Perhaps at other times I'd nodded off briefly. Dreams are also hallucinations. Figures who appear are archetypal, and details are symbols. In my reading, I found references to frogs, snakes, and cockroaches, but nothing about cats. Marcus's white suit must be significant. His cigar was obviously phallic. And the red rose stood for love. But what about the cats?

"Death is the undiscovered country from whose bourne

no traveller returns." Yet – Christ and Parnell had been seen after death. Kennedy had also been spotted in a wheelchair. All were archetypal figures. As was Marcus. Hamlet's father had ordered him to murder. Jung also said that some people are destined in their own lives to complete tasks which have been left undone by an ancestor. Was there something in the past which needed to be put right? Something to do with the Rosenthal case? If I found out more about it, Marcus might leave me alone.

As Molly suggested, I sent an author's request to the *NY Times Book Review*, and began researching in the college library. Although it was only 1912, the case was described as "The Crime of the Century". Yet nowadays it wasn't in any of the major encyclopedias.

From our perspective the big event in 1912 was the Titanic sinking in April. In the same year, Captain Scott perished on the way back from the South Pole. And Hiram Bigham, a junketing American politician, accidentally stumbled on a lost city in Peru. President Taft, a Republican, was the incumbent. But it was election year and socialist Eugene Debs campaigned from prison. Theodore Roosevelt split the Republican vote and, when shot campaigning, finished his speech with a bullet in him. Then an ex-Princeton professor and reforming governor of New Jersey, Woodrow Wilson, declared himself a candidate and won. I noted other details – in 1912 only three states allowed women to vote. And the same year L L Bean started his mail order service to protest the lack of proper waterproof boots. The catalogues still came in the mail.

Meanwhile I had classes.

I was no wonderful teacher as Chuck claimed but desperately nervous – yet OK once started. Except for Teri Scales, the obnoxious girl who had twisted my arm to get in, the students were quiet enough, but they'd liven up later. It was a case of getting to know one another. For the literature seminar I'd talked about Irish writers in the eighteenth century and how unusual Maria Edgeworth was in being a successful woman. But what had they made of *Castle Rackrent*? It might be remote to them. Anyhow, I'd see.

Some of the students had Irish names: Riordan, Kelly, Lynch. They looked Irish too – heirs of the immigrants I'd been thinking so much about lately. Only two males in a class of fifteen. I'd prefer women only, but there was nothing I could do about that. There were five men in the writing class, to ten women. Just as well, otherwise they'd take over. Men always did. Two of the women were older – Continuing Education students, from which the college derived a good whack of income. They were wives of rich men, returning to "school" now that their children were gone. I felt a rapport with them. The only trouble was they thought that writing was easy.

Everyone did. Even Oonagh, my mother. My first novel had bought our Dalkey house. But the money came too late for her. She'd only read the typescript. Afterwards she gave back the fat Xerox box without comment. We'd been chatting in the kitchen, waiting for the kettle to boil.

She shook it. "You have to humour it!"

Oonagh was so funny. Why were we always at odds? We just never got on since my adolescence. Was it my fault?

I pinned her down. "Well, you didn't like the novel?"

"The characters were insipid."

I said nothing.

Oonagh saw to the tea. "You said you were writing about your childhood."

"I changed my mind."

There was another silence.

"You should use your childhood, Annie. Write about what you know."

"But you mightn't like that."

"A writer's capital is her childhood." She looked at me sadly. "I gave you your childhood."

That was true – a mixture of gaiety and grief. But it wasn't all her fault. Our father had died, so we moved all the time.

But insipid characters?

Write about what you know?

What does anyone know? I only knew we'd disappointed each other. People don't realise how hard writing is. They think it's fun, not grinding, lonely work. A prison sentence. I didn't protest, although I'd hoped for her approval. The truth is too painful to write about. Besides, people pay more for junk.

And now my students expected the world. Oh, you could learn technique all right. But who'd want to? Somewhere I'd read that, of all the occupations, people most wanted to be novelists. Why not stockbrokers or deep-sea divers? They didn't know what it involved. Still, it was my job to teach the craft. After a few introductory remarks about structure, I assigned the next session's homework. It was very basic – exercises in plot, descriptive writing, and dialogue which were discussed in class for the first few weeks. By degrees I saw people individually, helping them get started. Then the classes were taken up with their individual stories. They each had to read their effort in class and it was then discussed. They had to write at least two for a pass grade. Some people found this difficult, but I usually got everyone through. Writing's a craft, I told them, you have to stick with it. The art of writing is rewriting.

But then something else happened. Here I was, pursued by a ghost. And, to compound my difficulties, I'd jumped from the frying pan into the fire – from Fergal to Chuck. I fell for him completely. How could I complicate life? Was I just terrified of being alone? Or flattered? He was wirily handsome and, as I said, a Jack Nicholson look-alike. Also there was something about his muscular tennis-player's wrists which got me. He reminded me of Humphrey Bogart in a trenchcoat. Maybe all our fantasies are clichéd and that's the appeal of movies – they tap a sort of collective unconscious. Did I yearn for curling blue cigarette smoke and piano playing? I'd probably choke in a Casablanca bar. I hated cigarettes. Although I didn't mind Chuck's. After all I lived with a pipe smoker.

Our first date was to the Crabshack for dinner. It's on Main Street and usually patronised by visiting parents. Their buffet salads are good, but that's about all. I forget what we had, but remember sitting over coffee, talking about his wife. It was the usual spiel – she doesn't understand me.

"Zelda's from Georgia." He laughed shortly. "A southern belle. We married in college."

"People change," I said.

He shook his head. "They sure do."

"Any kids?"

"A boy, Billy – he's nine. What about you?"

"We couldn't."

"Oh, you had a problem?"

"No, it was Fergal. But it didn't matter to me."

"Why not?"

"I dunno." Then I heard myself say, "Maybe I couldn't love anyone."

"I don't believe that."

"I was emotionally worn out before we ever met." I didn't tell him about the years of living with Oonagh, worrying about her when she disappeared.

"We'll have to revive you." He touched my wrist and a shiver shot up my arm. I swear it was Cupid's dart. I was hooked.

I told him about Fergal's irresponsible schemes. How he tilted at windmills and was a sucker for every stray cat. And Chuck told me more about Zelda. She was a wonderful homemaker, but had taken to the bottle. Lately she had "found herself" through the Women's Movement and Alcoholics Anonymous, but had then left him. At first he'd been shocked, but now their separation was by mutual consent, and they shared custody of their son.

We had liqueurs – always dangerous – and then someone in the restaurant objected to his smoking. He refused to put his cigarette out although it was a No Smoking area. The person kept objecting, and Chuck went white with anger. He had a quick temper, but I didn't think more about it.

So we went back to my apartment. We sat on the balcony over more brandies – I found a bottle in the landord's cabinet. And there were the right glasses – Americans are well equipped. Alcohol wasn't good for me, yet I went on drinking, intoxicated by the company and the warm sweet night.

I remember Chuck swirling his brandy in the glass and looking at me distractedly. "Writing anything these days?"

I told him about researching Marcus. "I've dried up on novels."

His brown eyes glinted. "Do you research a novel?"

"Sure, I dig around in the library. Read histories, newspapers, that sort of thing. But this actually happened." I told him a bit about the Rosenthal Case.

"Was William K Jerome the DA?"

"No, Charles Whitman. A man with political ambitions."

"Whitman got a mention in Doctorow's *Ragtime*. There were gunmen with colorful names – Gypo something."

"Gyp the Blood." Chuck's field was modern American literature, so I mentioned another fact. "Stephen Crane used Becker as a model for the brutal policeman in *Maggie, A Girl of the Streets*."

Chuck frowned. He had an interesting wrinkle between his eyes when puzzled. "But *Maggie* was published long before 1912."

"It was in the crime encyclopedia."

"Hmm. I'll check it out."

There was a silence as Chuck looked into his glass. "Ever have affairs when you're researching?"

I laughed. "No."

"Then how can you write about love?"

Next thing his arm was around me.

I didn't pull away.

"You're so beautiful," he whispered.

"What?" I laughed aloud. Maybe that was it – flattery. Fergal never said things like that. To him I was skinny.

"May I?" Chuck kissed me before I could refuse.

Who said alcohol increased the desires, but inhibited the performance? In this case it was the golden oil, the magic lubricant. I responded, of course, without thinking of Aids, pregnancy, anything – except getting my clothes off. Suddenly we were undressed and making love on the balcony mat.

How was that for folly?

Afterwards, Chuck pulled on his pants and lit a cigarette. "I feel like a new man."

The night air was damp, so I started to dress, mumbling, "We've been hasty."

Chuck laughed. "I'm clean, in case you're worried."

"Clean?"

"I've been tested – for HIV. Syphilis. Gonorrhoea. Athlete's Foot – you name it."

"Well, eh, no, I'm not worried. I don't have it – them – either."

We sat there, looking at each other awkwardly. How did it happen? And what were we to do now?

Then the phone rang.

Pulling my sweater on, I got the receiver. "Hello?"

"Anne?" A deep Kerry accent.

Fergal.

There were the usual trans-Atlantic time lag pips which made us speak together.

"Hello," I said again.

Then from a distance. "Sorry, Anne. Have I woken you up?"

My husband – at a time like this. "No, I wasn't in bed."

"What time is it there?"

"About nine."

"How're things going?"

"Fine."

"You're sleeping better?"

"Yes," I lied.

"Did you get my letters?"

"Yes, thanks."

"I rang Molly."

"Sorry, I tried to get back to you," I lied again.

"The flight was OK?"

"Yeah." It seemed in the distant past now.

"How're the classes going?"

"Not too bad. Well."

"Listen, I'm sorry about – "

"Oh, forget it."

"No, hear me out. I'm sorry for being such a shit."

I said nothing.

"I shouldn't have said that. You know, I didn't mean it."

Did I?

"Anne, are you there?"

God, why couldn't he be consistent – go, if he were going?

"Anne?"

"Yes?"

"Let's call a truce. You keep on the American job, and I'll come over at mid-term as usual."

What about that girl? Or had she dumped him?

"Anne?"

Chuck hovered in the background. "Who's that?"

I cupped the receiver, mouthing, "My husband."

"Anne, is someone there?" Fergal sounded desperate.

"No!"

"Pax then?"

"Let's talk another time."

"You said it was only nine!"

"Yes, but I'm tired."

Chuck came over with my glass, saying at the top of his voice, "I've topped you up."

"Anne, there's someone there."

"No!"

Click. The line went dead.

He'd hung up on me.

Fergal would know what to do about Marcus. But he didn't ring back. And neither did I. I suppose I should have, but I dread rows. It was ostrich-like, but there you are. Everytime the phone went, I thought it was him. But it never was.

About a week later I got a padded envelope in the mail. It was full of household dust, which immediately made me sneeze. Was it a joke? I didn't think so. Fergal knew I was having an affair. But so was he. I thought of mailing the dust back with my wedding ring inside, but didn't. Instead I put him out of my mind and concentrated on work and enjoying life.

Middle-class Americans don't realise what an idyllic life they lead. By now the Irish would be in coats, but here you could wear shorts till November. They had closed the pool, so Frances, whom I continued to see, came to my apartment for an *aperitif.* She didn't drink, so had diet coke or iced tea, while I had champagne or explored the different wines. One could afford to live in America – one was allowed to, not taxed out of existence like the Irish.

I'd become fond of Frances, and gave her a key in case I was late home. I dreaded solitude. Marcus might appear at any moment.

I was always hearing things.

One day there were noises. But it was only the cat on the balcony. It crept in, miaowing.

"Hungry again?" I asked.

BC padded placidly into the corner and sat down in the middle of its tail.

"OK, fussbudget." I put out some food – there was a cupboard full of the special dry food and two shelves of smoked salmon snacks. It would only eat one brand.

BC sniffed it fussily.

At first I'd been dismayed that BC went with the apartment. Its litter bin was on the balcony and at first this upset me, but it wasn't too noticeable. Cats have personalities – like people, there were good and bad. BC was self-absorbed and left you alone.

Another day I heard whistling.

Christ, who was it?

Was it Chuck? Or had someone else got in?

It was low whistling – coming from my bedroom.

I froze. No, don't be ridiculous, I told myself – GO SEE WHO IT IS.

I crept up the hall.

Oh God. Should I call out the window?

Grabbing a vase, I waited behind the door.

The whistling kept up.

I tiptoed into my bedroom.

This time it was a radio clock. The digital face was lit.

Whew. It had come on somehow. I went over and pulled the plug.

Idiot.

CHAPTER NINE

***

BELIEVE IT OR NOT, THAT CRAZY IRISH BOY FROM THE PLANE PHONED the English Department, asking for my number. Maybe it was the season for the middle-aged? Anyway I had told Sarah about him, and she got rid of him. She was good at that.

But one morning on my way into the Department, she waved a yellow WHILE YOU WERE OUT note. "Message for you, Anne!"

I thought it was the boy again, or Fergal, but scrawled on it were the words – *Marcus O'Neill called. Arriving Philadelphia 4.35. Flight number 1750.*

I stared at it in dismay.

This Marcus was my Cousin Bud – a Paul Newman double, only better-looking. He was like someone sent up from central casting for a lead in a soap opera. But, arriving Philadelphia? And today? Did that mean he was staying with me? There'd been no invitation. And how the hell did he know I was here?

I turned to Sarah. "When did he call?"

"About an hour ago. Long distance."

He was last heard of in Las Vegas. There was no way of getting in touch with him, of telling him not to come. He'd probably already set out. "Did he say anything else?"

Sarah stared at her monitor. "He wants you to meet the flight."

"But I have class."

She went on with her work, shrugging. "There's a good shuttle service."

I collected some papers and went downstairs. A visit from Cousin Bud was something to concentrate the mind. His father, my mother's brother, had died a few years ago. He was an old man in pyjamas and dressing-gown who chain-smoked in a veterans' hospital. He'd had a lobotomy, a fashionable cure for mental illness in the forties. Did he really need it? As a child I'd seen a photo of him in a military academy uniform and thought he was hurt in World War 2. But he never fought. He spent most of his life in a Brooklyn Vets hospital.

Why did I never go see him? Ogie used to bring him cigarettes. But I'd seen *One Flew Over the Cuckoo's Nest* and feared meeting someone with half a brain. Now it was too late. Our family was always doomed.

And why couldn't I get on with Oonagh? Why was there so much anger between us? And now I couldn't get used to her being gone. If death could happen, anything could. It had seemed so preposterous when she died. Just ludicrous. She was too strong a character. But she'd gone to sleep one night and never woken up. "To cease upon the midnight with no pain." It was an ideal death but, at the time, I'd held on to sanity by a thread. I remember reading the death columns, thinking that every family listed was suffering the same loss. It was a daily occurrence, all around you. But you lived as if it would never happen, as if you could somehow survive life. As if it weren't a tragedy.

It was too late for my mother and uncle. But I could be kind to Bud, a waif of the storm. He was my schoolgirl pinup. I stuck snaps of him, baby-faced in army paratrooper's gear, on the inside lid of my desk in boarding school. Jumping out of airplanes seemed romantic then. At the Bay of Pigs he was put on alert, and sat in a plane ready to take off for Cuba. But the invasion was called off. He said he was scared shitless and only volunteered for the army to get out of reform school. He had been married twice before he was twenty-one. The first wife was a cheerleader, the second a professional pool player who found Jesus. He ran away from her, drifting round the country, in and out of jobs. He'd been a weightlifter and a male model. A beach lifeguard and beachcomber. Finally he ended up in Las Vegas as a card dealer – Ogie and I stayed with him that fateful summer of '69. With his friend, Sonny, I witnessed his third marriage to an unemployed country and western star. Afterwards we brunched in the Desert Inn where Bud worked on the crap tables. For the honeymoon night Ogie and I moved into Sonny's apartment. In the closet we discovered rows of fur coats. They looked hot – in the criminal sense.

What would I do with Bud now?

Where would I hide Chuck?

It was Bud's way to arrive unannounced. About ten years ago he turned up in Dublin, looking for a little bit of heaven in the shape of an Irish colleen. Instead he got the flu and spent most of his time in bed or lounging around in vest and track suit bottoms. Amazingly, he'd got work as a male model, but couldn't do it. He was too sick. I remember he groaned constantly. The house reeked of Vick's Vapour Rub and chicken soup. Fergal played hours and hours of chess with him, at which Bud was a wizard; somewhere in his career he'd been in prison and so had the time to practise. The US election was on, and I stupidly argued with him about politics. I was for Mondale, which incensed him. He called me a commie, and I called him a redneck. I suggested he might be happier staying with my sister. But we patched it up when he presented me with a bunch of flowers. When he was feeling better, we dragged him to a play at the Abbey. He was polite but groaned constantly again, so at the interval I suggested he go to a disco in Leeson Street.

The next morning I asked how he'd got on.

"Got meself a pretty little redhead," he said in his Gomer Pyle accent.

"Great. Where did you go?"

Bud smacked his lips. "Up against a wall."

"Oh! . . . " I was shocked. With his looks, he didn't have to buy love. "Sorry, I meant, what *disco* did you go to?"

"Looked in one o' dem doors. The chicks were too young."

"But you're not *that* old."

"I'm old enough to be their dad."

Now he was visiting again. Again unannounced. Well, this time I wasn't going to be drawn into discussing politics. He'd consider Clinton a draft-dodger and Hillary a freaky feminist. Also I couldn't play chess and wouldn't cook. How long would he stay this time? And how did he know I was here? It had to be Ogie. But it was a bit much, expecting to be met. There was no way I could get to Philadelphia. I couldn't just leave my classes. What was I to tell the students? "A long-lost cousin turned up?" No, I rang the airport and left a message for him to take the shuttle.

That evening a fifty-year-old version of Bud stood outside my door in Bella Vista with several large suitcases. He was tanned with solid steel-grey hair and steel-blue eyes and still wore a beautiful fringed leather jacket, western boots and huge stetson. "Coz!"

He always called me that. "Eh, it's great to see you, Bud. How did you get in?"

"Rang all the bells. Sweet-talked some little old lady." He took his hat off, bear-hugging me in Ogie fashion. "Must be five years."

"Eight," I said quickly. "This is a lovely surprise." But I looked in alarm at the suitcases.

Puffing, he hauled two in from the corridor, looking round swiftly. "Say, this is pretty nice."

"I'm renting."

"Still, not bad. Thur's money in writin'."

I dragged in the last case.

Inside we sat on one of the couches. Then, groaning as of old, he pulled off one boot, then the other.

"Would you like a drink?" I asked.

He held up a hand. "No alcohol."

I'd forgotten he was teetotal – a recovering alcoholic. "Tea or coffee then?"

"In a mo. First things first. How's Fergie?"

"Fergal is fine – Fergie's the Duchess of York."

"Duchess of New York?"

"Never mind. How'd you know I was here?"

"Ogie." Groaning again, he pulled off his socks and sat wiggling his toes. "Phew! That's better."

"They're new boots? Do you need some elastoplast?"

"Naw." He examined his raw heel. "Ogie said you were a college professor now." He shook his head in admiration.

"Only visiting."

He whistled. "They pay you to visit. Not a bad deal."

"There's nothing much to it." I nodded uneasily at the suitcases. "Eh – are you moving East?"

"Sure thing." Still perusing his feet, he chuckled ruefully. "Hadta get my ass outa Vegas in one hell of a hurry."

"What happened?"

Opening his hands, he stared at them, palms down. "They threatened to break ma fingers."

"Who?"

"The Mob."

"The Mob?" I sat bolt upright. "You mean it still exists?"

"Sure, it exists." He looked at me pityingly.

"But does it have power?"

"Power." He whistled. "Are you serious? They own Vegas."

"But they're not on the East coast."

"Whatja mean? They run Kennedy."

"The airport?"

He nodded. "And all the vending machines in New York."

"But you're not in contact with them?"

He shook his head grimly. "No siree! Can't do much with busted hands!" He cracked his knuckles nerve-rackingly.

I flinched at the sound.

He chuckled.

I was still alarmed. "But why'd they threaten you?"

"Thought I was graftin'."

It was like something out of Bald Jack's time. "But were you?"

He shrugged. "A guy's gotta live, don't he?"

What had I let myself in for?

"Look," he went on, "a pal in Atlantic City's promised to fix me up. Meantime – can I crash here?" His voice was urgent, his blue eyes deadly serious.

"Certainly," I heard myself say. "Eh – for how long?"

He shrugged. "A week, maybe two."

I stood up, relieved. I could manage two weeks. "That's fine. Let me get you something to eat now."

He settled for herb tea and oatmeal cookies. While I was getting them, he toured the apartment barefoot, commenting on the books and paintings. He looked scornfully at the faded and expensive oriental rug. "These professor types live well. But why don't they buy a new rug?"

"I think it's Persian, Bud. An antique."

"Hmm. Looks antic, OK. Persia, ain't that Ayraq where that Sodom Hussein comes from?"

I nodded.

"How much they chargin'?"

"Eight hundred a month."

"For wop rugs! Buy a new one and take it off the rent."

I didn't argue.

He stood in front of an abstract sculpture of a torso, shaking his head. "Where's the head?"

"It's an abstract."

"No tits either."

I brought his tea over and poured myself a strong scotch. "It won't upset you if I drink?"

He shook his head. "I work in a Casino."

While Bud drank his tea and munched cookies, I sat on the couch sipping. How the hell would I explain Chuck?

"There's just one thing." I cleared my throat nervously.

"Sure, whad?"

"Eh – I'm working now. I don't cook."

He waved a hand dismissively. "Leave that to Cousin Bud."

"And another thing." My tic started, so I put a hand up to stop it. "I – I have a friend."

His eyes lit up. "A friend? Great! Goodlookin'? Remember I'm a tits man!" He moulded lascivious breasts in the air.

"I mean a *male* friend. A new man in my life."

"He sweet-talkin' yuh?"

I nodded.

He munched cookies for a long second, before chuckling lewdly. "Hmm. Fergie's goin' to kick ass!"

I controlled my irritation. "Hardly. We're divorcing."

He took another cookie, shaking his head ruefully. "Divorce ain't nice. Been there three times myself. Fergie's a good man."

"I just wanted to explain the situation."

He held up his hand again. "No need. Cousin Bud's a big boy."

"Eh, my friend – Chuck's his name – may be staying over."

He waved an arm grandiosely. "There's plenty o' room."

"Eh, thanks."

Smirking, he wagged a finger at me. "It's Fergie's job to kick ass. So long as this Chuckie guy treats you OK, that's fine with Cousin Bud. OK."

". . . OK."

CHAPTER TEN

* * *

COUSIN BUD ALWAYS WORE BOXER SHORTS AND A SINGLET VEST IN the house. Otherwise, he was fairly unobtrusive. And, I have to admit, another voice to keep Marcus at bay. I was out during weekdays, but in the evening or at the weekends we chatted, avoiding any serious conversation – he talked about Fergal nonstop, urging me to call him. Our opinions on absolutely everything were different. The election was definitely out as a topic. The Democrats looked like winning, and he'd consider them all draft-dodging, leftie, commie hippies. I didn't want to repeat our previous quarrel. He'd take it as a personal rejection, and he'd been rejected by everyone else in life. Or so he thought. His parents, his foster parents, the army, his wives, and now the Las Vegas Mafia.

Usually Bud occupied the back bedroom or watched TV in the living-room, surrounded by a circle of empty coke cans. The curtains were always drawn "against the sun," he said, but I suspected he was nervous. Or hiding from someone. Because he never went out, except to walk the cat after dark, when he wore sunglasses and a hooded track suit. He gave me shopping lists for items which I picked up in the 711. But he did the cooking as promised – or what passed for cooking: TV dinners; or ordered in – Domino's pizza, Chinese, or Kentucky fried chicken. Lately he'd coaxed Chuck into chess, and the board was always set up in expectation.

On the weekend of Molly and Theodora's party, he went to Philadelphia "on business." I dreaded to think what this might be, so I didn't ask. Just nodded vaguely at his parting words, "You call Fergie now."

It was heaven to have the apartment to myself. To walk around without a dressing-gown. Chuck was coming over later to pick me up for the party. Before that I had work to do.

I was in the bath when the phone rang.

Damn. Who could it be? Fergal?

I struggled up and, grabbing a towel, ran to the adjoining bedroom. The receiver was by the bed.

It was someone selling light bulbs.

Perhaps Bud was right. I should phone home.

On impulse, I dialled Ireland.

No answer.

Where was Fergal? He usually spent Sundays at home, reading the newspapers.

Then his deep voice came over the answering machine. "Please leave your name and number and I'll get back to you as soon as possible."

Then the signal.

"Fergal, it's Anne," I said quickly. "Please ring back. My number is 765-2345. I'll be here all day, but I'm going out about six."

When you came to it, it was difficult to let someone go.

I went back to my bath, shampooed my hair and towelled it in front of the long bathroom mirror. The glaring light revealed all. Irish bathrooms didn't usually have mirrors, so you don't notice your lumps and bumps.

A scrawny hag looked back at me. Why do you turn into mashed potatoes in middle life? Was Chuck really attracted? Or was he just using me for sex? It was so long since I'd thought of myself in that light. Why had I wasted my life on Fergal? I'd imagined a future of speaking French or Italian – at least one language. I even had an idiotic obsession about translating Dante. But I never read poetry now. And was still held together with pins, psychologically at least. But now that I'd reached middle-age, what had I become? A hack. A hack with a failed marriage. And a facial tic. *"Mais ou sont les neiges d'antan?" Ou sont,* indeed? Why did I have such an overwhelming sense of being second-rate?

Because I was?

A middle-aged woman in search of fulfilment, a cliché of modern literature. Not to mention life.

What had I let myself in for with Chuck? He always came on strong, leaving me in no doubt about his intentions.

I didn't feel guilty, just good – no doubt as good as Fergal did. He was probably out with his girlfriend now. If he could be unfaithful, so could I. Why should I always be the hurler on the ditch? Afraid of life. As an alien, I was surely entitled to the benefits of US law. Divorce still wasn't legal in Ireland. The thought of Ireland irritated me. I didn't care if the whole country sank to the bottom of the sea. It was meant to disappear seven years before the rest of the world anyhow. Good riddance. It belonged there. A fascist backwater, a frog's hole of swollen egos and begrudgery.

My depression was gone. The routine of class preparation and researching Marcus left little time to brood. Teaching was now over till next Tuesday, so I could work on his biography over the weekend. Exercising with Molly helped me sleep better – although I still woke early. But I hadn't had any "dreams" for several weeks now. I was enjoying everything too much – work, the sun, swimming.

Having an affair was crazy. Still, it was fun going out with a new man.

My black pants and top lay on the big bed. Did they suit me? I had money for clothes, but no dress sense. I was bored to tears by shopping, china, cut glass, things which other women liked. Best not to think. To think, to worry, aye perchance to dream, there's the rub.

The phone rang.

Fergal?

"Hello," I said into the receiver.

It was Molly. "Anne, listen, I've got tickets for an afternoon concert."

"But the party?"

"Theodora has everything under control."

"I have papers to grade."

"Can't you skip it?"

I hesitated – Molly was hyperactive.

"Oh, never mind. See you at six-thirty!" And she hung up.

Other years I'd gone with her to lots of things, but this year I had Chuck.

I dressed quickly and graded some papers.

Then took a glass of wine to the balcony.

Outside the trees were in full leaf, and soon there'd be brilliant fall colours. But no time to contemplate them. The biography had to be drafted by Christmas. My Xeroxes were scattered on the table. I'd made a few notes already. If only

I could meet someone who remembered Marcus. So far, there were no replies from the *Times*. I'd written to Elizabeth also, asking for Marcus's journal, but nothing from her either.

I'd found out more about the Rosenthal case. The murder car, a grey Packard, had once been the property of John L Sullivan, the prizefighter. As well as hiring it, Jack Rose had hired the four young gunmen with comic book names – Gyp the Blood, Whitey Lewis, Dago Frank and Lefty Louie.

Hollering Herman was having a horse's neck in the Hotel Metropole on the stifling night of the murder. He was high on publicity and showing around newspapers with a story about him, when the gunmen called him out. After they fired, he fell dead on a cardboard fan which advertised the latest fashion in celluloid collars. He was covered with a hotel tablecloth.

One of the first reporters on the scene was the young, squeaky-voiced Alexander Woollcott from the *Times* – later the famous drama critic. Then came Harry Bayard Swope from the sleazier *World*. He had earlier taken the train to Newport to persuade the DA to allow Herman to testify before the Grand Jury. So the murder was no surprise to him.

At first the headlines didn't implicate Lieutenant Becker:

ROSENTHAL SHOT AND KILLED IN GAMBLERS' WAR
*Man who Started Crusade Is Called out of Metropole
Hotel and Left Dead on Sidewalk.*

SLAYER FLEES IN AUTO
*Police Pursue in Taxi and Lively Chase in Fifth Avenue
Follows, but Fugitive Makes Escape on 58th Street.*

Then Bald Jack Rose said Becker paid him to do the killing. Because of this, there were three trials and five men were executed.

I was fascinated by Marcus's world. Maybe it was from seeing too many gangster movies? Was Becker a scapegoat? His photo showed him to be dark, with unruly hair and heavy rather brutal features. But he had a dimple in one cheek and despairing eyes. Was it the face of a murderer or a victim?

A shadow fell across the page.

Marcus was climbing over the balcony railing. This time he was younger and heavier. He wore a straw boater and chewed gum like an overweight James Cagney. Also he wore white-face make-up. "That's the face of a killer."

I put my head in my hands. "Go away! You're dead!"

He sat in one of the wicker chairs. "Ah, don't be a dumb broad! Becker was crooked. All the cops were."

"Was Bald Jack telling the truth?"

"Sure, he was. Jack was a grand man." Marcus pointed at my mother's pearl brooch. "Jack gave me that."

I was horrified. "But Oonagh gave it to me."

"It was Nora's."

"Oonagh said you sold everything in the depression. How did this escape?"

"It was hot."

"Oh . . . You mean . . . ?"

"Stolen." He was sitting with his knees crossed.

"You associated with criminals?"

He spat out the gum. "How else couldya be a criminal lawyer?"

"But I've found out other things. You weren't an editor of the *Hartford Courant*. You only sold subscriptions for it."

He held up his hand. "Tut!"

"And even then you cheated – getting the same family to resubscribe."

He grinned smugly. "A good ploy."

"Cheating."

He wagged a finger. "Surviving." Then, sticking out his chest, he frowned indignantly. "I became editor."

"Yeah? I can find out."

"Do that!" Huffily he put on his boater hat and made for the door, but, as usual, didn't go. "You shouldn't go digging up muck."

"You want a biography." I slammed down the Xeroxes. "But you won't even tell the truth. So, go!"

He lit up a huge cigar, puffing gangsterishly.

"I said, go!"

He waved a hand. "Aw, shut yer trap!"

I had to get rid of him.

"I'm giving yuh a chance to make something of yerself!"

I went into the bedroom and slammed the door.

I must have fallen asleep then, because I found myself dreaming about Chuck. We were in the apartment, getting ready to go to Molly and Theodora's party. He was wearing tennis shorts with a sweat band around his head and carried a racket.

He looked down at his shorts. "Can't wear jeans to the Dean's."

Then Marcus padded up behind me, eyeing Chuck suspiciously. "Who's that?"

I ignored him.

"Is he getting up your skirt?" Marcus chuckled lewdly, pulling at my skirt which was suddenly black see-through chiffon. God, I was wearing no underwear.

The phone was ringing in the distance.

Fergal?

No. It was the apartment buzzer.

How long had I been sleeping?

I spoke into the intercom. "H-hello!"

"Hey, babe. Chuck!"

I buzzed him in and went down the corridor to meet him. He stepped from the lift, properly dressed and looking boyish in his preppy navy blazer, grey pants, Oxford shirt and college tie.

I rubbed my eyes sleepily. "You're looking smart."

"Thanks. I rang and rang. You asleep?"

"I – must've been."

Back in the apartment, I looked around for Marcus. "Eh – I'll get you a drink."

I went ahead of him into the kitchen and put on coffee for myself. As I turned, he embraced me again. "You're trembling."

"I have these . . . bad dreams."

He looked concerned. "It's indigestion."

"Whatever it is, it's wearing me out." I'd never told anyone about Marcus and didn't want to confide in Chuck now.

He patted my back. "You work too hard. I've never met anyone who worked as hard as you. Been grading papers?" He picked up a huge *Webster's* dictionary from the dining room table. "What are you doing with this?"

"Checking spellings."

He laughed shortly. "My secretary does all that."

I managed a smile. "Everyone doesn't have a secretary."

I gave him a drink and when the coffee was brewed, we

went out to the balcony where my books and notes were spread out.

"How's the biography going?"

I pointed to the pile of Xeroxes. "I'm still working on the Rosenthal case. I may go up to the New York Public Library."

"By the way, I checked on Stephen Crane and Lieutenant Becker. *Maggie, A Girl of the Streets* was published in 1893 – well before 1912. A few years later, Crane was writing a series of sketches on New York low life. One evening he met a young prostitute called Dora Clarke. While she was in his company, Becker arrested her, saying she had solicited. When Dora was tried, Crane testified for her."

"So Becker was a bully."

"It's more complicated. Dora complained of police harassment. She had once refused the advances of an officer because she thought he was black. But there were no blacks on the force." Chuck paused. "It was before affirmative action."

"And political correctness."

"You bet." He laughed. "Well, the whole station felt insulted – at one of their members being thought black. They were determined to get Dora. And, because Stephen Crane stood up for her, they got him too. So Becker was defending a colleague."

I was staring at Becker's photograph. "They didn't repay him."

"What do you mean?"

"They let him take the rap later – *all* the police were corrupt."

His wrinkle appeared. "Why do you care? Eighty years on?"

It was a good question. "I feel he was wronged."

Chuck shrugged. "Who said life was fair?"

"My grandfather had a part in it. It's all very suspect."

Chuck picked up a photo of Herman Rosenthal. "Who's this?"

"The victim – Herman Rosenthal."

Herman was dark and squat with thick lips and a smug smile. "He had a reputation as a welsher," I said, looking at it. "He once refused to pay track debts because betting was illegal. The court upheld him, but the other gamblers insisted he pay and lent him the money. He was a protegé of Big Tim Sullivan."

"Big who?"

"A Senator who was murdered around the time of the trial. People thought there was a connection. The gunmen's gang defeated his gang at the turn of the century."

Chuck's eyebrows shot up. "A senator ran a gang?"

"The Whyos – He was Tammany Hall." I rummaged in my Xeroxes. "Look here's a list of the jobs they'd do. They made a strange whining sound when attacking."

Chuck read it out: "Punching, $2. Both eyes blacked, $4. Nose and jaw broken, $10. Jacked out (knocked out with a blackjack) $15. Ear chewed off, $15. Leg or arm broke, $19. Shot in leg, $25. Stabbed, $25. Doing the big job, $100 and up." He put it down. "Doing the big job. Wow."

I put the list away. "In 1912, murder was cheap. There was a movement for reform. You've heard of Reverend Charles Pankhurst?"

But Chuck was looking bored. He nodded in the direction of the chess board. "Say, where's the lodger?"

"Philadelphia."

"You mean he won't be back?"

"Tomorrow."

He touched me. "Let's fool around."

I held back. "Now?"

"Is he abusing you?" a familiar voice shouted in the distance.

Marcus was looking in over the balcony from the grounds.

But I zapped him out. Christ, I wasn't asleep now. So much for all my sleep theories. It was a ghost.

"What is it?"

"Nothing."

I drained my coffee, glancing nervously at Chuck.

He finished his drink. "You're tense. Let me give you a massage."

"We'll be late for the party."

"Lots of time."

"But we should be there now."

He pulled me into the bedroom and slowly took off my carefully selected clothes. Then laid me on my back across the bed. His lack of inhibition always surprised me and now I was lost, naked on roller skates and speeding downhill. His taut, muscular body never failed him and afterwards he pulled me on top of him. But here I must close the bedroom door.

Chuck showed me the flaws in my upbringing. Irish women of my generation were reared on a diet of Romantic poetry and niceness. It was our fatal flaw. Also Catholicism – "Learn of Me, for I am meek and humble of heart." We weren't assertive, sexually or any other way. Consequently, we were brainwashed into thinking sex was something taken from us, not something we freely gave. Had I given enough to Fergal all these years?

As we left for the party, the phone rang.

This time it was my husband – I knew.

"Answer it," Chuck said.

I hesitated. "No, we're late."

CHAPTER ELEVEN

* * *

THEODORA OPENED THE DOOR TO US. "AH, YOU MADE IT."

I was embarrassed. "Sorry we're late."

She seemed irritated but embraced me warmly, while ignoring Chuck. "It's good to see you, my dear. Did Molly give you your glasses back?"

"Eh – no."

They were on the table, and she handed them over.

"Thanks, I wondered where they were."

Was I imagining disapproval? I was always leaving things behind – coats, books, now glasses. Theodora's a small, beaky woman in her early sixties, with thick pepper-and-salt hair, who looks like someone's nice aunt. Usually more formal than Molly, she was now dressed casually in black trousers and a blouse. Her competence had always impressed me, also her penetrating, violet-blue eyes, now fixed curiously on Chuck.

"Eh – you know Chuck Matthews?" I blurted.

"Yes." Theodora arched an eyebrow, smiling slightly. "I think we're acquainted."

He bowed. "Ma'am."

Did he have to call her that? Theodora wasn't rude, but there was something moralistic about her now, as if she knew we'd just been in bed. Molly had been the same. It was unfair of them.

"Come on in. We're having drinks." Theodora ushered us through the front room to the back of the house where the other guests had gathered.

The Georgian brick house was a narrow dwelling, modernised, but it still retained its eighteenth century character. The formal front room looked onto the street. The large back one was decorated and furnished in tasteful comfort, with scattered kilim rugs on hardwood floors. An old wood stove was now empty. Overhead a fan whirred. There were books, pottery and paintings everywhere – also some grandchildren's toys by the French doors to the garden. The other guests were seated on the comfortable corduroy chairs around the pine coffee table.

A woman Spanish professor, who was swarthy and chunky but elegantly dressed, was telling a story in broken American about a cat. "Poor Kitty, her diagaphram was all cracked. My daughter ees always crying . . ."

Theodora put a hand on her arm. "Just a minute, Paola, this is Anne O'Brien, our visiting Irish novelist. And Chuck Matthews from the English Department."

I smiled hello. As Theodora made the introductions, I repeated the other guests' names in an effort to remember.

It was a typical academic dinner party. Over the years I'd been to many like it, and always enjoyed Molly and Theodora's mixture of guests. Besides the Spaniard, there was Dr Finnegan, the college psychiatrist, a bearded and bald amateur Irish Literature critic, who used a walking-stick and had a reputation for drink; Sarah, the English Department secretary. There were was a chic young black woman – the new film professor. There were also two middle-aged women, friends of Theodora from the

University of Delaware, who were working on Irish Literature. I remembered their odd ways and even odder names – Dodo and Dee.

Chuck shook hands all round, bowing to Sarah, "Ma'am."

"Don't call me that!" she snapped. "We're not in the midwest."

He smiled goodhumouredly. "Girlie, then?"

She glared, while he plonked down on one of the brown chairs.

Seeing that Sarah was put out, I whispered, "He's pulling your leg."

But she turned her back.

Was she serious? It was a joke for God's sake. I tried again, but she still ignored me. Why get so mad about nothing?

"Who's for champagne?" Theodora went over to the drinks table. "Anne? And, Chuck, a real drink? Or champagne?"

"Have any beer?"

"We do indeed. It's downstairs."

"Let me." He sprang up.

"OK. It's in the kitchen refrigerator." And Theodora directed him to the basement stairs.

I'm not a party person and always managed to put my foot in it. Still smarting from Sarah, I turned to Paola. "Hello."

"You are from Eerland," the Spaniard queried loudly. "A writer, eet's true?"

I nodded, changing the subject. "What part of Spain do you come from?"

She sat up stiffly. "Please! I am in America from the age of eighteen."

What had I said now? There was a huffy silence, during which I noticed Dr Finnegan's hand shake as he lifted a drink. He had a red face with a ruined nose, but surely it was too early in the evening to be drunk?

"But I have not heerd of you," Paola shouted.

"You wouldn't. I'm more popular than literary."

"Very popular in this house!" Theodora butted in, handing me champagne.

I took it, reddening. "I write airport novels."

The Spaniard leaned toward me, puzzled. "But I no understand."

"Popular fiction," I explained. "Mass market."

She turned up her nose. "Ooh. I know only Jims Juice."

"He's quite an industry now." I sipped my drink.

"It's a pity." Dr Finnegan nodded in agreement, saying in a slurred voice, "It cuts him off . . .

"A pitee? I no understand." The Spaniard looked affronted.

"Well, you know, deconstruction and all that," I supported the doctor. Molly and Theodora always asked him when I came, as he was interested in Ireland. "They make him sound difficult."

The woman waved a hand effetely. "He no difficult. I know."

"That's my point," I said. "There's too much new-fangled criticism. And there are other Irish writers. Would you agree, Dr Finnegan?"

Dr Finnegan coughed. "Indeed, yes – "

"So zere are other Eerish writers?" The woman shrugged.

The doctor was now irritated. "You've interrupted. Let me make my p-p-point!"

She looked affronted.

"Joyce has brought the novel down an alley way," he went on in a teacherish voice. "There's a whole literature – O'Casey, Synge, Mervyn Wall – "

"But O'Casey – he no great."

"You're interrupting again!" The doctor looked affronted.

"So I interrupt!" She waved a hand. "Ha!"

Now his face seemed to swell, as if he'd break a blood vessel. "Y-y-you shouldn't interrupt!"

"Joyce dwarfs everyone else," I placated. God, were they getting into a fight?

"And so?" She downed her champagne. "Zat is ze way. Dere are giants and dwarfs, no?" The Spaniard turned impatiently.

Dr Finnegan didn't say anything more.

"It's the same in American literature," Chuck said jovially from the other end of the couch. "In every literature. One or two take over."

Theodora sat down beside Dodo and Dee, who were across the room. "Tell Anne about your letters!"

They wriggled nervously. Except for their age, they were clones. Dodo was a dumpy thirty-five-year-old, dowdily dressed in denim and docksiders. Dee was dressed the same, but she was about sixty.

Now they eyed each other anxiously.

"Zey are on the edge of a great discovery perhaps, no?" the Spaniard chipped in, again dominating the conversation. "You must explain."

Dee, the older woman, rubbed her hands worriedly. "But Paola, we *can't*."

"Can't! Wat is can't?" the Spaniard shouted. Redfaced, she turned to me. "Dey discover letters between Jims Juice and Sammy."

I was puzzled. "Sammy?"

"Samuel Beckett," Dr Finnegan got in, shaking his head. "I, personally, would have to – ah – doubt the authenticity of s-s-such letters."

The Spaniard waved a hand. "But dey were lovers, perhaps?"

I looked at Dr Finnegan. "I've never heard that."

He burped drunkenly. "It's well known that Beckett was hetero-s-s-sexual. And Joyce too."

"But it drive poor Lucia mad. Lucia love Sammy, you know," the Spaniard persisted.

"You're int-t-terrupting again!" the doctor snapped.

She reddened. "So, I interrupt!"

He looked outraged. "It's c-c-considered rude!"

God, was he senile? And was the Spanish professor deliberately provoking him? And having us on about Joyce and Beckett? No, she looked too humourless. So did the two academics. And Theodora was listening quite seriously.

"Tell dem *where* you find letters," the Spaniard went on.

"We can't. It might break copyright." Dodo hesitated, looked cautiously round and lowered her voice. "Anne is Irish. She might leak it to the press."

What were they talking about? "Eh – what am I meant to leak?"

Dodo and Dee exchanged more furtive glances.

Theodora went down to the kitchen. "You can trust Anne, Dee."

I smiled into my champagne. I'd heard of academic rivalry, but, being a reclusive writer, had never come across it. It's an occupational benefit – there have to be some.

"You tink she could be spy?" The Spaniard leaned toward the others conspiratorially.

At this Chuck roared with laughter. "Now, I've heard it all!"

A few people tittered nervously.

He grinned wickedly from the other end of the couch. He was certainly at ease in a social situation and made no effort to hide his amusement now.

The three women looked at each other. Dr Finnegan coughed drunkenly, then got into conversation with Chuck. The two of them went over to the drinks table, where the doctor poured more bourbon.

Theodora came back with another champagne bottle. "More drinks, anyone? Paola, finish the story about your cat."

The Spaniard waved her wrist again. "Ah, the vet he fixed him up. We now have nine kitties. Which I cannot turn away." She grimaced tenderly.

Theodora laughed. "That must cost you a bit."

"Ah, yes, we pay mighty beeg for food."

"And vet's fees?"

"Ah, but he give us beeg reduction."

Then the Spanish professor turned to the young black woman who wanted the name of the vet. I listened, intrigued at the awfulness of coping with nine cats. But they probably weren't like Ogie's.

"His office ees on Main Street," I heard the Spaniard say. "How you like Oldcastle?"

Michelle shrugged. "It's OK – a bit quiet compared to Berkeley."

"You like Berkeley?"

"I was a grad student there. I miss the intellectual life. But we're near New York. I can get there for my poetry readings."

"You are publeeshed?"

"Not yet. It's a bit confining."

The Spaniard looked puzzled. "Confining?

The younger woman nodded. "The end of growth."

That concept was new to me. And was she implying that Oldcastle was dull? It wasn't the metropolis, but it was an interesting college town. Obviously, our new professor felt too good for us. As she chatted on in this pretentious vein and the Spaniard broke in loudly, I nursed my champagne, determined not to overdo it. It was cool and since meeting Molly and Theodora, my favourite drink – it was too expensive in Ireland. The only trouble: it might bring on Marcus – anything could.

Then Molly came in with a tray of steamed prawns and hot sauce which she laid on the coffee table. She wore a tight black polo-necked sweater, which emphasized her large breasts, and a long red peasant skirt which made her hips look enormous. "More starters, everyone. Anne, darling, you're here!"

I was always darling to Molly. "Sorry we were late."

She flopped down beside me. "You're not the last! We're expecting another couple."

"Eh – you've met Chuck?" I held my glass in his direction.

She nodded curtly across the room. "We know each other."

Was I imagining her tone? I felt about fifteen, caught necking for the first time.

Chuck raised his glass. "Hi, there!" Then he came over, "Let me pass these."

"Thanks, you can take that plate around."

As Chuck politely served the guests, she nudged the other plate towards the young woman opposite. "Michelle, a prawn? You've met Michelle, Anne? She's our new film person. Anne's writing about her grandfather."

Michelle held a prawn in mid-air. "Oh, was he famous?"

"He was a criminal lawyer."

"The best," an Irish brogue said.

I blinked. Marcus was now sitting at the other end of the couch, still in his James Cagney persona and still in white-face.

Oh, God. I turned my back. That had tuned him out

before. But how long was this to go on? Could the others see anything? Obviously not. They were all too absorbed in their own conversations.

Michelle looked directly at me. "What was his name?"

"Eh, whose?"

"Your grandfather's."

"Oh – Marcus – "

"Quilligan O'Neill," Marcus snapped, picking up Michelle's drink.

"How interesting." Michelle leaned forward eagerly, oblivious of his presence. "That's my glass, by the way."

"Sorry." I put down the glass. She was accusing me of taking her drink. But it was Marcus.

"Anne's researching newspapers." Molly looked at me oddly.

Marcus stuck out his chest, gripping his lapels. "He had an interesting life!"

I struggled for control.

"He sounds fascinating. Was he Irish?" Michelle chatted on.

"And proud of it!" Marcus quipped.

As Michelle laughed, I turned my back to Marcus. "Actually he emigrated to this country. He was carried over as an infant in the 1860s – "

"'70s!" Marcus corrected.

"There's a dispute about his birth date," I added.

"You're the only one disputing!" Marcus snapped.

I concentrated my mind. "A biography might get me back to writing – "

"She's given up novels," Molly butted in.

"I've written five."

"And very enjoyable too!" Molly touched my arm. "Thanks to you, I know something about Irish history."

133

"Me too." Theodora joined our conversation. "I finished *Cromwellian Castles* last month, Anne. It was a great read."

I was embarrassed. "I suppose fiction's a sort of history. And history's a sort of fiction."

"What's this fiction crap?" Marcus muttered, greedily downing a prawn. "Don't you wanta make something of yourself?"

No one had heard him.

"What's wrong? Is the sauce too hot?" Molly peered worriedly at me.

I popped a prawn in my mouth. "No, eh – I've found some information in the newspapers. But I'll have to dig out other sources. Everyone's dead who knew him."

"Tell Michelle about Bald Jake," Molly interrupted.

"Bald Jack Rose – ." I looked nervously round for Marcus. What if he butted in again? But he seemed to be gone. "He was a witness in the Rosenthal Case."

Michelle looked blank. "I've never heard of it."

"No one has." I looked at Molly. "Can I have coffee?"

"Now?"

"Well – more champagne then."

Molly filled my glass, still staring oddly. Had she seen anything?

I gulped my drink, fingering Nora's brooch, pinned to my front. It was real, but Marcus was a dream figure. Dreams came from the imagination, which lay at the root of all knowledge. Fergal, the ex-philosopher, had once told me that. Also that images were acts of consciousness. I didn't really understand this. But somehow, I'd called the dream Marcus to life. He came in the same way as my fictional characters did – in bits. But why the hell did he pick on me? He'd come twice in one day. Was I very stressed? Why couldn't he torment his other descendants – Ogie or Cousin Bud?

The other latecomers didn't show, so dinner went on without them. It was served downstairs in Molly and Theodora's big country kitchen. People helped themselves to Mexican pork and rice from a small side table, and then took their places at the big round one. There was a vegetarian dish as well, some sort of bean concoction – which was a Molly speciality.

The hosts sat at either end, Molly retelling a story about their first meeting. "I was just divorced and I took the kids to Florida. Theodora was on the same flight."

"Never saw anyone with so many bags." Theodora laughed. "And so many crying kids."

I'd heard the story before, but loved to hear Molly tell it again. They'd fallen in love on that trip, moved in together and brought up Molly's six children who are now all well-adjusted and successful. I met the family my first year at Sweetmount. At first Theodora could be grumpy, but it never lasted. Their friendship had changed my life.

The doctor and the Spanish professor were seated apart. I was at Molly's end, with Sarah, Chuck and Dr Finnegan opposite. All through the meal, there were several noisy conversations going around the big table. I forget what we talked about – it was just a lot of loud fun.

The late guests arrived in the middle of dessert, but Theodora refused to let them in. Voices floated down to us – Molly protesting and Theodora saying, "No, Molly, It's ten o'clock! They can't have dinner now."

I looked at Chuck, thinking it lucky we weren't any later.

Reading my thoughts, he raised his eyebrows.

Everyone was silent.

"Well," Chuck said, during the lull. "I hear the dirty girl has been sending her missives again."

I was shocked at his choice of word. "Who're you talking about?"

Before he could answer, Sarah snapped, "It's not the place to talk about it."

But Chuck was unrepentant. "She's an MA student."

Dr Finnegan, who had switched from bourbon to wine, said in a slurred voice, "A young lady whom we suspect of sending poison pen letters. This time it's rather serious."

Sarah looked nervously up the table, as the Dean came back. "It's not exactly proved yet."

"We have her, dead on," Chuck insisted.

"Nothing is proved!" Theodora barked. "And please don't talk about it here!"

"You're int-t-terrupting!" the doctor muttered.

Chuck swirled his wine glass. "Hmm. The girl's mad, I can tell you that."

Obviously irritated, Theodora continued her conversation with Michelle, paying no attention to our end of the table.

"But who is this girl?" I asked again.

Chuck linked his hands behind his head. "Teri Scales – a crazy in the MA programme."

Sarah tut-tutted him.

"But she's in my class," I blurted. "She begged to get in."

Chuck looked alarmed. "Sarah, why wasn't Anne warned?"

Sarah didn't reply.

"She *is* crazy!" he insisted. "She was in my seminar last semester."

I turned worriedly to Molly. "Remember the girl in the hall?"

Molly nodded. "She'd read all the books?"

"Actually, she *has*," I said.

"Watch out! She's a pathological liar!" Chuck ignored

Theodora's now frosty gaze. "Teri Scales, what a name! It's onomatopoeiac."

"Why omomatopoeiac?" someone asked.

"She has dandruff!"

"Oh, Chuck!" Sarah protested.

"She does! She's scaly. Which makes her fishy."

The secretary looked sympathetic. "She comes from a deprived background."

"Yes," Chuck went on, "her father was jailed for having sex with his dog."

Theodora looked about to explode.

"On the front lawn!" Dr Finnegan swung so far back on his chair that it broke, dumping him unceremoniously onto the floor.

Everyone gaped.

"You OK, Doctor?" Chuck helped him up.

"Please be more careful!" Theodora rasped. An angry red line was moving slowly up from her throat.

Unabashed, the doctor quipped, "There are very good glues."

There was a titter of nervous laughter around the table.

No one dared look at Theodora, as Molly quietly got him another chair.

Chuck examined the broken one. "I know where it can be repaired. Leave it to me."

Theodora nodded grumpily.

Then Michelle went on, talking about Teri's father. "Let me get this straight. You mean he didn't even go inside?"

The doctor shook his head. "No, he did it in full view."

She shook her head, genuinely perplexed.

The doctor was obviously taken with the young woman, because he smiled up the table. "A disturbed personality. It's rubbed off on his daughter. She's classically self-destructive. I've been – ah – "

"Doctor, please!" Theodora stood up.

"Don't interrupt me. I've been treating her for various types of self-mutilation."

At this Theodora stalked from the room. "We'll have our coffee upstairs!"

Some of the others trickled after her, carrying their cups.

Chuck looked after them, chagrined.

I whispered up the table, "You're not serious about the dog?"

He nodded. "Ask Dr Finnegan."

The doctor bowed his head.

"God, no wonder she's disturbed. But who'd she write to?"

"It's not proved, Anne," the secretary broke in. "Someone was writing nasty letters all last semester. They suspected Teri. Then she gave the game away."

"How?"

Sarah spoke in a low voice. "A certain professor got a letter. No one knew about it. No one but the Chairperson and me. But then Teri bounced into the office, asking how was Professor So and So coping with his hate mail?"

"It still doesn't prove anything." Molly lit a cigarette.

"It certainly doesn't!" Theodora was back, looking small in the doorway, her face like thunder.

We all squirmed like nervous children.

"I can assure you she was the culprit." The psychiatrist's voice wobbled on. "She's – "

"Dr Finnegan!" Theodora snapped.

Chuck nudged him, but the doctor was oblivious. "She's bulimic too."

"Dr Finnegan!"

"You're interrupting!"

Someone laughed.

The doctor went on. "Last year she burnt herself with a cigarette and then smashed her hand with a hammer. Classic symptoms . . . classic."

Theodora came over to the table. "I'd like you all to stop this conversation immediately! Or else go home!"

The doctor was too far gone to notice. Chuck looked embarrassed, and everyone else nervous.

But Theodora stood her ground. "It's completely inappropriate to talk about a patient in this way, Dr Finnegan. Nothing has been proved against her. The college is still enquiring into the allegations."

"You're interrupting again," he mumbled.

Molly started clearing the table. I helped her, thinking we'd upset our host, but were all a bit carried away by champagne, and the doctor was footless.

Chuck stood up and tried to smooth the situation. "Absence of evidence is not evidence of absence – Darwin! Join me for a smoke outside, Dr Finnegan?"

The doctor shook his head drunkenly. "A sad case . . ."

"I'll drive you home, Dr Finnegan!" Theodora snapped.

"N-n-now?"

"Now!"

"What about c-c-coffee?"

"You can take it with you! You can all go!"

People stirred awkwardly.

"I want to go to bed!"

The doctor tottered up and hobbled out on his stick, helped by Chuck. Theodora marched upstairs to the front door, carrying his coffee, while we followed. Then Chuck drove the old man home, Theodora disappeared upstairs, while Molly bid a slightly embarrassed goodnight to the other guests.

I stayed, to help stack the dishwasher. Molly's irritated

voice floated down, "That's a fine thing! The Dean throwing out the guests!"

"I'm tired!" Theodora shouted.

"Well, go to bed!"

Then a door slammed.

As Molly came into the kitchen, I said, "I'm sorry we upset Theodora."

"Oh, she'll get over it."

"I wish we hadn't."

Molly put in soap and shut the dishwasher. "She overreacts. But she has to be fair to everyone – it's her job. Tom Finnegan's getting worse. He gets drunker and drunker, then indiscreet. He's so utterly unprofessional, it's hard to believe."

"He was raiding the bourbon all night."

"He always does." She looked at me worriedly. "And you were knocking back champagne."

"I was?"

"Yes."

Molly didn't really drink. She looked concerned now.

"Sorry. I have – dreams."

This puzzled her. "Dreams?"

"Hallucinations. A person – eh – appears to be there."

"What person?"

"My grandfather."

She laughed shortly. "The guy you're writing about?"

I nodded.

"You have a drink problem," she snapped.

I felt slapped.

"Think about it." She wiped the counter.

My first effort to explain such weird events and my best friend had called me a drunkard. What would other people say if I told them? Listen, a ghost followed me down here from New York. We were on the same flight. Now he hops up in the oddest places. What could they say?

Molly broke the silence. "You seem pretty cosy with Chuck."

Her tone took me aback. "You disapprove?"

She raised her eyebrows. "He's not very reliable."

"What do you mean?"

"I mean, he has a reputation."

"For what?"

"For violence."

I felt slapped again. "Violence?"

"Yeah. He hits women."

I was speechless.

She went on tidying up. Why was she saying this? She was obsessed with her damn battered women. She saw every man as an abuser. Lesbian feminists generally didn't like men, I knew. To them, even ordinary sex was abuse.

At last I found words. "Isn't that just as unfair as accusing Teri?"

"I don't think so."

"But has it been proved? A person's innocent till proved guilty."

"His wife left. And he's had affairs which ended violently."

"Women have complained?"

Molly nodded. "Not formally. But it's generally known."

I stood there, trying to take it in. "He was charged in court?"

She smiled knowingly. "Ah, no."

"Well, then?"

"He got out of it. He's cunning." She hesitated, before going on. "What about Fergal?"

"What about him?"

"He'll be upset about all this."

I paused before speaking. "It's all over with him."

"Just like that?"

I felt very weary. "No. I've come to the decision – gradually. He never gives me any freedom. He even resented me coming here. He says I'm obsessed with America."

"Well, there's nothing wrong with that." She squeezed my arm gently.

"I want to keep my Green Card."

"Of course you do."

"It was hard enough to get."

"Hmm. Well, Chuck's not reliable. I don't want you hurt."

But I was – by her accusations. Which I didn't believe. Not for one minute. "At least, Chuck's not politically correct. He smokes."

She smiled ruefully. "Well, that's a plus."

Still, I couldn't help wondering about Chuck's calling Teri "dirty". It was a horrible way to describe anyone, never mind a young woman from a disturbed background. True, she was odd-looking in that batttered hat and old clothes, but she always seemed clean. Perhaps it was just a male way of talking? Chuck looked so handsome and confident. He had white teeth and strong suntanned muscles. He was privileged and clever. The life and soul of the party, of any party. Could I really be in love with a batterer? I'd never seen any evidence of it. So Molly had to be repeating gossip. It was unlike her to exaggerate, but then she loved Fergal – everyone did.

It was the first real breach in our friendship. I ignored her warnings and saw Chuck at least twice a week for dinner. I never went to his place. But he came back to mine, and despite Cousin Bud's presence, sometimes stayed over. Our affair progressed but, to my relief, he never talked of the future. We lived in the present by night, while by day I buried myself in the past.

CHAPTER TWELVE

* * *

A WOMAN FROM UPSTATE PENNSYLVANIA REPLIED TO MY *TIMES* ENQUIRY.

Dear Anne O'Brien,

I am sending this letter which might help in your research. It's from my grandmother Lilly, who was the widow of Harry Horowitz, better known as Gyp the Blood. In the letter she mentions the Rosenthal-Becker case. It might confuse you at first, but there were two Lillys involved. The other Lilly was Louie Rosenberg's girl. He was the famous Lefty Louie.

As there were family tensions, I did not meet my grandmother till just before she passed away five years ago. I found her in a New Jersey nursing home, lonely and old. It is my great regret that I did not know she was alive. She died soon after this and I did not visit with her again.

Feel free to contact me, if I can be of further help.
Sincerely,
Shirley Freeman.

Lilly Horowitz's letter was written in an almost indecipherable spidery scrawl:

Dearest little Shirley,

Thanks for your recint visit. I'm sure sorry your ma never let us get together before. Truth is, I wasn't a natral at the mothering bisness. I was a party gal and it's hard for us to rock a cradle. But being a grandma, hell, well that's something. You asked about my life as a young gal. Well, that's your rite to know. So here goes.

We came from the old country to Brooklyn before I was born. My ma, that's your greatgrandma, had to get the permishon of some offishal in Russia first. They didn't treat Jews well there. But there was problems in this land of the free too and don't you ever forget it. After travelling overland thru China, to meet my papa, didn't he die of heart affecshon, soon after my birth. They died young then, hon. Times was hard. Well, Ma didn't even speak proper English. But she crossed the bridge and set up a dressmaking shop in Manhattan. I grew up on East 14th Street. My ma had big plans for me and was strict. I went to school and learned the basiks. But your old grandma was stagestruck. All the guys then were soft on Evelyn Nesbit and all the gals wanted to be hoofers like her. I was no differint. I dreamed of meeting a swell guy – like her arkitect pal who got shot. Or else riding a gold bike through Central Park like Lillian Russell. Meeting a Diamind Jim. I was a dreamer and my ma said a dreamer ends up bad. I tried for the Ponies at Wintergarden, but was too small – roly-poly, Gyp called me.

We met in 1911 at a picnic – managing picnics was his bisness. He was some guy – dark and handsome, except for a broken nose, kinda Indian-looking with a lock of hair falling over one eye to hide a scar. My pal Lilly and I went round together. We was both brunettes, and at first I thought Gyp liked her best. But the next nite he turned up with Lefty, and they took us both to a cabaret. Lefty was named for a tattoo on his left wrist. Gee, they was fun. And smart. You never hear it now but then everyone hummed "Alexander's Ragtime Band."

People had fun then, hon, but they brought in that damn Prohibishon thing which did nothing but harm, in my opinyen.

The four of us did everything together. We fell in love together, lived together, ate together, and then Gyp and Leftie even died together, but that's too sad to think of. I prefer to think of that first nite when we tangoed till dawn. Gyp was some dancer. But Lefty was good too. We did the Castle Walk and the Turkey Trot. Other nites too . . . in midnite roofgardens. Them were the days of "Sweet Italian Love" and "Up and Down Broadway". And there was the new Negro music played by the Clef Club. Did ya ever hear of them? – they rented the Carnegie Hall and set off a craze. Oh, remembering it now makes my heart skip.

But then I think of Gyp and get sad again. Poor Gyp. Did your ma ever speak about Gyp? Maybe she didn't know – it was before she was born. Well, I will. Gyp should be remembered as he was. He was the gentlest person I ever knew, and that's the god's truth. He went to a rabbinical school. His old man wanted him to be a rabbi – the thought makes me laugh. I mean Gyp, a rabbi? But there wasn't much chances for Eastsiders then.

And none for foreign born, especially Jews. You remember that, hon. A Yid was considered worse than Irish. And Italians was treated like dogs. And the coloreds, well, they counted for nothing. Life was hard on us immigrints so we should of stuck together more. There wasn't no place for kids to play. So young boys joined the gangs and went bad. But Gyp was no riff-raff. He just wanted the big-time so he hung round with Monk Eastman's boys.

His real name was Harry Horowitz but everyone called him Gyp – cos that's what the press nicknamed him – Gyp the Blood. "Gyp" was from gypsy. And "Blood" because he was a fancy dresser – he had a daily manikure and wore tailored suits and silk socks. Some folks said "gyp" meant thief, but it did no such thing. Gyp wasn't no thief. He was a picnic manager. Anything he did was bisness. Everyone needs a bisness. You ask your da.

Lefty was a gent too. His name was Louie Rosenberg. His family had a funeral for him when he was arrested. How's that for loyalty? To them he was dead. But at first we girls didn't know nothing about their other life. To us they was just swell dancers. My pal Lilly thought Lefty was a salesman. We met their crowd OK, but didn't know they was gunmen. Poker was no great crime to us. We were no kept ladybirds. We was married and respectable. Gyp was no pimp – a lot of guys were then, hon. They made gals work, but not Gyp. No, we had nothing but the best – fur coats and swell furniture and drapes. We wore our skirts to the top of our shoes which was real daring then. Gyp took

*me joy-riding up and down Broadway in those new
fangled automobiles. Then for chopsuey or lobster a la
Newberg. Or sometimes we'd go to the movies. The older
folks was still calling them "moving pictures" but we
called them movies. They was so exciting. Everything was
new. We saw* A Girl and Her Trust *and Lillian Gish in*
Way Down East.

*We was together seven months. Later when he got
taken in for the Rosenthal murder, the papers printed he
liked to beat up on people, but that was a damn lie. Gyp
never laid a hand on me. He was brought up respectable,
and anything he did was bisness. There were lots a
picnics in those days and people could get rough. Gyp
kept order.*

*You asked me about the Rosenthal case and
Lieutinant Becker. It was a long time ago, but it seems
strange that nobody's heard of it now. There was no sex
in it, I guess. Besides Helen Becker, the only women
involved were Lilly and me, and we were just kids. We
was known as the two Lillys and our pictures was in the
paper. A lawyer said it was prejewdicing the jury to call
the boys Gyp and Lefty so the Judge asked us what we
called them.*

"Mr Horowitz," I said quickly.

And Lilly copied me, "Mr Rosenberg."

*But Helen Becker was a lady, and they sure don't
make the histry books. She lost her baby during the trial.
I felt real bad about that. Charlie was her man, like Gyp
was mine. And boy was Charlie handsome. The cops
then wore high helmets, a double row of brass buttons
down their long belted coats, and the silk tassels on their*

batons. Some of them weren't bad. The city was all carved up between the cops and the gamblers – with the gunmen somewhere in between. Nobody thought anything of it. Graft was graft. Then Herman got shot. Hell, lots of gamblers got shot then, but they sure made a fuss about poor Herman. Aw, it was awful, OK, don't get me wrong, but it just wasn't worth poor Gyp's life, or Lefty's. The other boys didn't amount to much. Dago had no class – Italian. And Whitey Louie well, I didn't meet him much. Oh, Herman was OK. He was always good for a touch, Gyp said. He gave him and Big Jack Zelig a hundred dollars on 14th Street only a few months before. But Herman was a squealer, and some other gamblers wanted him croaked. So did Tammany. It wasn't Charles Becker – that's all I know, cos Gyp told me before he died.

Herman was pulling the plug on the police. So first they warned him with a bomb. But that didn't work so they were going to rough him up a bit and run him out of town. The boys got a call that they might be needed the next day. So they came in from Rockaway, and hung round waiting in a cafe on Second Avenue. Then they got another call to come to Bridgey Webber's place on the lower East Side. There they were supplied with guns and took some dope – opium. We all smoked then – but didn't drink. Around two o'clock they drove to the Metropole with Bridgey Webber and his sidekick, Harry Vallon, also Sam Schepps. Harry was an awful hatchet-faced crook – the lowest of the low. And he was drunk that nite. At the hotel he told the boys to go in and shoot Herman, but they refused. They liked Herman and were only willing to give him his money, teach him a lesson and tell him to get outa town – nothing more. *Gyp thought it was a beating-up party. He didn't want Herman killed. He fired a shot OK, but not the one that killed Herman. The gamblers done that.*

Gyp and Lefty and us two Lillys went into hiding. Oh, we hated leaving our lovely new apartments in Rockaway, but what could we do? We had to stick by our men. At first we went upstate to Parksville, Sullivan County, for about two weeks. We was treated like any young holiday couples. But it was all over the papers how we were spotted here and there – why one paper said we'd been seen in Mexico! All the time we were staying in a regular boarding house. Then Lefty thought we should move, so I rented an apartment in Brooklyn. We got more furniture on the installment plan ($5 down and $1 a week) from Meagher's on Park Row. Things looked nice and neat. Gyp was real neat.

But the boys didn't want us involved, so they sent us back to our mothers – mine lived on 98th Street and Lilly's on Grand. But we visited often. They was great times. The boys was happy watching movies from the staircase of their building and humming the songs along with the nickelodian. Gyp loved music.

Us girls sure had fun giving the cops the slip. We took an elevated train a few stops and then hopped in a car with one of Jack Zelig's boys. The police couldn't follow, cos by the time our tail caught us we was gone. They was real dumb. We could spot them a mile off.

One of the cops was female, the first in New York. She was Mary Sullivan, a couple a years older than us. She was trailing Dago Frank's girl, Rosie. Rosie was a street walker, but that didn't worry us too much cos we didn't know anything about walking. It was her squealing and her pal which was objecshonable. Her pal was supposed to be cutting a deal with the D A's office, but we knew she was a stool. She thought she was fooling everyone by smoking cigarettes and drinking water, pretending it was gin. Rosie kept asking us where the boys were so she could tell her pal. I don't know what they took us for. I said Gyp and Lefty had gone to Mexico and was sending for us and we'd all be rich.

Then the landlord said he wanted married people in his premises and we must be ladybirds. This killed the men.

"He thinks we're not respectable!" Gyp yelled.

I never saw him so mad. So we went back to the Brooklyn apartment, and the four of us was together again – another pal, Jack Kramer, did the shopping across the road. I took over the cooking, and it was like old times.

But a cop overheard me say on the phone that we lived over the New Brighton laundry. One evening Gyp was playing the harmonica after dinner when the cops busted down the door.

"Hold your fire!" Gyp shouted, immediately putting up his hands. "Don't shoot!"

He didn't want anyone hurt. Like I say, he was gentle. The boys and us all started crying then, and they had to pull us apart. So much for the histry books.

It's best not to know the future. We was all taken in, but they soon set us girls free. Lilly's ma and mine demanded to see us. I tried to get Jack Zelig's help, and he was about to testify for the boys, but was shot too. They found my address in his pocket. We only saw our men once more in court and before they died in Sing Sing.

"Just always remember two things," Gyp said. "I love my gal. And Becker had nothin' to do with hiring us."

So that's my story, hon. I wish I'd been older, old enough to change Gyp's wild ways. I often think, what if he'd gone straight? He might of got sense and gone into protecting the unions. Not that I've any sympathy for unions. They was all commies and unAmerican, but then bisness is bisness.

You wanted to know what happened after Gyp, hon? Well, nothing but hard times. There was a rotten foreign war on and I met a soldier boy for awhile. I cheered him off at the boat and then got one letter. He was killed like Gyp. But all things end, even a war. On Armstice day, New Yorkers poured into the streets, shouting and singing and dancing. I kissed every man in uniform. But then life got back to routine. Maybe too routine. I worked in Macys awhile. But life was rough without a man. One day I met a guy from Gyp's old crowd and got tied up with him. He was no gentleman, so I walked out. But my old love for the stage had never died, and I got a small part in a vaudiville show. But then I had your ma, and couldn't feed her. So I tried fortune telling and got caught. I was sent to jail. So that's how she was brought up in foster homes. Yeah, I disappeared for years and she can't forgive that. My old ma was right – I ended up bad. I know what yer saying now, pitying your old grandma and all. But I had Gyp. Maybe in the great beyond we'll all be humming, "Come on an' hear . . . come on an' hear . . . "

I'll stop now. I'm sure feeling pooped after writing so much.

Come see me, hon.

Fondly,

Your grandma,

Lilly Horowitz

CHAPTER THIRTEEN

* * *

LILLY'S LETTER WAS AN ACCOUNT BY A CONTEMPORARY, AND included the last testimony of a dying man to his wife. Surely it was proof that Bald Jack had lied? But had Marcus known? I couldn't help but be touched by the fate of the young gunmen, and planned to get back to New York soon for more research.

Meanwhile my classes were going well.

But the odious doctrine of PC had found its way through the doors. It was amazing – the kids were afraid of words. In the fiction seminar one day, there was a hushed silence because I called the wonderful Edna O'Brien character, Baba, a bitch. Everyone had looked aghast, as if I had blasphemed or something. But how else could you describe her? She was an anti-character and anyone who has read *The Girl with Green Eyes* would agree. It wasn't sexist, I explained quickly, because a man could be a bitch too, but this didn't help.

When I called someone an ass, it really puzzled them. I had to explain that in Ireland ass referred to idiot, rather than a part of the anatomy. Someone else was offended by the frequent use of "boy" in Irish literature. But in Ireland you're a boy till you're fifty. At least, I told myself, there were no blacks in Irish literature, so nobody could be upset about that. But a negro singer is portrayed negatively in *Dubliners* and in James Stephens's novella, *The Charwoman's Daughter,* Yeats is described as "the young black poet, buzzing like a bee."

When we were reading this, a puzzled black girl asked me if Yeats was also black?

Before I could answer no, another genius piped up with, "It's dated to call him 'black'."

"Why?"

"Why not African-American?"

"Because he wasn't!"

I explained that "black" had other meanings. Yeats wore a "black" coat and hat. Or you could be a "black" protestant, although this was probably not the meaning here.

The infamous Teri Scales had turned out to be a terrific asset to class discussion. She was amazingly well read and almost irritatingly knowledgeable. She always sat beside me, her battered hat pulled down on her lank hair, her thick glasses down on her nose, her fat legs bulging out of unattractive shorts. Sometimes she chewed gum, bursting the bubbles loudly. But I was grateful for her. She was never afraid to ask a question and always the first to answer mine. The others were more clod-like, but generally did the reading – except for one boy who never turned up.

His name was Nick Coyle. He had macho muscles and always wore a baseball cap in class, that's on the rare occasions he came. Also he had a habit of snoozing. I didn't know what to do about this, so ignored it.

When I told Chuck, he said, "Tell him he's failing."

"Can I do that?"

Chuck laughed shortly. "Sure. You snooze, you lose!"

"I'm probably boring him."

I once threw a book at a student. Really, I was angry

because I was boring myself. But he woke up very startled, and I didn't know what to do, so I roared at him for losing my place! He apologised profusely.

Well, I wasn't the most stimulating teacher and nowadays had more sympathy with people falling asleep.

One day there was an altercation.

It started when Teri raised her hand with a question about a story set in Northern Ireland. I expected something political, but no.

"What are chilblains, Dr O'Brien?" she asked.

"You don't know?"

She shook her head, picking a pimple.

I checked the class. "Doesn't anyone know?"

Fifteen blank looks.

"You get them on your toes, from poor circulation in cold weather. I sometimes get them when I'm writing." But I was still perplexed. "You mean, no one has heard of them?"

No one had.

"Every Irish schoolchild gets them. Or used to!" Then, I added stupidly, "You've a higher standard of living than the rest of the world. We have to plug draughts and get by with three pairs of socks."

They looked intrigued.

Then Teri added, "Yeah, and we use 7.9 t.o.e. per capita compared to Western Europe's 3.2."

I was puzzled. "T.o.e.?"

"Tonnage oil equivalent. We're using up the planet's resources. It's gross – this classroom's so hot we have to open the window."

It was true. Even in deepest winter, you never needed a sweater. It was almost unbearable to wear wool. You sat in a pool of sweat. Then I said, "Why do you think you went to war in Kuwait?" – a fatal mistake.

155

At that Nick Coyle stirred to life. He glowered from under his cap, muttering, "We kicked Iraqi butt."

"You must come to our Democratic rally tomorrow," Teri went on, picking up on my liberal stance.

"Where is it?"

"On the Mall at noon."

The boy suddenly jumped to his feet, yelling, "We kicked Iraqi butt. They took our oil!"

Dead silence.

"And we killed a hundred thousand!" Teri quipped.

He thumped the table. "We kicked butt! We kicked butt!"

I put up my hand. "Stop it! Please!"

But Teri paid no attention. "A hundred thousand died. Innocent men, women and children."

"Please, Teri!"

"My brother died too!" the boy screamed back. Then he began sobbing wretchedly.

It was awful.

"It was his job!" Teri was pale but insistent. "He was a soldier."

Nick gripped the table, his knuckles showing white. "He was my brother!"

I stood up. "Just a minute – "

Teri looked smug. "You think he was on a picnic?"

"Stop it, Teri." It was getting out of control. "Eh – we'll call a halt for today."

I gathered my books. Why had I mentioned the war? You weren't supposed to mention politics or religion, but it had come up naturally.

As the class filed out, I caught Nick at the door. "I'm sorry about your brother."

He was still breathing heavily and wouldn't make eye-contact.

"It must be very hard for you."

"I never expected to hear talk like that," he said stiffly. "Not in a class like this."

"But people have opinions. That's democracy. How was your brother killed?"

"Sand in the helicopter engine," he growled.

"I'm very sorry."

He didn't answer.

"It's hard for you. And your parents."

"He never saw action – they never even sent the body home."

I couldn't think of anything to say. Of course, I'd been against the Kuwait War, the Falklands War, the Vietnam War, all wars. But war was a vague, far-off thing to me. And if I thought of those who died, at all, I thought of them as men. But soldiers were children. Like this boy.

"Is that why you've been missing class?" I asked kindly.

He dug both hands in his pockets, staring at the floor. "I've had to stay home with my mom."

The kids had the most ingenious excuses for not doing work: relatives having strokes, parents divorcing, fathers having heart attacks, lightning viruses. A grandparent's funeral was very popular. A boy had once told me on a Monday that he'd be absent on the following Monday for a grannie's funeral. I'd innocently asked what they were doing with the body till then.

But I believed this poor fellow. He was depressed. That was why he was so sleepy. He had been heading for an F, but now I had to get him through the course.

"Could you come a little more often?" I pleaded.

He nodded sullenly.

"Have you decided on a paper?"

"Yeah, I'm doin' Somerville and Ross."

"You know a bit about them?"

He shrugged. "Sure. I seen 'em on TV."

The Memoirs of an Irish R.M.?"

"Yeah. That's it."

"Well, if you need help, let me know."

"Aren't they two Irish peasant writers?"

"Not quite."

We talked for awhile in the corridor about the two comic geniuses. He listened politely. It was his big ambition to visit Ireland, as his grandfather had emigrated from Cork – that was why he had taken the class. Everyone in America came from somewhere else. Yet they were so isolated from the rest of the world.

CHAPTER FOURTEEN

* * *

WEEKS PASSED, BUT COUSIN BUD SHOWED NO SIGN OF GOING, AND I hadn't the heart to tell him to. Whenever he could, he persuaded Chuck to play chess with him. Or else he talked endlessly about his past life, his time in reform school and prison, the army, his ex-wives. He was a world-betterer in a way, and his stories had a moral twist which he applied to the young. Or their sex life. Or his. Or mine.

One day Molly invited us to lunch. Typically, Bud wouldn't come, but agreed to drive me over – I let him use the landlord's Mazda to keep it tuned. He wore hooded sweats and sunglasses. I felt it was a disguise.

America has beautiful trees. It was now distinctly fall, and the leaves had turned brilliantly in the grounds of Bella Vista, and all along the route. We passed a student walking in the usual black tights and micro miniskirt. I was thinking how lovely it was to be young, and how all fashion is a throw-back.

Bud looked in the rear view mirror, puzzled. "She workin'?"

His meaning took a minute to sink in. "No, Bud, she's a student."

He groaned, shaking his head. "But she's wigglin' her ass."

"Oh, Bud – "

"A college student dressed like that! What's the world comin' to?"

Where had he come from?

He looked sideways at me. "You and Chuckie takin' precautions?"

"It's Chuck. And what do you mean? I'm a bit old to worry."

"I mean, don't get herpie."

Did he have to be so personal?

But he chuckled, before launching on one of his many stories. "This chick pulls back at the vital minute. 'Wait!' she screams, 'I got Herpie!' 'That's OK,' I shouted back, 'I'll fuck Herpie too!' I never heard of the damn disease!" He broke into laughter, wiping tears from his eyes.

I laughed too. "You mean Herpes?"

"Yeah! I thought Herpie was a guy."

"Did you get it?"

"Naw. But *you* might. Is Chuckie clean?"

I cleared my throat. "He seems to be."

Bud shook his head. "You never know."

"Bud, we're in love."

It just popped out.

"Ha! He said that?"

I nodded.

"Said that to a chick once meself. I was nineteen and in the army. Couldn't pay her, so told her that. 'You'll pay,' she screamed after me. 'Just you wait!'"

"Did you?"

"Sure. Got the clap. Yuh screw, yuh get screwed." And he shook his head again, chuckling sardonically.

Molly was working in her garden and, seeing Bud in the car,

asked him to join us. But he immediately fled. She looked after him, slightly puzzled. "What a handsome man."

"I'm afraid he's not very sociable."

"Hmm . . . one of those."

I followed her inside and downstairs to the bright and pleasant kitchen. There was a Quaker austerity to the old red quarry tiles and plain pine furniture. Yet the stove and preparation area were utterly modern. The wooden table was already laid, with coloured napkins and old green wine glasses.

Theodora wasn't there.

On the counter-top was a note from her, which Molly read out. "Sorry, called out unexpectedly. My love to Anne."

Molly studied the message, puzzled. "Wonder what happened?"

I knew – Theodora was irritated with me. "I'm sorry we upset her at the party."

Molly shrugged. "Oh, she overreacted. No, it's probably something unexpected. There's a bit of a fuss going on at the moment. Remember Michelle, the new film professor?"

I nodded, remembering the pretentious young black woman at the party.

"She wants us all to start marching, because last weekend there was a Ku-Klux-Klan rally."

"Here? In Oldcastle?"

"Oh, a few rednecks from the next town. They come in every year. But this time they rallied outside Michelle's house. It's a college house, rented to new faculty, so they couldn't have known she lived there. But she didn't take it too well."

"But shouldn't we support her?"

"Best to ignore it. The fuss is all because of PC. The English Department has written a formal letter of objection to the Dean. But Michelle still talks about leaving. She's refused to participate in Affirmative Action to recruit more black students. She says the college is racist."

"But it must've been terrifying to have a mob outside the house."

"Yeah, all three of them. Plus two neo-Nazis."

I was aghast. "Nazis are allowed?"

"Free speech is protected by the Constitution. It's better to know what's out there."

Still it was weird. But Molly had strong opinions, so I concentrated on my lunch. It was her famous hot and sour soup, bread and a salad. The soup was HOT, and there were Nasturtiums in the salad.

We'd started eating, when she jumped up. "Forgot your wine."

I shook my head. Molly didn't drink at lunchtime. "I won't, thanks."

"Oh, have a glass of wine."

"No."

"A beer then? Beer's a food?"

I shook my head.

Molly looked chagrined. "I'm sorry for what I said last time."

"What?"

"About you having a drink problem."

I laughed. "I probably do."

"How're you feeling these days?"

"Fine." I didn't want to go into my hallucinations again.

We ate in awkward silence, which she broke. "Are you free this evening? I need someone to fill in at the Shelter?"

I shook my head. "I have to prepare for class. Perhaps Friday night."

"Friday's the concert, remember? What about tomorrow night?"

I was going out with Chuck. "Sorry."

Molly slurped her soup. "Do you get *any* time these days?"

My spoon was at my mouth. She was referring to me spending time with Chuck, who had now become an unmentionable subject between us. "Not much."

"You're backtracking completely?"

"Backtracking?"

"Yeah, quitting. You used to write a lot more."

She made me sound like a lazy adolescent. "But burn-out's real."

Molly looked sceptical.

"I'm tired," I persisted. "I've written five door-stoppers."

Molly looked amused. "But you can't pack it in!"

I sipped my soup calmly. "Why not?"

"Because I enjoy your books!"

I laughed at her exuberance. "Nice of you to say so."

"I'm not being *nice*! I've never tried to be nice in my life. I'm being honest."

I broke off bread and buttered it. "What are they playing on Friday?"

But Molly wasn't to be deflected. "It's the critics, right?"

"Partly."

"But surely you expect criticism?"

"Sure, it's free speech." I bit into my bread.

"Then why get upset?"

I shrugged. Then noticed Molly was fixated by a mark on my wrist.

"What's wrong?" I asked.

"What happened to your arm?"

"I burnt it."

"Are you sure?"

"Yes! Taking a frozen pizza out of the oven."

She looked at me suspiciously.

Suddenly I knew she thought Chuck had done it. "I'm – always burning myself."

There was another silence.

"It drives Fergal crazy. Listen, I know you don't like Chuck, but – "

Now she looked worried.

"He's *not* violent," I protested.

"Hmm." Molly stared into her soup. "Well, he's in serious trouble. Teri Scales has accused him of harassment. Sex for grades. She was in his seminar last semester. A committee has been set up to investigate her charges."

This was too much. I put down my spoon. "She's kept pretty busy, isn't she? Writing letters. Now this."

"It's serious, Anne."

I was tired of Molly's interference. "A disturbed girl accuses a professor, and she's believed."

Molly reddened too. "The college has to take it seriously. He could be in real trouble. I thought you should know."

We ate in silence for a few seconds. She was my friend, I knew she was. And she was telling me this because she cared about me. Yet I was angry.

Molly served dessert, gobbling one large helping of apple pie. Then another. She always ate too much when she was anxious. And now she was worried about me. "How's your research going?"

"I got an interesting letter about the Rosenthal case – from one of the gunmen's wives. The trouble . . . is, my grandfather turns me off."

"You knew him well?

"No, he died in 1935. It's just – oh, things my mother said."

Molly looked sympathetic. "All families have skeletons."

I hesitated, then went on, haltingly, "My mother hinted that she was abused."

Molly didn't even blink. "It's all the fashion nowadays," she said matter-of-factly. "Did she get into the clutches of a therapist?"

"No, I'm sure."

Molly frowned. "She say exactly what happened?"

"No. And I didn't ask."

"Child abuse gets the headlines now. Of course, it's always been there."

Suddenly I pictured my mother as a lonely dark-haired child in a light cotton frock, walking up a long road to meet me.

"You're very absorbed today."

"Am I?"

"Yeah – in another world."

Marcus's world. Last time I had confided in Molly, she'd called me a drunkard. And now she was insinuating things about Chuck. "I can't rake things up."

Molly took another slice of pie. "Why?"

I stared at my plate. "I dunno."

"Your family?" she said between bites.

"Oh, my sister wouldn't mind." I paused. "My brother went to Australia."

"You feel bound to protect the reputation of the dead?"

"I suppose."

"That's a bit vain." Molly put down her spoon. "Why should he get away with it? Wherever he is." She waved at the ceiling.

"You believe in heaven?"

She shrugged. "People create heaven – or, more frequently,

hell. Look, it's a biography – you could always leave out that aspect of your grandfather. After all, there's no proof."

"Just my mother's word."

When I was thirteen, Oonagh said angrily out of the blue, "If HE ever touches you, tell me! Just tell me!" HE was my father. I thought Oonagh mad then, yet understood exactly what she meant. She was obviously recalling her own childhood. It must have started when she was thirteen. A motherless child in thirties Florida – missionary country, she always called it. Irish priests went out there to preach the gospel, in the same way as they went to Africa.

"I should stick to my historical romances," I said.

Molly put coffee in front of me. "That's new, calling them romances. Why not fictionalise your grandfather's story?"

I creamed my coffee. "He . . . disturbs me too much."

"You're disturbed about something that happened sixty years ago?" Molly sat down again.

"I regret not knowing. I could've done something."

Molly put her elbows on the table. "What?"

I looked into my cup. "Had my mother analyzed or something."

She stirred her coffee. "First, it's only a hunch. And second, I don't know why *you* feel guilty."

"It's more than a hunch."

She raised an eyebrow. "Your identification with your mother's odd."

I looked up sharply. "What do you mean?"

"It's just like you're the victim. Have you ever had therapy?"

"Now and again, but never carried it through."

"It isn't all it's cracked up to be," she went on. "You were what's called 'an adult child.' Your mother dumped on you."

I'd never thought of it like that.

"My daughter Sue's into therapy in a big way," Molly went on. "Her marriage just broke up." Molly lit a cigarette. "You don't mind?"

"No."

"Theo makes me go outside. But she'll never know. Anyhow, Sue married very young. She and her husband were teenage sweethearts, both seventeen. He lived next door." Molly looked wistful. "We seemed to attract the whole street. I think of our house, full of all those kids, all screwing each other."

"She thinks you should've stopped her?"

Molly shrugged. "Yep. She blames me. And – accuses her husband of molesting her."

I didn't know what to say.

"She seems to hate all men." Molly hesitated, then went on in a pained voice, "She was raped. We were involved in desegregating a swimming-pool in Virginia. We had young black men staying in the house. One of them stole into Sue's bedroom . . ." Molly's face was white. She inhaled deeply. "You're supposed to protect your kids."

It sounds naive, but I never knew Molly had problems. All her children seemed so normal, so well-adjusted and successful.

"Then . . . perhaps I should've stopped her marrying so young," she went on, shrugging. "But it seemed to be a healing relationship. With kids, you're blamed whatever you do. I'm resigned to taking the rap. But you're blaming yourself for things before you were even born."

I stared into my cup. "I was in God's pocket."

Molly laughed. "That's a nice way of putting it."

"We were told that as children." I drained my cup. I'd

167

forgotten the expression. I thought I'd forgotten so much about childhood, but it always stays with you. Oonagh had never recovered from hers.

"Well, I'm dying to read about Baldy Jack."

"I'll have to write it first."

CHAPTER FIFTEEN

* * *

DIFFICULT TO ADMIT, BUT THERE WAS A CHANGE IN MY RELATIONSHIP with Molly and Theodora – especially Theodora. Oh, I'd never been as close to her as to Molly, but now she seemed to disapprove completely and was always away somewhere when I called. Molly remained friendly. But neither seemed to understand that I was an adult and divorcing Fergal.

I couldn't understand their lack of understanding.

Molly and I still exercised together, and they had me over for an evening meal occasionally – always without Chuck. He was now completely *persona non grata*. It seemed unfair that they should dislike him so much. He was a devoted father, I'd discovered. Of course, he came from a monied and conservative family – he was Charles Matthews III, he jokingly told me. And his father had been a friend of Nixon, while Molly and Theodora were embattled liberals. But this couldn't be the reason. No, it was because of Teri Scales's accusations.

She was only getting a hearing because of the puritan climate of the times. It was ridiculous. Fergal, after all, had been my teacher when we met, although I'd been somewhat older than Teri. But he had married me. Was that sexual harassment? If so, I hadn't minded. So, even if Chuck had made a pass at Teri, was there something criminal about it?

When I asked him about his upcoming committee investigation, he laughed it off as nothing. Teri Scales was bright; he'd given her an A because she deserved it. Not for sex. Christ, had I ever taken a good look at her? Could she attract anyone?

I had to agree with him.

While I didn't dislike the girl, she made me nervous. She was neurotic and a well-documented troublemaker with a frightening naivety. How could anyone believe that Chuck would be interested in her? She was pathetically unattractive.

Just like the Rosenthal case – one person's word against another.

But her latest effort at self-dramatisation topped everything. She claimed that a man dressed up as a pirate broke into her apartment and woke her from sleep, demanding sex. She refused so he chased her, burning her with a cigarette. Finally he relented when she cried, telling her if she went into her bedroom, took off her T-shirt and came out topless and paraded in front of him, she could escape further injury. In the bedroom she managed to lock the door and call the police. They came, but could find no evidence of a break-in, or of anybody being there. There were no fingerprints or footprints. Nothing. Only Teri, locked in her bedroom, sobbing hysterically in a state of shock and with a burnt behind.

It was a masochistic fantasy. She'd previously injured herself with a cigarette, and had been treated for this behavioural aberration by the college psychiatrist.

Behavioural aberration – was I beginning to think like that? Maybe it was time to get out of America?

We were in bed together when Chuck scoffed at her latest story. "A guy dressed as Zorro chases her?"

I sat up. "A pirate."

"A pirate! Zorro! The Shadow! 'Who knows what evil lurks in the heart of man? Eh-heh-heh-heh!' My Orson Welles imitation."

"But why make it up?"

"She's one sicko girl. She was longing to be caught!"

"But the story's not against anyone personally."

"Oh, no! She's only personal about blackmailing department members. And now she's ruining me."

"No one will believe her," I said.

He got out of bed. "I'm not so sure. This was a crummy girls' school. There's a lot of old-fashioned thinking. The Dean had me in yesterday. Someone in the Provost's office pushing for my resignation."

I couldn't repeat Molly's opinion of him. It would only upset him.

"But I won't resign." He paled in anger. "God damn their eyes – as Josh White brilliantly put it!" He looked at me suddenly. "You believe me, don't you?"

I put my hand on his arm. "Of course."

The other consuming issue was the counter-march against the Ku-Klux-Klan. The campus was split down the middle. To march or not to march, that was the question. Most of the staff were sixties' liberals who had fought for Civil Rights. Even I had been thrown out of a café with Ogie on our trip of long ago. Now a black woman was accusing us of condoning bigotry. The Klan had a right to parade, Chuck said, agreeing with Molly and the ACLU, and it was wrong to give them any importance. He confided in me that the new film professor was a fake, and I agreed. She wasn't seriously put out by the Klan, just attention-seeking.

But when I repeated this to Molly, she blew up completely.

"He thinks all the blacks should be run out of town?"

"No, of course not . . ."

Although she had been on the same side as Chuck in this, anti-PC, she seemed to hate him more and more. I put it out of my mind and concentrated on my book.

Molly was right, there was no need to get bogged down in protecting the reputation of the dead. Oonagh had wanted to explain her personality. But she needn't come into the biography. The Rosenthal case was enough. It had made headlines. All America was riveted by the corruption in a big eastern city, and it was reported as far away as London and Paris. The New York District Attorney, Charles Whitman, was an ex-schoolmaster, a Republican with presidential aspirations. With hair parted in the middle, he looked half like a pre-Scott Fitzgerald character and half like Edward Carson, with a lantern jaw, cold eyes and a letterbox mouth. A famous drinker. Initially he'd refused to listen to Rosenthal's complaints about police intimidation. But Harry Bayard Swope had persuaded him that it would impress Whitman's rich reformist friends. Police reform was the politically correct issue of the day.

So, on the murder night, Swope dragged Whitman out of bed and down to the station. The DA stormed in, throwing down his boater, and then grumpily examined the police blotter. His suspicions were aroused by two odd events: 1) No policeman had taken down the correct automobile number. 2) A young café singer, who had reported the correct number, was now in jail.

"Release that young man at once!" Whitman snapped. Next he was accusing the police of the murder. "Rosenthal is killed and with him dies his evidence."

A complete turnabout, and the newspapers were full of it:

WHITMAN PROBES CHARGES
Issues Subpoenas for Men Named as Knowing Inside Facts

Becker came into the station also, saying, "I would give anything in the world if this had not happened. It robs me of any chance to clear myself of this man's accusations."

Hardly the words of a murderer.

The four gunmen had fled – upstate, according to Lilly's letter. The subpoenas were for four gamblers who had all been on an annual gamblers' picnic, the Sam Paul outing, the previous weekend. Immediately after the murder, Bald Jack had lain low for several days. But when the other gamblers started talking, he surrendered. All the other gamblers were arrested, except Sam Schepps who'd disappeared.

At first Rose cleared Becker, saying, "I was never his stool pigeon." But, when confined with the other gamblers in the Tombs, he changed his story, saying the policeman had ordered the murder, repeatedly asking, "Is the job done yet?" If not, Becker would plant a gun on them and arrest them for carrying an illegal weapon. Rose now claimed to be Becker's collector and listed his other grafting activities, giving dates and accounts of protection money collected. His story was corroborated by the other gamblers who were all given immunity.

At midnight on July 29th, Charles Becker was arrested at Bathgate Avenue police station. He'd been transferred to desk duty there and was now suspended. When charged, he pleaded not guilty and was confined to the Tombs along with the gamblers – which drove them into a frenzy. They asked to be transferred to another prison, and were. From the beginning they were VIP's.

Marcus was quoted in the *Times*: "I have only praise for the manner in which District Attorney Whitman has pursued this inquiry. He is the best judge of the value of the evidence at his disposal, and I venture the prediction that he will be able to force a confession from Becker within the next two days which will make the entire police structure of the city collapse like a house of cards."

Was he incriminating the NYPD? Graft was part of the "System". But here was the real, rather than the imaginary, grandfather. He seemed to be sucking-up to Whitman and, when asked why Rose hadn't confessed earlier, was lawyer-like, saying his client was afraid of the police.

But had justice been done?

Helen Becker had believed in her husband. It was over eighty years ago but, if some new evidence could be found, the case might be reopened. History was full of injustices. The Mudd family were still trying to clear the name of their doctor ancestor of involvement in the Lincoln assassination. Bruno Hauptman's widow had held press conferences to assert her husband's innocence of the Lindberg kidnapping. And recently I'd seen the Rosenbergs listed under *In Memoriam* in *The Irish Times* of all places. But the Rosenthal case was so long ago. Was anyone left alive? Was Lilly Horowitz's letter evidence? The trial had been reported fully in the *World* which was on microfilm in the New York Public Library's extension on 43rd Street.

At Hallowe'en I took the Amtrak back to New York, intending to combine research with a visit to Ogie. As I came out of Penn Station at 8th Avenue and 34th Street, four slight youths dawdled by the entrance. Two wore Fedora hats and two had dark, oil-slicked hair. All were sallow-skinned, and all wore similar dark suits.

As I passed, they set out after me. They could be muggers. But I was determined to be unafraid, and set off up Eighth Avenue to Times Square.

At the next intersection, I looked back.

Dammit, their heads bobbed among the crowds. They were following me.

I hurried on.

This was pure paranoia.

It always happened to me in cities. I had to think of other things. Anything – the nippy air, the smell of roasting chestnuts. New York's breezy canyons are always thrilling, but an underworld exists beneath the steam-hissing streets, something like Dante's Inferno – the underworld of the homeless. On a trip to the city last year, the Women's Room in Penn Station was so crowded with unfortunates that Molly bought fifty dollars worth of hotdogs and distributed them – she's like that. The destitute frighten me. We have our own national disgrace in the Travellers. But New York has emptied the mental hospitals, and the sick just roam the streets.

By 39th Street, I'd lost the four youths.

Crazily they reminded me of Gyp and Co. Since reading Lilly's letter the gunmen had come alive in my mind. They'd all been young Eastsiders. In 1912, Eastsiders were usually Jewish immigrants. A generation earlier, the term referred to the Irish living in the tenements below 14th Street. Like most gangsters, the four were slight young men, dandies of around five foot and weighing about a hundred and twenty-five pounds. Gyp was the only one to make posterity. What chance had they had in life?

I passed panhandlers with paper cups held out for coins. One pale young man, covered with HIV brown spots, sat on the pavement. His eyes were closed and a pencilled sign read: PLEASE HELP A HOMELESS NAM VET.

I gave him ten dollars, and walked on. Then glanced over my shoulder – no sign of them.

I'd been stupid. My paranoia was caused by all this misery. In the world's richest country, young men died in the street. Had things advanced at all? Lately I'd been reading the city's history. In 1912 it had four million. Nearly half of these lived on Manhattan Island, the rich in fantastic luxury, the poor – immigrant Irish, Jews, and Italians – in utter squalor. Although they came to America, yearning to "breathe free", most of the Famine Irish had not gone much further inland than the east coast cities. Odd, considering they'd mostly been rural labourers. But in America, they became the urban underclasses which were even more violent than now.

The Five Points was the worst area – five streets met in a square which is today's Columbus Park. From 1820 there were settlements of Irish there, and by 1840 it was a hopeless slum, which even the police feared. After the Famine we moved to squatter settlements in Central Park and Upper Manhattan.

But by 1912 we were into Ward politics. The historians say we changed American history by the parish mentality of our representatives, who made sure of votes with buckets of coal and bags of groceries. The Democratic Party's New Deal was an extension of this. But the bad result then was Tammany.

Marcus was a Tammany lawyer, I was sure. His law office was even in Park Row, one of the original Five Points streets. No wonder my grandmother hated the city. She probably had to associate with criminals. Also it was hellishly hot before air-conditioning. Hand fans were part of life. Herman Rosenthal had fallen dead on one.

I reached Times Square. As always, it was teeming with

crowds. From the island, I looked down 43rd Street, imagining the vintage automobiles and horse-drawn carriages of old photos. In 1912, it was a sleepy city square. It was hard to see it as "the great white way", the home of the theatre, of Rector's and Shanahan's restaurants – hangouts of Floradora girls like Evelyn Nesbit, hopefuls like Lilly Horowitz and other "broadminded broads from Broadway".

> *Tell me, pretty maiden*
> *Are there more at home like you?*
> *There are a few, kind sir,*
> *But simple girls, and proper too.*

In 1912 Laurette Taylor was a hit in *Peg O' My Heart*. Broadway was part of the Tenderloin, the area with all the good pickings. Herman Rosenthal had been helped move uptown from the lower east side by Big Tim Sullivan. The world of entertainment was close to the world of crime. How many Irish Americans knew that their ancestors had staked out territory in the city? You thought of them as rosary-muttering Catholics, but many were thugs who used fascinating slang: the term "copper" comes from the copper star the police wore. A "leatherhead" was another word for policeman. A "lobbygow" was a gambler's sidekick. Everyone had a nickname. By the time of the Rosenthal case, the gangs had reigned for nearly a hundred years. There were the Plug Uglies, the Bowery Boys, the Hudson Dusters, the Whyos and the Eastman gang from which Gyp and Co. came.

The four sallow-skinned boys were now dawdling outside a fast food restaurant across the street.

Damn. They *were* following me.

But no, I must control myself.

177

I crossed to the top of 43rd, where Herman Rosenthal had met his fate, and looked up at the buildings for some sign of the Metropole Hotel.

A man in shirt sleeves stopped beside me, craning his neck too. "Lookin' for someplace?"

"The Hotel Metropole was somewhere here – in 1912."

He gave me a funny look. "1912? Naw – that was always Rossoff's."

"Rossoff's?" It was the name over a private hotel with a sign, NO VACANCIES.

"Was it called the Metropole in 1912?"

He shrugged, moving nervously on.

Well, it was a long time ago. I went into the hotel lobby and asked a man behind reception if this were the scene of the Rosenthal murder.

He also eyed me suspiciously, shaking his head and saying in London cockney, "Never 'eard of it, luv. But there was another murder here . . ."

Then he was called to the phone.

But a girl behind the counter looked up. "Was that murder written up in a magazine?"

I nodded. "Yes."

"This is the place."

I wanted to ask her more, but the owner was now back and gave me a "get lost" look. New Yorkers are good at that. So I thanked the young woman and, on the way out, stared intrigued at the marble staircase. Had it been there in 1912? Had Rosenthal lain dead and covered with newspapers on the outside steps? Adjoining the hotel was a café. It looked like part of the elegant old hotel. Was that the place from which Rosenthal had been called out? I went in, sat by the window and ordered coffee and a muffin.

When I had finished eating, an old-fashioned grey car

chugged up the street outside. It was for a Hallowe'en parade, I thought. After all, it was the night of the pumpkins. But then four slight young men piled out and stood around grimly. I froze – they were the boys who were at Penn Station. Now I could see them more clearly. One had a broken nose and a scar over his eye. Gyp. Then an older, rubbery-faced man got out of the front and walked up the steps. He wore a boater and high celluloid collar and had one hand in his pocket.

It was Bald Jack.

Then voices called menacingly, "Come on out, Annie."

Suddenly a dark squat man came down the hotel steps, holding a newspaper with a photograph of himself. But Bald Jack ignored him and pointed his gun at me.

"No!" I shouted, ducking beneath the window. "No!"

But it was too late. Shots rang out.

Bald Jack had missed me.

Then the car took off again with the gunmen jumping onto the running board.

I looked up to see a waiter standing over me.

"You OK, Ma'am?"

My voice shook. "I want to report a crime."

He looked at me oddly.

"But didn't you see them?" I pointed out to the street. "A man tried to kill me."

Nervously he edged away. "You need more cawfee, Ma'am?"

"Coffee?" I'd drunk all of mine. And eaten the muffin. But people in the cafe were staring. Had I shouted? "No, just bring the bill."

Then I fled, dashing up the street and into another Times Square fast food café. For once I was grateful for the vulgarity and clamour of my surroundings. I needed the babble of the living. Caffeine gave me heart palpitations, but I drank two more cups, staring out at the jostling crowds – all races passed, brown, black, yellow. A huge black man in white chef's apron and hat passed like a character in search of a play. This crossroads of the world was the scene of a turning point in Marcus's life. What if Herman hadn't been shot? Then Bald Jack wouldn't have gone to Marcus for help. Marcus wouldn't have got him off. He wouldn't have been rewarded politically, there wouldn't have been a scandal and he wouldn't have retired to Ireland. My grandmother might have lived. But such speculation was useless. Now other ghosts besides Marcus haunted me. The gunmen had looked so young. Were they innocent? No one had cared about them. Yet, they were someone's sons. Had they descendants?

CHAPTER SIXTEEN

* * *

WHEN I GOT TO THE NEW YORK PUBLIC LIBRARY'S ANNEX ON 43RD Street, the other scholars were already busy. I was still shaking, and the company was comforting. With others around, I felt safe.

I ordered the 1912 copies of the *World* on film and spent the day squinting at readers and making notes of pages to Xerox later – that's their system. It was a sort of "You Are There" sensation to see press reports of the actual trial – The People versus Becker. All were anti-Becker. He refused to plead, so the court entered a plea of Not Guilty. He also refused, throughout, to testify, or admit graft, thinking he'd be cleared and could return to his job. The papers described him as having lost weight, his grey suit "hanging loose".

There were drawings of Judge Goff, an Irishman, who presided. Also of the lantern-jawed Whitman, prosecuting. He summed up the case, ending with the statement, "I charge that Becker plotted the crime from last May!"

Bald Jack looked sinister, almost evil. Maybe it was the lack of eyebrows as well as hair. When he testified, there were some initial questions about his relationship with Marcus.

Q. In Connecticut you knew Marcus Quilligan O'Neill?
A. Yes, he is my lawyer.

Q. And was that when you were apprehended for murder?

A. I was not apprehended. I surrendered.

Q. What were your relations with O'Neill in Connecticut?

A. He was my press agent, while I promoted prize fights there.

Q. You took the box receipts several times, and you and O'Neill decamped, didn't you?

A. That is positively a falsehood.

Q. Did you gamble in Connecticut?

A. No.

Q. Your relations with Marcus Quilligan O'Neill have been very intimate?

A. Yes, in Connecticut only.

How intimate? Had Marcus fixed the witnesses? He had acted for Sam Schepps too, another gambler. That nasty character had corroborated Rose's story, and was a vital witness. Yet he'd been at the scene of the crime.

I flicked on, taking notes of the relevant pages. The defence argued that Rose killed Rosenthal in a private feud. They claimed that he later made up the story, incriminating Becker, when incarcerated in the Tombs. But the jury, mainly white collar, delivered a guilty verdict – *beyond reasonable doubt,* as instructed by the judge. Yet there was no physical evidence. Only circumstantial.

There was a photo of Lilly Horowitz crying at the gunmen's trial.

Two years later there were newspaper stories about Marcus's diplomatic scandal, all damning.

A photograph of Marcus with his wife and child, boarding a New York ship, hopped out. They were all bundled against the weather. He looked pompously overweight, while my grandmother was grave-eyed with a big hat. My forgotten child-uncle was about four. Why were there no other photographs of this boy who had disappeared into death? He should be remembered on someone's mantlepiece.

Squinting at the viewers, I heard a menacing chant, "Come out, Annie."

I didn't look up.

"Come out! There's someone here wantsta talk to ya!"

Marcus sat at a desk across the room. Even more alarming, a bald, rubbery-skinned man in a boater whispered in his ear, while pointing to me.

It was Jack Rose again.

"We gotta croak that broad, Marcus. She's a squealer," he snarled and ducked out the door.

Marcus ambled over, again in his white-faced, Cagney incarnation.

I looked up nervously. "You're in all the papers."

He chewed gum. "Oh, yeah?"

"Did you get rid of Sam Schepps?"

"Whaja mean?"

"Becker was convicted in advance by the press!"

"Tha's poppycock!" He grabbed my notepad. "Gimme that! I've heard enough. Jack's not too happy either!"

I held onto it. "He tried to kill me!"

"Yeah, he's gone out to round up the boys."

"The boys?" Desperately, I changed the subject. "You gave up law after the Rosenthal case?"

Marcus screwed up his eyes, still chewing.

"Was it because of Becker?" I persisted. "You felt guilty about him?"

"Guilty?" He laughed slowly. "Naw. I needed the cash. Diplomacy was a better number."

"How did you get Rose to confess?"

"Told him he'd burn."

"It was a trick to save him?"

"It was my job to save him."

"Wasn't there a pay-off?"

Marcus looked reflective. "You don't get involved emotionally. It was business."

"But an innocent man died."

"He was guilty."

I looked over at Marcus. "Did Whitman owe you?"

"You bet he did," Marcus spoke out of the side of his mouth. "I got him into the Governor's mansion."

Then Bald Jack came back with a small weasel-faced man. They both wore boaters and had white standup collars. Rose pointed me out, and the small man came for me.

"Plug her, Jack?"

"Do it good, Sam!" Jack croaked.

It was Sam Schepps – Rose's sidekick.

"Help!" I screamed to Marcus.

But he turned his back. "I told ya to let things rest."

I screamed again, but it was no use. Bald Jack was coming for me with a gun.

Marcus grinned. "You wouldn't let things be."

"But it was all your idea. Help me!"

He looked back coldly again. "It's your time to die."

Luckily just as Sam Schepps reached me, a bald librarian shook me awake. He stood over me, staring and shocked. "What is it?"

"Nothing. I was dreaming."

"Dreaming?" He looked dubious. "You were screaming."

I blinked. People were looking.

"You want a glass of water, Ma'am?"

"No, I'm OK. Sorry – sorry . . . "

I gathered my stuff and left, ignoring the stares.

184

I was too shaken to take the subway or get into a cab, so I walked uptown, past the Lincoln Centre, through crowded evening streets to Ogie's. The sky was mean and rain had been forecast. But I didn't care, the city was beautiful and the walk would steady my nerves. Anyway, I wanted to be late, so Ogie'd be home from work and I wouldn't be stuck with the children. All the way, I thought about the case. One thing was clear: Becker was tried in advance by the press. Statements were attributed to him which he could hardly have made. Things like: "I'll croak that Jew squealer, Rose."

And Helen Becker haunted me. She had never remarried but worked as a New York public school teacher into old age, never giving up on her husband's case. But what was the truth? Marcus said he thought Becker guilty. But many other people at the time believed in his innocence. The Mayor. Also the Police Commissioner with the marvellous name of Rhinelander Waldo. Bat Masterson, the famous westerner – by then a New York sports editor – believed in his pal Becker. And down the years, many others. Until everybody forgot.

For all of its contemporary fame, the Rosenthal case wasn't remembered today. There was no hook. No beautiful woman or rich society murder. Just a crooked cop who got his come-uppance. Still, it was perfect tragedy. Becker's fatal flaw was greed. He'd got rich on protection money. Even his refusal to testify was motivated by the fear of losing his pension. Or perhaps he loved his wife too much and wanted to provide more of life's comforts than he could afford. His last outing with her was to see their new house in the Bronx.

The story had structure. There was exposition, conflict, leading to the crisis of his conviction and then the long dénouement, during which he came to accept his fate and was a support to other prisoners, including the four young gunmen. He died begging for his name to be cleared.

> *"Good name in man and woman, dear my lord,*
> *Is the immediate jewel of their souls;*
> *Who steals my purse, steals trash . . ."*

This time Ogie answered her basement bell. She was flushed and wore an apron.

I got the usual big hug. "Come on in. How's Sweetmount?"

"Oh, fine. It's so good to see you." As I held onto her, tears suddenly came.

"What is it?" She pulled me on in, took my coat and sat me down on the living-room couch.

I struggled for control.

"Are you overworking? You are, aren't you?"

"No. New York just wears me out. I spent the day in the library. I'm almost blind from old newspapers." I rubbed my eyes and cleaned my glasses.

Ogie looked concerned. "Have some wine. I bought it in your honour, if you wouldn't mind opening it." We went into the kitchen, and she handed me a bottle and opener. It was Gallo Dry Reserve.

I uncorked it. "My favourite. Will you have some?"

"A half a glass."

We sipped our wine. The house was amazingly peaceful. Jessica was reading on the stairs in fancy dress, ready to go trick or treating for Hallowe'en. There was no sign of Jason.

I put down my glass. "I've got something for you. I copied it in the library."

"What is it?"

"It's from the *World. Shingle* – the annual of Yale Law School. They described our grandfather, 'Mark' as a 'reporter, editor, journalist, orator, politician, statesman, jurist,' who spoiled his chances of being President of the United States by being born in Ireland in 1873."

Ogie's eyes bulged. "President?"

I had to smile. "They're being satirical."

I went on. "'Mark' was the first senior President of the Kent Club and a 'speaker of force and ability' on the inter-department debating team. They said that the transition from the public schools of Boston was just as big a jump as that from Park Row lawyer to American Minister."

"Gosh."

"He was certainly energetic."

Ogie read the Xerox silently. I sipped my drink, reflecting that, as Marcus was steam-shipping to the Caribbean, Becker was rotting in Sing-Sing. While in Europe the First World War was brewing over Serbia and Bosnia. Weird, how nothing ever changes.

"Can I copy this for the children?"

"Keep it. I got it for you." I changed the subject. "Cousin Bud turned up in Oldcastle."

"Yeah." Ogie grimaced. "He called for your number. He's not staying with you?"

"For awhile."

"Is that OK?"

"Oh, he's company. I can't throw him out."

Ogie got up and drained some potatoes. "He wanted to stay here, but I've no space."

I said nothing about his problems.

"I'm so excited you're working on Marcus." Ogie looked over earnestly. "If I can help with the typing – anything. You just say."

187

I nodded. "I'm OK for the moment. Remember, I mentioned the Rosenthal case? Well, Marcus had an important role in it."

"Hey, Jessica! You hear that! Your ancestor was an important lawyer!"

The child grunted from the stairs.

Ogie shook a basket of chicken in the fryer. "It's only fried chicken."

"Lovely."

The tension had gone completely. When dinner was ready, Jessica was sent upstairs for Hans who'd been reading to Jason. They came to the table laughing and joking hungrily. Jason was in blackface which, Hans whispered, wasn't very politically correct, especially as there was a little black boy coming after dinner to trick and treat. He helped serve the children and us from the dishes of potatoes, corn-on-the-cob and hot corn muffins which had been miraculously produced. Soon everyone was eating happily. Even the children seemed nicer on this second visit, both to me and to each other.

When Ogie told Jessica to eat slowly, Jason quipped, "It's no use tellin' her that."

Ogie was puzzled. "Why not?"

"It's like tellin' God, don't let me die."

Hans took a leg of chicken from his mouth and peered suspiciously at it. "This isn't cooked, Ogie."

"What?"

"It's raw."

She was speechless.

I looked nervously from one to the other. Was there to be another row, after all?

"Are you criticisin' ma cookin'?" Ogie spoke southern again.

"But it's – raw." He passed her his plate. "See for yourself."

Ogie peered at the gnawed leg, breathing heavily. "It ain't raw!"

"Well, in that case, I'll pass!" He knocked a tall pepper mill over as he stood up. The noise startled the children. But he went to the sofa and sat down with his newspaper.

The silence was deafening. Even the children were quiet and ate nervously. It was the lull before a storm. I righted the pepper mill, glancing fleetingly at Ogie.

She was still staring speechlessly at the chicken leg. "Prince Charming!" she shrieked, getting her breath at last. "Prince Charming!"

"Ogie's a party poop, Anne." Hans rustled his newspaper wearily. "Forgive her."

I was afraid to answer. One look at Ogie's purple face was enough to stir queasy memories of her tantrums of twenty years ago. Numbly I nibbled my chicken. Hans was right, it was pink. Would we get salmonella poisoning now? It would surely be simple enough to pop it in the microwave for another few minutes, or under the broiler. But that might offend Ogie who looked about to burst.

Then Jason started coughing.

Ogie immediately stiffened. Her eyes bulged, showing white, as the child coughed and got redder and redder.

"A glass of water, Jason?" I coaxed, pouring out some.

He kept coughing.

"I want water!" Jessica shrieked.

"You gotta drink milk, Jessy," came from Hans.

"I hate milk! Pass the water, Mom!"

Ogie stared at her choking son, white with fear.

"Mom!" The girl banged the table.

Ogie pushed the jug across the table, spilling water all over.

Oh God, he can't be choking, I prayed, as Jason went blue. But his eyes were rolling back in his head.

"Oh, my God!" Ogie thudded from the room, gnawing her index-finger. "I can't handle this!"

Hans looked up from his paper, but didn't move.

I went into slow motion. Time seemed to stop. Thump the child in the chest. Just under the ribs. But first look in his mouth. Perhaps it hadn't gone down far.

"My God!" Ogie screamed again from the bathroom door, "why hast thou forsaken me?"

I prised the child's mouth open. A piece of chicken skin was stuck in his throat. Please God, don't let it be a bone.

I pulled it loose.

The child coughed and spluttered. Then got his breath and broke into gasping sobs.

It had happened so quickly. "You're all right, pet."

The father rustled his newspaper, frowned and read on.

The tough little boy was crying. Tears made white rivulets down his blackface. He rubbed his eyes with grimy fists in the pathetic way children do. Children are so beautiful. Instinctively I hugged him, looking nervously around to the parents. "Should he lie down?"

Ogie was still in the bathroom doorway.

"He's all right, Ogie." I kept my voice level, smoothing the little boy's blackened forehead.

Briefly he stopped howling, then started up again.

I gave him a tissue. "Now, now. You're the brave boy, aren't you?"

Hans read on.

Typical man. I wanted to grab the paper and hit him with it. For God's sake, didn't he realise his child had almost choked?

Then Ogie came over. "Oh, my God. Is he OK?"

"He's all right," I repeated firmly. Trembling, I pointed to the incriminating chicken. "This was stuck in his throat."

"My poor baby." Ogie took the child in her arms.

Although Ogie put the cats in the bathroom that night, I still slept badly and awoke before the rest of the household. I'd had no dreams, but the choking incident had flattened me. Also the quarrelling. But at least the child's narrow escape had shocked Ogie out of her anger. Like the last time, she and Hans had laughed and chatted normally, as if nothing had happened. Later on they got a kick out of Jason's black friend coming in whiteface. His mother delivered him and, when the children left to trick or treat at the upstairs apartments, the three parents laughed together – so much for PC. Still, it intrigued me that Hans and Ogie always bounced back so quickly from such ghastly rows. Hans was so detached. How did Ogie stick it? Men are all the same – ignore something and it hasn't happened. But then Ogie wasn't easy either.

Did she have to work? Children needed security, stable parents. It was all I ever wanted as a child – an ordinary life with an ordinary mother at home. It was the same for these children. Oonagh had to work to feed us, but what about Ogie? Maybe things would be safer if she stayed home? Her children would know what to expect. They were probably disturbed. Who wouldn't be with quarrelling parents? And the children weren't the worst, when you got to know them. Jason had even kissed me goodnight – I nearly fainted.

In the morning I helped Ogie with the children. They ate breakfast noisily, then left with Hans. We lingered over coffee.

Ogie was in her kaftan, her white hair wild. "Hans and I were talking last night . . ."

I stiffened. Were they divorcing?

"We're making wills. And we wondered if you'd consider being the children's guardian?"

I was taken aback. "Oh, my goodness! Well . . ."

"There'd be no financial strain."

"I'd be honoured. It's just that I'm not that good with children."

Her eyes widened. "But you're gifted with children."

It was the nicest thing anyone had ever said to me.

"They'd need someone like you – if we weren't here."

I stared at her. "Fergal would be better." He still hadn't rung. "Listen, you're not *dying* or anything?"

She waved a hand, smiling. "Oh, no. This is just in case. Now let's get off it. Whatcha doin' today?"

"The library. Then home."

"You don't wanta go shopping?"

I hated shopping, but didn't say so. "I can't."

"But we're right near Zabar's."

"Maybe I'll go there on the way to the library."

As I left, there was a drug addict snorting coke in the basement yard. He ran when he saw me. I walked down Broadway to Zabar's to buy bread for Molly. All the way, the homeless held out paper cups for coins. One man sold me a pencil. Outside the gourmet deli, another man ransacked a garbage bag, as a limousine the length of a house pulled up and a chauffeur jumped out for groceries.

CHAPTER SEVENTEEN

* * *

AFTER ANOTHER DAY AT THE LIBRARY, I TOOK THE TRAIN HOME.

New York always gave me a funny *déjà vu* feeling – as if I'd lived before. After all, it's not so crazy, the Buddhists believe it. And we carry so many other lives in our genes. Once on Clare Island, off the west coast of Ireland, a funny thing happened. I was in a pony and trap, going to the quayside for the boat back to the mainland, when I was overcome. I couldn't stop crying. I don't know – maybe the mode of travel had somehow transported me to another life.

But the same thing happened again – twice. In Kilkenny I found the house my grandmother grew up in. Although I'd never been in the city before, the house drew me like a magnet. Fergal and I had stopped on the way to Cork. He was hungry and looking for a place to eat. "Let's walk up this street," I said, not knowing why. He followed me grumpily until I stopped at a gaunt Georgian house in the centre of town. I was certain my family had lived there.

I was right.

The house had a plaque to my grandmother's uncle – a Healy who'd been a semi-famous opera singer. Then in Kerry, in a place called Blennerville outside Tralee, I got that *déjà vu* feeling again. I'd no idea why it should happen there. But later I read that Blennerville was a point of departure for Kerry emigrants to the USA in the last century. Marcus's people, the Quilligans and O'Neills, had come from Kerry, so must have departed from there. Maybe it was just a strong feeling of empathy with the thousands who crossed the water never to return. Or maybe a racial memory. You inherited other things from the genetic soup, so why not a memory gene? It made sense.

Marcus didn't reappear in the library. Or his murderous henchmen. Despite the nervous-looking librarian, I was learning to live with Marcus. But his visitations were wearing. I didn't consider another analyst, but maybe sleeping pills. Or perhaps next time I should confront him. Kill him, before he killed me.

It was late when I got back. I'd planned to ask Chuck over, but couldn't as Bud was still up. It was difficult to have a love life with a half-dressed cousin always skulking in the background with his chess board. And he still showed no sign of going, although I'd hinted that the apartment was only leased till Christmas.

As usual, he was slumped in the front of the TV with a coke, and in his boxer shorts and Nike runners.

There was a red rose on the hall table. "Who sent this, Bud?"

He shrugged. "For you. Must be some beau."

I examined the card. No message, just a telephone number. Not Chuck's. Who else would be sending flowers? Not the Irish boy on the plane! Damn, how had he got my address?

"When did it come?"

"Yesterday."

I felt weary. "That kid on the plane."

Bud eyed me suspiciously. "A kid? Pretty busy, ain't ya? And pretty late. What kept yuh?"

Controlling my irritation, I got orange juice from the fridge. "Late?"

"*Late,* dammit!"

Had he gone mad? The juice was acidic from being too long in the fridge, but I drank it anyway.

"Yer dinner's waitin'."

Now I was being bullied in my own home. I kept my voice calm. "I didn't know you expected me."

He pulled a box of fried chicken wings and deli coleslaw from the fridge. "I got dinner in."

His "cooking" was beginning to pall. "I'm not hungry."

He looked outraged. "What's wrong with chicken, dammit?"

"Nothing. I'm just not hungry."

"Dammit, yuh need to eat!"

"I hate coleslaw – all we ever eat are takeaways," I snapped.

Immediately he grabbed the coleslaw and dumped it in the trash. Then he put the chicken back, banging the fridge door. "You're picky! The pickiest goddam broad I ever met."

"Look, Bud, firstly, I ate on the train."

"Well, that's OK then!"

"And secondly, I'm a grown woman. I don't – want to be called a broad."

"Oh, yer into that feminineism."

"The word's feminism. But it's nothing to do with that!"

"I was married to one o' them feminines. Now she misses ole Bud." He stood with arms folded, roaring on, "When the shit hits the fan, you'll need ole Bud. I was goin' to call the cops!"

I was startled. "The cops?"

"Yuh know I can't!"

"But why would you?"

He jabbed the air with a forefinger. "Cos, you said you'd be back early!"

I was getting angry now. "I got a *later* train."

"You coulda called!"

"I could! But I didn't! I had work to do. I'm not like you. I can't sit around. And I please myself in my own home. If you don't like it, go!"

It was said now.

He rounded on me. "So yer throwin' me out!"

I sighed heavily. "No – but please – just look after yourself."

"Now you just listen to Cousin Bud!" He calmed down a bit, but started pacing. "You're my blood relation and you got me worried!"

"What's worrying you?"

He still paced up and down. "That Chuckie's a creep."

"You needn't concern yourself with my private life."

"I gotta gun if he gets rough."

"What!"

"I gotta gun for protection." He gritted his teeth.

"Well, get rid of it! And stop this paternalistic behaviour. I can take care of myself."

"That's a joke. You left the cat out!"

"So what?"

"It's not meant to be out all night. You can't take care of a cat. How can you take care of yourself?" He slumped miserably into a chair. "And Chuckie's a cheat."

"It's Chuck, Bud. And what do you mean?"

He folded his arms and roared, "He *cheats* at chess!"

I sighed. It was an obsession between them. "You're not just a bad loser?"

He groaned. "Oh, I'm a loser, OK. But that sonofabitch's been cheatin' since we started."

"But how can you cheat at chess?"

"He'll try and sneak a pawn off the board. He thinks I'm dumb – not educated, so he'll do something stupid like that!" He laughed in exasperation. "But I'm a professional, Coz!"

Why was everyone so down on Chuck? First Molly, now Bud. "You mean a professional cheater?"

He groaned. "I work in a casino, for God's sakes. I spotted him from the first!"

I went into my bedroom, calling, "Please mind your own business, Bud."

"Fergie plays a clean game!"

I slammed the door.

All night I tossed and turned, my stomach upset from the orange juice and Cousin Bud's gun. I wasn't having a weapon in the house. He'd have to get rid of it. What if he got angry over a chess game and shot Chuck? How had I got myself into this mess? And would I ever get rid of him?

I was beginning to miss Fergal. He was so easygoing – except for his drinking. Oh, he preached at me, but never bothered about the mote in his own eye. Why was there one law for women and another for men?

The next morning Bud was up before me. As I came into the kitchen, he was fussing around in an apron. There was flour everywhere. The *Fannie Farmer Cookbook* was on the counter.

I nodded – all I'm capable of in the morning.

He was back to his old self. "Cooked yuh some bacon. And biscuits from scratch."

"Thanks, Bud."

"First rule. Don't fry bacon, naked."

I laughed, as he served me from the stove. It was a cholesterol cocktail of bacon, eggs and sausage. But I cleaned my plate to keep the peace. As I was deep in the *Times*, he interrupted. "How'd yuh get on in New York?"

"Fine. I saw Ogie."

"How's Ogie?"

"Terrible. I mean, fine."

"She has two kids now?"

"Umm."

"See any shows?"

I shook my head. He kept quizzing me, so finally I gave up trying to decipher Christopher Lehmann-Haupt and told him about researching the Rosenthal case.

Bud shook his head, frowning. "Never heard of it."

I told him about how Bald Jack, a known criminal, was believed, and that it didn't seem right.

He shrugged. "Deals are cut all the time. You heard o' Sammy the Bull?"

"No."

"Salvatore Gravano. He's rattin' on John Gotti now."

"Who's John Gotti?"

"The Gambino family boss. They've been tryin' to nail him for years. He's called the Teflon Don, cos nothin' sticks. But now Sammy the Bull's sellin' out the mob." He shook his head ruefully. "The Mafia won't like it. It ain't done to turn state's witness."

"What did the – eh – Teflon Don do?"

"Ordered the execution of Paul Castellano. There were four gunmen involved – Gravano was probably in on it too. But Gotti supervised."

"There were four gunmen in the Rosenthal case too. Why was Castellano murdered?"

"Look – it's a jungle out there. Castellano probably wanted to get Gotti – for drug dealing. Castellano banned drugs. So Gotti got him first."

Times hadn't changed much. "Will Sammy the Bull go free?"

"Get probation or do a short term." Bud let out a short laugh. "But they'll nail him."

"The Mafia?"

He nodded.

"Bald Jack Rose lived till old age."

Bud laughed again. "He probably took care of things."

"What do you mean?"

"I mean he tied it up. Took care of the opposition."

"Well, the gunmen were all executed."

"It might be different for Sammy the Bull." Bud took a coke from the fridge and opened it. "They never forget. They got Kennedy."

"The Mafia?"

"He insulted them so they got him."

"I thought it was Lee Harvey Oswald?"

He shook his head. "The Mafia delivered the votes and Jack was ungrateful. He set Bobby on them. It was an insult."

Everyone has a theory about Kennedy. To the Irish he was the emigrant dream come true. To the feminists he was a horror and a sexual athlete. But I cried for a week when he died and, even now, his ringing voice brings a lump to my throat.

Cousin Bud was shaking his head dismally. "They never forget."

Suddenly it dawned on me. "They're after *you*? That's why you have the gun?"

He looked furtive. "Naw, I'm small fry. Besides they'd never find me here – a small college town."

"Bud, will you do something for me?"

"Sure, Coz."

"Get rid of that gun."

He nodded. "Eh – don't worry. I told yuh – I'm small fry."

Small fry? Hadn't I troubles enough with a ghost, Chuck, and a broken marriage? Now I was harbouring a male chauvinist cousin on the run from the Mafia.

The next day Bud told me he'd been promised a job in Atlantic City. He had a pal there, pulling strings. Something should come up soon. Maybe the end of the week. I wasn't sorry at the prospect of having my apartment back. My relationship with Chuck was suffering. It was difficult to relax. And oddly, Chuck never suggested going to his place.

But day followed day, and Bud didn't go.

The next week, I got another rose. But this time the card had a message: *If you want to know who framed Becker, call 215-456-7899.*

It was a Philadelphia number.

But it couldn't be the Irish boy – he knew nothing about the Rosenthal case.

"Bud, look at this!"

He read the card. "Aw, it's a joke. Someone's putting you on."

"But why?"

"Why would anyone care about some dumb cop who's been dead for seventy years?" He gave me the card. "Yuh some crazy baby."

I ignored that description. "People care about the truth, Bud. 'Who steals my purse, steals trash.'"

"What?"

"It's from *Othello*," I explained.

"From who?"

"*Othello*, a play by Shakespeare, the famous – "

"I heard o' him!" he snapped. "I ain't that ignorant!"

I read the card again. "It says, 'framed Becker.' Our grandfather might've done in an innocent man."

He grinned. "Innocent, huh?"

"How can you be so cynical?"

"And you so dumb? Yuh live in the clouds, Coz. Yuh go around with weirdos."

"Weirdos?"

"Like Chuckie."

"You promised to shut up about him!"

Bud held up his hand. "OK, OK. But this town ain't – "

"What?"

"Real, dammit." Then his voice changed. "I never went to no college."

I sighed. "You still could. I was a mature student."

He chuckled. "Mature?"

"Stop that!"

He straightened his face. "OK, Coz. But I can't help thinkin' Fergie's a great guy. Yuh got a life, dammit. Yet you're chuckin' it for Chuck. Yuh don't know the world. Yuh don't know how filthy it is. Yuh act so shocked. Our grandfather mighta done in someone innocent. He mighta taken graft." He waggled his hips. "Well, Coz, one way or the other, we all take graft."

"I don't."

He shrugged and picked up the card that came with the rose. "Who's this nut?"

"I don't know. You call the number, Bud. No one understands my Irish accent."

He laughed. "Sure. But I love your Irish accent. Wish I coulda found myself a colleen."

If I said anything, I'd be inviting him back to Dublin, so I waited as he dialled the number then and there. My heart raced while it rang.

Then it was answered by a wheezy, "Yeah?"

I suddenly grabbed the receiver from Bud. "This is Anne O'Brien. You sent me roses."

"Yeah." A pause, then an old man's voice said, "Saw your letter in the *Times*."

So that was it. "But why did you send me roses?"

There was a pause. Then the old voice again. "For Bald Jack Rose."

At last I was finding out something. "You know something about him?"

Another pause. Then a wheezy, "Sure do."

"The Rosenthal Case?"

"Yeah."

"You have new evidence?"

There was a silence. Then the old voice went on, wheezing noisily, "Can't talk over the phone. We're being listened to from space!"

Dammit, a nut. I was about to hang up but Bud stopped me.

"Why don't you come up to Philly?" the old man said.

Bud nodded in the background, so I agreed.

The old man gave me an address. "Near the market. I run a typewriter shop. Ask for Harry."

I had finished teaching for the day, so Bud and I drove up. Although it was early afternoon, the traffic was terrible. There was an accident on I-95. A trailer truck had jack-knifed on the highway, and a majestic black man lay on the dividing wall with a white towel up to his chin. If he was dead, the towel would have covered him completely. But his face was in such deep repose, it was worthy of an old master.

When I said this to Bud, he muttered, "Poor sonofabitch."

We found the shop easily enough. It was in the old part of the city and crammed with ancient and dusty typewriters. As we entered, a bell rang and an old man on two walking sticks was shouting at a burly black youth, "Get out! Out!"

The old man wore tracksuit pants, a wool hat and a down vest. The boy, in hooded sweatshirt and huge Nikes with velcro fasteners, hovered ominously.

The man waved a stick. "Offa my property."

He looked frail and ancient. His dark eyes had deep black circles round them. Bud took my arm, holding me back. For a second, as it looked like the boy might pull a knife.

They were eyeball to eyeball.

Then the boy turned and stalked out.

"Trash!" the old man yelled after him. Then seeing us, "He mugged one o' my customers last week."

"I'm Anne O'Brien. I've come about the Becker case."

He looked us over.

"This is my cousin."

Bud held out his hand. "Howdee, Sir."

The old man shook it, looking him over cautiously. "Come on in."

We followed, as he hobbled to a dingy and even more dusty back office. It was crammed with more machines – did people still use typewriters? I looked around curiously. On the wall there was a collage of old sepia snaps, going back to the turn of the century. The old man heaved himself into a rickety chair in front of a roll-top desk and indicated we were to sit in two others.

"What's your interest?" he wheezed.

"I'm writing a life of my grandfather."

"She's a well-known writer," Bud interrupted.

"He was a lawyer on the case," I continued, frowning at Bud.

"Gonna put this in a book?"

I had to tread carefully now. People were very suspicious of being in books. "If you don't mind."

"Naw, I want the truth told." He swivelled around and put the telephone in a drawer. "They're listnin'."

"The FBI?" said Bud.

"Outer space."

Still he wheezed out his story coherently: "The Rosenthal case is a few years back. No one remembers it now, and not many cared then – hoods was two a penny. No one liked Becker much either. So what if he was to croak. The city was better off without him. Helen Becker, now she's my interest. She was some lady. I was an errand boy and general helper workin' for Sam Schepps' jewelry store on Broadway." He sighed heavily. "Dey worked kids then. Bought and sold 'em. It was July, a hot afternoon, musta been 1914. A lady with a veil came into the shop and was shown into the back room. It was Mrs Becker. She was meetin' Jack Rose there. Because of the heat I was sent out for some ginger ale. As I brought it in, I heard her say, 'Jack, for pity's sake, tell the truth. It's the only hope to save Charlie.'"

The old man paused for breath. "Jack was an odd-lookin' dude. Never forget him. 'Do you want me to swop places with Charlie, Helen?' he said.

"Then my boss, Sam, saw me and hushed him up. 'Sweep the shop, Harry!' he ordered me.

"So I left, but the door was ajar, and I heard her beg some more. But it was no use. In the end she came out through the shop. Troubled an' all as that lady was, she stopped and smiled at an orphan boy. 'You goin' to school, Harry?'

"No one ever smiled at me. But she did – said my name too. When I went in to clear the glasses, I heard the two men talkin'. 'It's a pity about poor Charlie, yeah, a real pity,' Schepps said. 'Dey won't find out it was a frameup, will dey Jack?'

"Bald Jack put on his hat. 'Naw. The DA can't go back now. He wants to be President.' And he walked outa the shop."

I stared at the old man. "But you never came forward?"

He coughed chestily. "I was eight years old."

I had my witness. But he was old, very old. And crazy.

CHAPTER EIGHTEEN

* * *

CLINTON WAS ELECTED, AND WHEN FERGAL DIDN'T FLY OVER FOR Thanksgiving, Molly and Theodora said it was as well because they'd be busy with their family, and couldn't throw their usual party for him. Maybe they were trying to make me feel better. I felt bad about Fergal, but still too weary to take the initiative. A worse blow was Chuck's decision to spend the day with his wife. I persuaded myself it was for his son's sake, etc – but if you're infatuated, you'll tell yourself anything. Anyway, I couldn't desert Cousin Bud or Frances. So the three of us orphans went to a restaurant.

The next day Chuck came over for a drink. He was achey after tennis, so we didn't make love. He looked tanned and handsome with his strong wrists and beautiful white teeth. But he stared gloomily into his vodka and tonic. The committee investigating Teri's charges had hauled him up, but hadn't yet given a verdict. So it was hanging over him.

"They won't believe her," I said calmly. "Not with those poison pen letters."

He gulped his drink. "I'm not so sure. You women have it all sewn up. A few years ago, I was reported by a little bitch for saying Louisa May Alcott wrote girls' books."

I laughed. "What else are they? I loved them as a girl."

"There are boys' books too. Is that sexist?" His tone was misogynous, but who could blame him?

"Did they find the phantom cigarette burner?"

He guffawed. "Of course not!"

I had experienced Teri's tantrums and manipulation, so was completely on Chuck's side. And, despite the Anita Hill case, the Department was too. Except for Sarah and a few feminist fanatics, there was no sympathy for Teri. She was considered too dangerous a troublemaker.

But the whole business was depressing. It put Chuck in an awful mood. When I got a chance to escape for the weekend, I took it.

Marcus's aged niece, Elizabeth, had replied at last. She admitted having Marcus's journal and invited me to Washington. My interest in the Rosenthal case had been recharged by meeting the old man in Philadelphia. Elizabeth might know something too. Or there might be something in the journal. It was easier to think about the past than the present.

I got up at dawn the next Friday to catch the college shuttle – Sweetmount sent a car down to a weekly seminar at the Folger Shakespeare Library in Washington. Four of us waited in the dark at the Fieldhouse, only to find it had gone without us. Finally one of the girls drove, giving me, a Chinese student and Dr Finnegan, the drunken college psychiatrist, a lift. He was on his stick and panicked at being left off, so I shepherded him up the Mall to the Library of Congress where he was to do some research. I expected to be mugged on that open space which was designed by Stanford White's firm, McKim, Mead and White – White was the murdered architect in the Thaw case. They'd also designed the Lincoln Memorial. And the Marble Arch in New York's Washington Square, and the General Sherman statue outside the Plaza hotel. I was clogged with facts about the early century.

I spent the day in the National Archives before taking a cab to Georgetown. As we passed neat brownstones and ritzy shops on narrow streets of the suburb made fashionable by the Kennedys, I was excited about meeting my cousin. Except for Ogie and Cousin Bud, I had hardly any relations. What would she be like? And what would the journal reveal? As a retired law professor, Elizabeth seemed comfortable. Her apartment building was modern, characterless concrete like Bella Vista, except that it was a semi-retirement home for the well-heeled old. It was overheated inside with the usual motel smell of stale perfume, but there were plush red carpets and rubber plants galore.

A hefty, crew-cut security guard sat at a lobby desk. His huge stomach bulged sack-like over his belt as he stared at a portable TV.

Dragging his gaze from the screen, he buzzed Elizabeth for me.

"Sorry, Ma'am, Miss O'Connor ain't answering."

I put my briefcase down. "But I'm expected."

Lazily he buzzed again.

No answer.

It was rude to stare, but what on earth did Americans eat? You didn't see such obesity in Ireland.

"Naw, she ain't in, Ma'am."

What now? I groped in my shoulder bag for Elizabeth's postcard and studied her old and spidery hand. Had I got the day wrong? I was getting everything wrong these days. *I'll be glad to see you on Friday next. Take a cab from the station and I'll refund.* No, there could be no mistake.

"When'll she be back?" I asked.

He shrugged, staring at the TV. Great hulking shapes in helmets hurled themselves at each other, as a commentator's voice rumbled and shrieked.

"But she invited me."

He swigged coke. "Dey forget."

"Can I wait?"

"Sure." He nodded toward a lobby couch. "Take a seat. I need clearance to letja upstairs."

Wearily I plonked down. Clearance? Did I look like a thief? Americans are all mad. The armed guard in the National Archives had asked if I had explosives. What if I'd said yes? But where was Elizabeth now? It'd been a tiring day, missing the shuttle and then escorting the doctor who already seemed drunk. Perhaps his mind was going? Was that why he behaved badly at the party? He had panicked again when I left him. But I wrote down the name of the subway station where the group would meet to ride back – the Smithsonian. Had he made it?

Although Washington was easier than New York, I was weary from the strain of cities. The National Archives was Kafkaesque – with its motto "The Past is Prologue". I was shunted from floor to floor all day. You had to sign in at every office, and almost undress to look at anything. Everyone was eccentric. An archivist finally found a file on Marcus's diplomatic appointment, containing letters for and against him. There was one interesting item:

I am informed that Mr Marcus Quilligan O'Neill, a member of the bar here, is being urged for appointment to a Federal position. I have known Mr Quilligan O'Neill for some years, and have always found him honorable, upright and reliable.

He was counsel for Jack Rose during the time of the

investigations and prosecutions growing out of the murder of Herman Rosenthal, and I believe that he was largely instrumental in persuading Jack Rose to tell the truth and become a witness for the State. Mr O'Neill's course was thoroughly professional and, I believe, in every way commendable.

I am, with kindest personal regards,
Most cordially yours
Charles Whitman.

It was dated 1913, so the first trial was over. But Becker hadn't yet been executed. To gain political kudos, Whitman needed the conviction to stick. Whitman had been a Republican, but was here recommending a Democrat. He was obviously repaying a debt.

There was also a letter from Marcus, referring to his role in the affair.

I understand that Charles S Whitman, District Attorney for New York, has written to you concerning the part I have taken in making possible the reform movement he is now conducting in New York. Although Judge Whitman is a member of the opposite party, I am gratified that he has seen fit to express his confidence in me as a lawyer and a man.

Police reform was the issue of the day, and Whitman was later elected governor of New York for his efforts.

But there was a telegram from a bishop:

AS AN AMERICAN CITIZEN I PROTEST AGAINST THE
CONFIRMATION OF THE NOMINATION OF MARCUS Q
O'NEILL TO BE AMERICAN MINISTER

To be damned by a bishop might be in Marcus's favour. Another letter described him as a self-made man who had done well in the metropolis. He was "big-brained, big-hearted" and would do honour to any office to which he was elevated.

I looked at my watch. Too late for the lift back now. Anyway I had to see Elizabeth. She'd promised me the journal and I'd wait – all night if necessary. She had to return sometime. But why was the old woman so difficult to track down? She was ex-directory. And why hadn't she answered my letters? My mother hadn't liked her much. She'd told me horror stories about Elizabeth. Of being afraid to fall asleep in her house. Of Elizabeth's strange unbending Irish Republicanism. Of her rage when Oonagh accidentally spilt the grass from Elizabeth's fiancé's grave – it was stored in a little vase on the mantelpiece. He had been one of the rebels who took over the Dublin Post Office in 1916. Later he was killed in the Civil War. Perhaps then, she *had* been in the IRA? Elizabeth had once swooped down to Florida and sacked the Irish nanny Marcus was about to marry. The girl had retaliated by taking back a new frock she'd bought for Oonagh. It was one of my mother's saddest stories.

Maybe now I'd find out more about Oonagh's childhood.

Two frail old women passed on walkers. They examined their mail disappointedly. Old age couldn't be much fun. You might end up with an imaginary child as Frances had. But there was no choice – you either died young or got old. Amazingly Elizabeth had gone to the Caribbean with Marcus in 1914. How could anyone be that old? What would she look like? Was the porter saying she was senile? Not necessarily. You could forget things without being senile. I did all the time. Still, what had I let myself in for? My obsessions were ruling my life. I should go back to Sweetmount now and console Chuck. But I couldn't go on until I'd found out more about Marcus. Had he sent an innocent man to his death? His journal might hold a clue.

A lanky old man joined me on the couch. He was stooped and wore a black French beret and a cream cord Norfolk jacket.

"Hi." His watery china-blue eyes lit up. "Say, you someone's kid?"

I was amused. "No."

"You driving someone to the doctor?"

"No – I'm – "

"Ah, the dentist, then?" He had a high reedy voice. "I know – the eye doctor!" He crossed his long legs and gripped his chin.

"I'm Elizabeth O'Connor's cousin."

"You driving her?"

"No, visiting."

"But no one visits here. They only come to take us out." He looked into space. "Sometimes in boxes. But I shouldn't complain. Lizzie's cousin . . . I must have cousins . . . " His voice trailed off.

Had he Alzheimer's? He looked OK – sort of wiry, like an aged James Stewart. But there was plenty of life in him. Where had I read of octogenarians playing football? It had to be in the *New York Times*.

He shook his head sadly. "What was I saying?"

"That you must have cousins."

He sighed mournfully. "I can't remember."

"Mine's forgotten me too," I joked.

He searched my face. "Who's yours?"

"Elizabeth O'Connor. The porter says she's out."

"Aw, Gerry's an airhead!" He stood up wobbly. "Lizzie never goes out. Come on!"

The guard was still lost in the game, so I followed the old man to the elevator. We took it to the first floor. But on the plush corridor, he looked vague again. "Now, where were we going?"

"To Elizabeth O'Connor's apartment."

He hit his head with his fist. "Of course! Sorry, my dear, I can't remember from one minute to the next. They tell me I was five years in hospital."

Next thing he was crying.

I touched his shoulder gently. "Listen . . ."

He sobbed loudly. "I get so terribly depressed."

What could you say?

He mopped his face with a big white hanky and bounded limpingly ahead over the soft red carpets. We passed down a corridor of doors and, stopping at the end, he banged on one. "Elizabeth!"

No answer.

"Elizabeth!"

"She isn't in," I said.

"She's in all right."

Then a cracked voice answered, "What is it, Claude?"

"Someone to see you." He looked enquiringly at me.

"Anne O'Brien," I said.

"Miss O'Brien's here!"

The door inched open and a tiny old woman peeped out. Her skin was yellowish with brown age spots and her pale blue eyes watery behind thick horn-rims. She was stooped, and her head stuck out tortoise-like. Her thick blue-rinsed hair was crimped into a thirtyish Marcel-style perm and she wore a black and white, spotted, silk dress with a neat white collar. "Well, Claude?"

"Elizabeth, your cousin's here."

She smiled sourly at me, turning up her hearing aid.

So that was it. I cleared my throat awkwardly. "I'm Anne O'Brien, your Irish cousin."

The old woman stared me up and down, purse-lipped.

I put a hand to my tic. It certainly wasn't a royal welcome. Had she been avoiding me? "Eh – I sent a card."

"I couldn't read it!"

"Sorry." I found her own postcard. "You sent this."

Frostily she glanced at it, then stretching her neck out, snapped, "If you're coming about heirlooms, I have none."

"I – "

"That Oonagh Max keeps pestering me. I've told her repeatedly, I have nothing."

"But you have a journal."

"I have nothing. No christening gowns."

"Can we talk, then?"

"No china!"

Claude leaned on the door. "She's a nice young lady, Lizzie."

"Nothing!"

"I've come a long way," I added.

Elizabeth held the door, as Claude pushed against it, pleading, "Lizzie, why don't we all have a nice drink."

"I won't be bullied!"

I looked defeatedly at the old man. "I'd better go."

He rolled his eyes up. Then turned to the old woman. "Look what you've done. She's leaving."

Elizabeth suddenly looked outraged. "What?"

"I'll go," I said.

She unchained the door. "You're not coming in! After all this fuss!"

She was a Red Queen.

As I stepped inside, Claude attempted to follow but she slammed the door. "Thank you, Claude!"

I stood there awkwardly, looking round the comfortable apartment. At least I was referred to as a guest, but the woman was bats. I broke the ice. "He was a character."

"A pathetic failure!" Elizabeth limped up steps to the living area.

"Leave your coat in the closet. You can bring your bag up to the guest-room."

The closet was neat. Rows of old ladies' shoes had been placed on a rack and old-fashioned hats arranged on a shelf over the coats.

"He thought I was someone's child." I carried my bag up the steps.

"You are a child to him!" Elizabeth perched on one end of a big green couch, like some old bird.

"He gets depressed," I said.

"He's a whiner. He tried to commit suicide once. Put his head in the gas oven but forgot to turn it on."

I held back laughter.

"He's one of those . . . You know – "

"No?"

"He dresses up in women's clothes."

"Oh . . . " I composed my face, concentrating on my surroundings. The living area was nicely furnished in an antiquey way. There was an oval mahogany table with dining chairs. Landscape paintings hung on the wall and framed photos stood on the table. The carpets were thick underfoot. Anti-macassars protected the green velour winged-back chair. It matched the couch on which Elizabeth now sat with her feet barely touching the ground. A room-length picture window framed the river. "You're lucky with the view."

Elizabeth smiled sourly. "Your bedroom's the first on the right."

The guest room had a mahogany tallboy and two old-fashioned mahogany-headed beds covered with lumpy eiderdowns. Towels and a face cloth had been left out. So I was expected. Why then had the old woman acted so oddly? She mustn't like visitors. She certainly didn't like Ogie.

I tidied up and went back to the living-room, where Elizabeth was now turning cards onto the coffee table. She looked up begrudgingly. "Would you like a sherry?"

"If it's no trouble." I sat opposite her. At least one member of the family drank.

"Hmm." Elizabeth pulled herself up, groaning.

I hopped up. "I'll get it."

"I'm not that decrepit!"

As she hobbled out to the kitchen, I fiddled with the photos on the coffee table. There was a middle-aged woman and two teenaged boys. Who were they? Noises came from the kitchen: the fridge door was opened; then ice clinked in a glass; something was poured from a bottle. Then more clinking as Elizabeth came back, dwarfed by a precariously wobbling tray.

"Let me!"

"Thank you, I can manage!" She slammed down the tray. It held two glasses of what looked like orange juice and a bowl of peanuts. "There's no sherry. Is vodka all right?"

"Fine." I put the drinks on the coffee table.

"No! No!" The old woman frantically waved her arms.

"What is it?"

"Up! Up!"

I looked up at the ceiling. "What's wrong?"

"The glasses – you'll ruin the table!"

"Oh . . . sorry!" I replaced the glasses on the tray.

Huffily Elizabeth took two coasters from a drawer and put them meticulously on the table. Then she placed the glasses carefully on them and laid the peanuts on the coffee table halfway between us. Then hid the tray under the table.

I held up my glass. "Sláinte."

My cousin had had an Irish Republican background, but was not amused. Gingerly she sipped her drink before returning it to its coaster. Looking guardedly at me, she slid both a little closer to her. "Well! If you haven't come for heirlooms, what do you want?"

I took out a notebook. "To talk."

Elizabeth breathed in sharply. "You're not a spy?"

I was getting exasperated. "I'm just curious about my grandfather, Marcus Quilligan O'Neill."

She breathed more easily. "Uncle Mark?"

"You knew him?"

"I could hardly avoid it."

"The *New York Times* says you went to the Caribbean with him."

This brought a smile of reminiscence. "He called me his secretary."

"It must've been exciting. You went by sea?"

"There was no other way."

I scribbled on my pad. HIDING SOMETHING – WHY?

"What are you writing?" She peered over.

"Eh, nothing." I put a hand over the pad. "A pen focuses my thoughts." I had a list of questions. "It must be hard to remember so far back. You knew the family well. Nora – did you like her?"

"Yes, I liked Aunt Nora."

"And the children?"

"I don't remember them."

That was surely a lie? "Danny was a saint."

"What?" Elizabeth broke into phlegmy coughing.

I watched in alarm as she tried to speak, then went into another long chesty spasm. Was she choking too? But, when the old woman got her breath, I realised she was laughing.

"Danny, a saint? *Who* told you that?"

"My mother. She said he was, you know – the white-headed boy."

"He was nothing of the sort!"

"But he died – "

"He was spoilt! He had a fat pudgy face." Elizabeth puffed out her cheeks. "And a mean little mouth, like this." She pursed her lips.

I couldn't help smiling. "Who spoilt him? Nora?"

"Yes. He was horrible."

There went another myth. The angel in the little white coffin who had died on his first communion day. What other family lore had been transposed? Was myth-making a basic need of mankind? A way to make unpleasant things palatable? I'd heard everything from Oonagh, who had heard it from someone else. Perhaps truth lay somewhere between two extremes.

I cleared my throat. "Did Marcus ever speak of the Rosenthal case?"

Elizabeth turned over more cards. She stared at each before laying it slowly in place.

"It was in 1912," I went on. "A policeman was – "

"I know," she rasped. "It's not important now."

"But it interests me."

The old woman looked up. "Why?"

"Because Charles Becker was innocent. I have a letter from Gyp the Blood's wife. And I found a witness."

Smiling cynically, she turned over another card. "You found a witness?"

"Yes. I suspect Marcus's role. Tammany was involved."

The old woman stared at her cards.

I tried again. "Marcus gave up the law afterwards. Do you think he was unhappy about the case?"

Elizabeth had completely clammed up.

Nervously I reached for the nuts. "A lot of people at the time believed Becker was a scapegoat. That Tammany let him take the rap."

No response.

I nibbled more nuts. "A gangster called Zelig was shot before he gave evidence. And Big Tim Sullivan, Marcus's cousin, died mysteriously a year later."

"He wasn't a cousin!"

"It said – in Marcus's obit."

"It's incorrect."

"Well, people thought he was murdered."

Elizabeth glared now.

I felt nervous. Perhaps I'd said too much. She was angry about me accusing Marcus?

"Pass me those nuts!" she snapped.

"Sorry!" I pushed them across the table.

The old woman took some. "They have to last the weekend!"

I'd been eating compulsively, but nuts do that to me. Now I felt like a greedy child. But everything Oonagh said about Elizabeth was true. She'd terrify a child. But why was she so cagey about the Rosenthal case?

The silence thickened.

"Now you're drinking too fast!"

"I'm sorry." I put down my drink and reached automatically for a nut, but pulled back.

"You'll ruin your appetite. I have snacks for later."

I nodded.

Elizabeth picked up her cards, then, carefully measuring her words, said, "You have theories about Tammany. Marcus. Jack Rose. Big Tim. But they didn't send Lieutenant Becker to the electric chair. He was convicted by a jury." She spoke slowly in her thin old voice. "*Two* juries."

"Well, juries can be wrong."

"They've never come up with a better system!"

"You've heard of the Birmingham Six? The Guildford Four? They were imprisoned in the wrong."

"I know nothing of Irish affairs."

"But you did once."

She looked cagey. "Are you blackmailing me?"

"No!" I was afraid to say anything more. They'd got it so wrong, those old Republicans. Because of them we were suffering in Ireland today. I scribbled: SHE'S HIDING SOMETHING ABOUT IRELAND TOO.

"Who sent you?"

I threw down my pad in exasperation. "No one! I'm curious about my grandfather."

The old woman stared in disbelief, then said in the same slow voice, "But he's been dead for nearly sixty years."

"I'm still curious."

She went back to her cards, turning them over slowly and pausing over each one.

"What was he like?" I asked.

No answer.

She was an unpleasant ogre. "Look," I said. "You said you had a journal. We know nothing about our past. Our American past. Oonagh never knew her mother. There's just this – gap."

Still no answer.

"Why should only kings and queens have ancestors?"

She didn't answer, so I walked over to the window. Outside the river flowed strongly. I couldn't tell this mean old hag the extent of my delusions. Then I heard myself say, "Marcus haunts me . . . "

This made her look up. "He wouldn't haunt anyone."

I held back.

"Uncle Mark was generous. The life and soul of a party. But he married, and then didn't care about anyone . . . " the old voice went on dreamily, "except her."

"Nora?"

She nodded. "He never got over her death . . . typhus is a terrible death."

"Oonagh said it was flu."

The old woman looked grim. "No, typhus, from the dirty drains of Dublin."

I watched the river. "But he loved his children?"

"I suppose so. He seemed fond of your mother."

I couldn't reveal my suspicions about that relationship.

"The others gave him trouble. Eithne went off to boarding school. I paid for that. He'd sent me to Smith College. So it was repayment."

"I didn't go to college till I was thirty," I heard myself say. Why was I whining like this? "My father died."

"How's your mother?"

"She died – six years ago."

"Oh?" She turned another card, grimacing. "Uncle Mark was a toucher."

"What do you mean?"

"He pawed you. I never liked that."

So that was it. My mother had never liked to be touched either. Perhaps that was all she meant?

I sat down again. I wanted to shake the mean little woman. Why wasn't she concerned for Oonagh now? Why hadn't she had some interest in her as a child? Nobody in the family cared. Nobody except Ogie. She was warm. You had to give her that.

I picked up the framed photos of the woman and the two boys. "Who are these people?"

"My niece, Hanna, and her two children."

"If she's your niece, is she my cousin?"

The old woman nodded. "I suppose. Why's it important?"

I controlled my irritation. "We're just descendants of two people who sailed to a new life. We share a past, genes, but I didn't know she existed."

Elizabeth smiled sourly. "There's nothing to know. She married a nogood who left her with a broken nose and two children. She's coming over tomorrow. I'll call now and make sure." Fussily the old woman picked up the phone.

I was fed-up. I wasn't going to get anything out of Elizabeth. No journal either. And by the looks of it, no dinner. Anyway I wasn't hungry, just feeling dangerously sleepy. "I'd like to go to bed now."

She slammed down the receiver. "I'm sorry you're exhausted."

"It's been a long day."

"Would you like a snack?"

I stood up. "No. Perhaps you'll come out to dinner later?"

"I won't go out!"

"We can go tomorrow night if you'd prefer."

"But I'm giving a party then!"

I walked toward the bedroom. "Then I'll leave early."

"Well, that's a nice thing! YOU'RE THE GUEST OF HONOUR."

It took a minute to sink in. "What?"

"The party's for you!"

"I might eat too many nuts."

"I'll put them away!" Hugging the dish indignantly, she

hauled herself to her feet and hobbled after me to the bedroom area. "We'll have an early night. That's an excellent idea."

That night I dozed dreamlessly, awakening in the dark with a hot wind blowing in my face. I felt awful. Dammit, it was only two am. Would I have to lie awake the rest of the night? All I needed now was to see Marcus. What madness had brought me here? How would I stand a whole weekend? Maybe all writers were mad. Doomed, according to the analysts, to observe life rather than live it. I hated staying with people and especially hated being at the mercy of this old crone. How could we be related?

The thermostat was too high. Thinking she'd have a fit at the waste, I got up and crept around the apartment, looking for a way to turn it down. I tried the living-room, the kitchen. Then opened the study door and flicked on the light. There was no sign of the switch. Amazingly the room was lined with books – paperbacks, old bound novels and legal text books. My eye rested on a rolltop desk. A key was in the lock, as if Elizabeth had recently been using it. What if she kept our family papers there? On impulse, I went over and opened it. It was full of old envelope files, which looked like yellowed records. I flicked through them quickly, but nothing.

I opened the drawer and immediately saw a file with "Uncle Mark" scrawled on it. Trembling, I took it out and sat down, accidentally bumping into a standard lamp which crashed to the floor.

I righted it.

Had Elizabeth heard?

I waited, but no noise came from her room. The file contained letters from Nora and a faded manuscript – the journal. There were photographs of my grandmother and her children. An old fan and locks of baby hair. So these pathetic relics were what Elizabeth refused to give. As a direct descendant, they were mine. Or Ogie and Bud's.

Then a door opened.

Feet shuffled down the corridor.

How would I explain my presence here? I was caught with my hand in the till. Again on impulse, I took the journal from the file, shut the desk and tiptoed behind a curtain.

The light flicked on.

Through the curtains, I saw Elizabeth come in, stare at the desk, then slowly peruse the room. She was stooped over her stick, and wore a hairnet tied under her chin and an old-fashioned wool dressing-gown. Also her teeth were out. She shuffled over to the desk, opened the drawer, checked inside, then locked it, pocketing the key. Dammit. Now I wouldn't be able to return the journal. As she inched up the corridor, I anticipated her next move – she would check my bedroom. So I crept behind her back, fleeing ahead of her to the living area and, curling into an armchair, pretended to be asleep.

I only just made it.

The old woman's slow steps were again on the stairs. She thumped her stick, calling into the dark, "Are you there?"

I stood up groggily. "What is it?"

"Why aren't you in bed?"

"I got up to read."

"You can read in the dark?"

"I nodded off."

She snorted in disbelief. "Then why is the light off?"

"It must've gone off," I lied, flicking it on.

"You should give up coffee," she snapped.

"Can I get you anything?" I asked shakily.

She ignored this. "Did you hear anyone in the study?"

"No."

"You weren't in there?"

"No."

"Hmm! Well, go back to bed."

"It's too hot there."

"Well, turn down the thermostat!"

I followed, as she puffed and panted down the passage to my room. She found the switch immediately. "There! It's at sixty. Now please don't wake me again."

When she had gone, I closed the door and got into bed. God, I was a thief, stealing from the old. My obsession had led me to this.

Marcus's journal was written hurriedly in a large inky, almost illegible, scrawl. Nervously I began to read:

I write this memoir for those who will come after and to set the record straight on certain things. I am the third child and eldest son of . . .

I couldn't make out the next word.

Then Marcus appeared before me. He was barefoot and had the bottoms of his trousers rolled up.

I had planned to kill him, but now couldn't move. "What are you doing?"

He walked up and down. "Having a grass bath."

I'd read somewhere that he was accused of running around Washington barefoot.

"It's great for the corns. We did it in the old country."

Would I ever get any peace? I tried to read the journal.

"You can't read that!" He grabbed at it, but I held on. "I want you to get certain things straight. Do you have a pencil and paper? You can take dictation!"

I looked away. "Who says I'm writing about you?"

He looked outraged. "But you are!"

224

I didn't reply. In this crazy nightmare, I was being shoved around by a ghost. A ghost who now sat opposite in affronted silence.

"But, I'll have to rake up things."

"I'll tell you what to say!"

"Jack Rose lied."

"Ah, Jack was a grand man." He cleared his throat, saying solemnly, "I want a place in history."

"You have one – sort of."

"Not the one I want."

"Go away! Please . . ."

"Don't say that!" He looked terribly sad.

I closed my eyes, but he didn't go.

"Look, I can't protect ya, anymore. Jack's after you."

"What?"

I was trembling with fear. Was Jack really after me?

For the rest of the night, I dozed dreamlessly and finally got up before Elizabeth. I fixed her tea and toast and brought a tray to her bedroom. "I didn't see any coffee."

She looked small and vulnerable in the big double bed. "Never drink it, dear."

She shakily put in milk. "You're kind, my dear."

The dressing-gown hung on the bed-end. If I got the key, I could put the journal back. Maybe sneak a look at the rest of the family papers?

"What are you thinking about, dear?"

"Nothing."

She chatted on, telling me her household help came in twice a week for one hundred dollars, otherwise she managed alone. Her niece came once a fortnight to do the shopping, but was too busy with her own family to do anything else for her. You couldn't expect a single mother with two sons to have any spare time, she explained pathetically. I said nothing.

"My niece phoned last night. She's bringing over some food for our party. She was supposed to help me tidy, but the boys have swimming."

"I'll help you."

She smiled coyly. "But you're the guest of honour."

The tidying took most of the morning. First I was handed a new dustpan and brush and ordered to do the corners before vacuuming. I never did my own corners and these looked OK. "Can't I vacuum them?"

"After the corners are done!"

After vacuuming, I dusted the furniture. Then scrubbed the bathroom. Whoever was paid a hundred dollars weekly to clean wasn't earning the money. There was the trash too. Directed by Elizabeth, I carried bags to the chute. She hopped ahead along the corridor like some gnarled gnome, pressing an ear at every door.

I was puzzled. "What are you doing?"

She put a finger to her lips. "Shh! Checking everyone's alive. At our age, you're never sure."

Back in the apartment, she announced, "Now there's laundry. Just a few napkins and linens. Would you mind, dear?"

I shook my head. "Of course not."

"The clothes basket is in my bathroom."

Passing through her bedroom again, I searched her dressing-gown pocket for the key.

It was gone.

Dammit. Where had she put it? I looked round the room, but it was nowhere in sight. Now, what would I do about the journal?

I carried the clothes to the basement laundry. And while they were in the machine, I went back upstairs, where Elizabeth was spreading cheese on crackers.

"Here, dear! You do these." She pushed some crackers at me.

As I began spreading, she shrieked, "No! No!"

"What's wrong?"

"You're putting on too much!"

"Sorry!" I spread the cheese more thinly.

Elizabeth pulled open the fridge and stared dismally. "There's no Perrier water."

"Let them eat cake?"

"Cake?"

"Tap water."

The old woman collapsed into chesty laughter. "Let them eat cake . . . !"

We were getting on better.

At last everything was ready – napkins, food, us – and we awaited Hanna and the other guests. Elizabeth passed the time with her cards.

"I'm sorry Daniel died so young," she said, looking kindlier. "And your grandmother. I stayed in her house. It was a happy house. A house that loved children."

A house that loved children? Could Elizabeth throw any light on what had happened later?

"I'd like to see Killiney Bay just once more before I die."

"The Vico Road?"

"Yes, I used to walk up there with my fiancé. He was killed."

"I heard."

"I'll die before you, dear," she went on dreamily.

That was true. But what could you say to someone so old? How did you console them for death?

She threw the pack down. "But you won't live out your life!"

My heart missed a beat. So that's what the cards said. "Won't I?"

She smiled dourly. "No. You'll be blown up."

"Oh, how?"

"In a nuclear explosion, dear."

I breathed more easily. "But it's looking better now."

The old woman wagged a gnarled finger. "Mankind is doomed."

There was no sign of Hanna and her children. But two other members of doomed mankind hobbled down the corridor to our Mad Hatter's tea party. I opened the door to Claude of the lobby, and another old man called Cyrus Van Dam.

"THIS IS MY GUEST OF HONOUR," Elizabeth shrieked from her couch, "Miss O'Brien from Dublin."

Cyrus Van Dam was stuffier than Claude, a WASP of the old school and a retired law professor like Elizabeth. He was dressed in a three-piece striped suit and had white hair and a pale patrician face. He greeted me with antique courtesy. "You're welcome to Washington, my dear. Lizzy's been so excited about your visit."

Claude wobbled up the steps. He had changed for the occasion into a wrinkled white summer jacket. A cravat was now tucked sportily into his open shirt. I followed them to the living area, trying to catch Elizabeth's eye for a signal as to whether to pour drinks. But none was forthcoming. Wait, I told myself. You had to be careful with the old. You couldn't patronise them. Hanna would be here soon. She'd know how to cope with the old woman.

She squinted back. "What are you staring at?"

I was confused. "Nothing."

The three old people knew each other well, and the conversation kicked off nicely on a discussion of memory. The topic preoccupied them. Claude had forgotten an appointment, and Cyrus had just read *The Man Who Mistook His Wife for a Hat*.

"I sure wouldn't want to get like that," he lamented.

"I forget things all the time," I said.

Cyrus looked alarmed. "What sort of things?"

"Tennis scores, things like that. I tend to forget book titles too. And phone numbers. Unless I write them down."

Claude was sympathetic. "And you're so young."

"Oh, stop talking rot!" Elizabeth finally screamed. "Get up and offer my guests a drink! Go on, you're years younger than anyone here!"

"Sorry!" I felt myself redden. Here I was, trying to respect Elizabeth's role as hostess, but had ended up looking lazy. You couldn't win.

Elizabeth and Mr Van Dam drank gin and tonic; Claude wanted ginger ale. When everyone was happy, I fixed myself a drink and sat down again.

Immediately Elizabeth thrust the snacks at me.

I took one. "Thank you!"

"Anne!"

"What is it?"

"GET UP AND PASS THE SNACKS!"

I passed the plate around.

Elizabeth glowered. "You're the youngest here!"

"I'm not that young!"

The old woman's glare followed me. "Of course you are!"

I held back laughter. In a minute I'd burst.

Then there was a knock on the door.

Hanna?

But an old lady on a walker was outside, dressed for a party.

"Tell Miss O'Connor, Mrs Peterson is here," she said rather grandly.

I went to the bottom of the steps. "It's Mrs Peterson."

Elizabeth held a hand to her ear. "Who?"

"A Mrs Peterson."

"She can't come in!"

"What?"

She clutched her glass. "She'll drink everything in the house! And eat all the nuts!"

"Oh . . ."

The two old men exchanged glances.

I went back to the door. "I'm afraid Miss O'Connor's gone to bed."

The latecomer shuffled off sadly.

When I was back sitting down, Cyrus asked politely, "Have you come to America permanently?"

"Eh, no, I teach here for four months of the year."

"What do you do with the rest?" Claude butted in.

"I write. Or used to. At the moment I'm researching the Rosenthal case."

"The Rosenthal case. How interesting." The old man took out his pipe. "I haven't heard it mentioned for years."

My heart leapt. At last someone was familiar with the case.

"Mind if I smoke, my dear?"

"I do, Cyrus!" Elizabeth snapped from the corner. "You want to kill us all!"

He pocketed the pipe. "Yes, Charles Becker was an unfortunate policeman. The case was mentioned in a memoir – written by a professor in Harvard. He accused the judge of bias."

"Yes, he was Irish – "

The old man nodded. "And famous for being anti-police."

"Becker was probably guilty of graft," I interrupted. "He had a reputation as a bully."

Elizabeth looked huffy. I ignored her. "How do you go about getting someone pardoned?"

"You need new evidence, my dear."

"I have documents."

Elizabeth peered suspiciously.

"And if I found someone who's prepared to testify?"

The old man fiddled with his unlit pipe, then delivered a lecture. "There's no fixed procedure. If the defendant is alive, a motion is filed with the highest court that ruled in the case for a reconsideration of its opinion, based on new evidence. With the defendant dead, as in Becker's case, the judicial proceeding is over. However, the governor or president may be petitioned for a pardon, again based on new evidence, that the judicial proceedings were fraudulent."

"But Jack Rose lied."

"Can you prove it? You see, my dear, cases are decided on certain principles of justice. And it is well established what those principles are. They are based on the assumption that the jury has deliberated in good conscience, and that their deliberations relied on evidence that a judge decided was admissible."

Then I told him about the old man in Philadelphia.

Cyrus puffed on his empty pipe. "Hearsay, my dear. Besides, there is no one to rebut him. And remember the jury might well not have believed him. And a judge will be reluctant to subsitute for that jury."

"Two juries!" Elizabeth interrupted.

The old man went on. "And the executive even more reluctant."

Then I said, "But I have another document."

Elizabeth perked up. "What document?"

"A letter from Gyp the Blood's wife. He swore that Becker didn't hire him."

Claude sighed. "But we are back to the same argument. The jury might not have believed her."

"What would I need then?"

"New evidence – which would be impossible after so many years."

At this Elizabeth erupted. "I'm sick of this conversation!"

Claude coughed politely.

Elizabeth yawned exaggeratedly. "My guest's exhausted."

I shook my head. "I'm not."

"You are!"

At this the two old people politely took their leave. "If I can do anything else, my dear," Cyrus said at the door, "please don't hesitate to call me."

I promised to.

When the door was closed, Elizabeth looked relieved. I thought she'd want to flop into bed, but no. "Now we can have a decent drink!"

As we drank more, I picked up the photograph of Hanna's two sons. Why hadn't she come? I'd never meet her now.

Elizabeth coughed. "What are you doing with that?"

I put down the frame. "You have handsome grandnephews."

She looked amazed. "Have you not noticed they're Hispanic?"

Later I tucked her into bed. Then I rang Amtrak and discovered there was a train in an hour. There was no chance to find out what was wrong with being Hispanic. Or put back the journal.

CHAPTER NINETEEN

* * *

I READ IT ON THE TRAIN:

*I write this memoir for those who will come after and to
set the record straight on certain things. I am the third
child and eldest son of James O'Neill, schoolmaster, and
Julie Quilligan, both of County Kerry, Ireland. My
father's people came from the Gap, near Beaufort,
County Kerry, and mother's from Bantry in County
Cork. Like all the Irish, they were well educated and had
a deep love of learning. Although English was their
main language, they could also read and write in
Gaelic. They were unusual in this, as most of the Irish
spoke a mixture of English and Gaelic, but could not
read or write their native tongue. This was not the fault
of the British, or the Tallystick, but of the Irish
themselves, who wanted their children properly
equipped for life. For we were bred for two things:
eviction or emigration.*

*In 1869, when I was six years of age, my father was
dismissed from his school and my parents decided to test
their fortune in the United States. I remember silence
and grief, but do not recall if the neighbours gathered
for an American wake. This was the custom, as an*

emigrant then left forever. I remember an old uncle coming to the boat with us. We took a Cunard Steamer from Cove, then called Queenstown, boarding with lonely young men and women and whole families, leaving for a new world. As we pulled out, drums drowned the keening and wailing from the quaysides. To this day, I cannot see a ship without tears for all the mothers who did not see their children again. We all went: O'Regans, O'Reillys, Quirkes, Quilligans and Quinns – often to a fate worse than that which we left.

The O'Neills were not the hungry Irish and travelled with two servants, leaving behind a slate-roofed house. Yet the memory of the Famine had cut deeply into the souls of my father and mother. They talked of what they had seen to the end of their days: whole families barricading themselves in their cottage to await death; children dying by the side of the road; a nation mortally wounded. All of their generation had a deep hatred for the English. Indeed it was for expressing such sentiments that my father was dismissed.

I remember the journey in flashes only, flashes of terrible seasickness. New York was sighted in two weeks. Its harbour was full of ships, waiting for clearance like us. Immediately, uniformed men jumped aboard, looking for unlucky victims of yellow fever or leprosy. Then, after many delays, we finally entered Castle Garden in the Bowery, a place of great madness, confusion and ducking under the wire. There was no Lady Liberty to greet us, only grim-faced doctors who made us walk the plank of inspection with our tattered brethren as they searched for the tell-tale signs of consumption which is the curse of our race.

Manhattan was not yet an island of skycrapers, but of church spires. But the sight was unforgettable to a child who was used to fields and mountains. It teemed with people of every nationality – Italians, Germans, Chinese, and us Irish. Horses clattered on cobbled streets lined with brownstones. Everywhere was the smell of manure and rotting fruit. We immediately crossed the river to Brooklyn where my father had been promised employment as a school teacher. This job did not materialise, so we soon used the last of our money. Our servants left and we were now poor immigrants, reduced to sharing a house with three other families. From being "the Master" in the old world, my father now found his skills useless, so succumbed to drink and despair.

After a while we moved to Boston, Massachusetts, where we had relatives. But this was another city, and factory work was too much for my father. My mother took in washing to support the family. Also she cleaned the houses of the rich. We were no longer "the Master's children," but "the scrubwoman's children." My father was a broken man. Two of my sisters and a brother died of consumption. Life was hard. Along with the Jews, we Irish were considered as vermin. Only the coloreds were less. Everywhere you saw the sign: NO IRISH NEED APPLY. But my mother was undaunted by this, telling me that the same words would be written on the gates of Hell. I went to parish schools and at nine got a paper route. At fourteen, I became a grocer's delivery boy and at sixteen was apprenticed to a carpenter, becoming a journeyman at eighteen. In my free time I boxed in unofficial fights. I also played baseball, which became a passion of my life.

My father had now left the family. I loved my mother dearly and was ambitious to improve her life. The Democratic Party was the party of the poor, and for the

Irish the only way up. We either joined it, or took to crime, or sometimes both. As I grew older, much of my free time was spent in ward politics, and by degrees I became a good stump speaker. Although I had little formal education, my mother had inspired me with a love of learning. I was an avid reader and burnt the midnight oil on the works of Dickens, Scott and anything I could beg or borrow. I dreamt of being a writer like them, but settled for journalism. I became sports correspondent for the Hartford Courant. *Later I moved to the* Waterbury American, *where I was known as "Legs" because I would walk anywhere to get a story.*

In 1896 I met William Jennings Bryan. The great Commoner was touring Connecticut in the presidential campaign, and speaking for the introduction of a silver standard for our currency. The American *was an uncompromisingly "Gold" paper, and it was well known that Bryan hated the press, especially the Eastern press. But when he came to Waterbury, it was necessary that he should be interviewed. For this the managing editor picked me.*

"Now, Mark," he said, "Bryan will probably fly into a rage as soon as you introduce yourself as a reporter for this paper. But stick to him. This is your chance to test the full force of your blarney. Go to it, but don't forget that you're representing an anti-Bryan paper. Don't truckle to him."

I set out, soon realising that my editor had put a "tail" on me to check that I gained access to Bryan. Well, I managed to lose my sleuth, and at Bryan's hotel room, sent in a card from an opposition paper. I was immediately admitted. Once inside I confessed this to Bryan, who was fanning himself on the couch. He was then without the receding hair or portliness of his later years. At first he went on fanning, silently staring at me. Then he shook with laughter. It is hard to describe the electric presence of that great American, whose wonderful baritone voice attracted thousands to the end of his life. Today he is remembered for the Scopes trial in which he defended traditional religion. But Bill Bryan was much more than this. Like most men, he had many sides. He was a great reformist and pacifist, a founding father of today's Democratic party whom history will honor for his courageous oppostion to that cruel first war. He quarrelled with Wilson for sending young men to die and for this was considered as a traitor to patriotism.

Well, we got on famously that day and I was granted an hour's interview.

"Mark," the great Commoner said, shaking my hand in farewell, "you have given me an hour of unalloyed delight!"

"Mr Bryan, I fully realize your purpose in this great campaign, and with all my heart I trust the outcome will be what you deserve."

My story was a scoop, and gained me a reputation as a newsman. Of all my careers, I regretted abandoning that trade which has sustained me in these last years of my life. But I was hungry to make more of myself and had already decided on law school. This required money, as I was then the sole support of my mother and my younger sister's children.

At that time some New York gamblers, including Jack Rose and Herman Rosenthal, formed a coterie in Connecticut. I met them in a local bar and was soon offered a share in a baseball team. In those days, betting was a passion among young men and a good way of making and losing money. We soon progressed to prize fight promotion as the National Athletic club then allowed exhibition fights. These fights were mainly fixed. At one such event, the gamblers had as usual arranged things – their man was to throw it. But he was genuinely knocked out and lay down at the first punch. The house rioted and the sheriff was called and confiscated our takings. So Jack Rose and I high-tailed it out of town.

My hopes for law school were now dim. But with the financial help of the gamblers and a cousin, I finally entered Yale, having passed an entrance exam. The university was then a Yankee bastion with few Irish. To support myself, I worked as a night hotel porter. I was then nearly forty years old and mingling with boys twenty years younger. A great chasm separated their world from mine. To avoid ridicule, I reduced my age by ten years. As a large blustery Irishman, I was still the butt of jokes. But I persevered, graduating and winning a medal for oratory in 1902.

At first I practised in Connecticut, mainly representing the poor against the police. The Tammany Club, which had just been started in Boston by James Michael Curley, gave me many cases. But I was still anxious to better myself and moved to New York in 1906. There I was recommended to Tammany Hall and joined the law practice of Dan O'Reilly, who employed me as an assistant on the Harry K Thaw defense team. The nation was riveted by this case. I remember Harry K Thaw's cold bird-like eyes and Evelyn Nesbit's demure and innocent act. Here was a young gold-digger who had baited two men, husband and lover, telling the former she had been ravished and the latter she had been flogged. Was she telling the truth? I think not.

She even outwitted the brilliant W K Jerome.

Everything about her was staged to gain the sympathy of the jury and the press. Was Thaw guilty of murder, or had he merely defended the virtue of his wife? To most people of the day he was a hero, while his victim, Stanford White, was vilified.

For weeks, I sat in that courtroom, looking for one good person. And there was only one: Howard Nesbit, a frail young man who was Evelyn's younger brother. He had come to New York "to do whatever he could to clear the name of Mr White." In this he was unsuccessful. The law has little to do with justice. Harry K Thaw was a rich man's son and so got off on an insanity plea and was committed to an asylum, from which he is now free.

Through the years, I had always kept in touch with the tragic politics of my native land and returned there in 1910 to speak at Wolfe Tone's grave. While in the country, I met and married my wife, Nora Healy, the daughter of a prominent Parnellite, who was Mayor of Kilkenny. We were very much in love and deliriously happy. My wife came with me to New York, but hated the heat, the frantic pace of life and the nature of my work. My offices were on a street known for prostitution and gambling. Although we were soon blessed by a son, she missed her country and family. Living in New York was expensive, so it was necessary to make more money as my wife was used to much and often visited Ireland. To keep her love was the aim of my life and the cause of its most shameful deed.

This was my part in the Becker-Rosenthal case. In July 1912, Jack Rose, my old partner, called to my apartment in Riverside Drive, asking for help. My wife at first thought we were being held up, so sinister did Jack look to her. He was pale and bald, with no lashes or eyebrows, and a habit of rubbing his hands together like Uriah Heep.

I quickly ushered him in, nodding to my wife to leave us.

Jack looked around from under hooded lids, saying in a low, deadpan voice, "You gotta nice place here, Mark."

I feared what was coming.

"Mark, remember the time we fixed fights?"

I nodded. For that I could be disbarred.

"Mark, you gotta help me. I'm wanted for the murder of Herman Rosenthal."

"Are you guilty?" I immediately asked.

"Yeah, but he was a rat squealer. Becker wanted him croaked."

"This is serious, Jack."

"But you owe me, Mark."

This was true. Years ago, he'd cut me in for a take in the prize fights. Without him, I could never have graduated from Yale. In my world, a man returned a favor. Besides, at first I believed his story. Everyone knew the New York police were corrupt. Becker, the Strong Arm Squad leader, was a well known grafter. Rosenthal had squealed, so there'd be no trouble in persuading a judge and jury of Becker's guilt in this affair. Reform was in the air, and everyone wanted a scapegoat. Judge Whitman's career would rise on the issue and mine with it. So I made a deal with Whitman: immunity for my client, who in return would swear an affidavit that Becker had ordered Rosenthal's killing.

Rose's testimony needed a corroborator. A vital part of the prosecution's case was a meeting between Becker and Rose in Harlem, when they allegedly planned the murder. This became known as the Harlem conference.

Sam Schepps, another gambler, had attended this meeting, so I schooled him as the "third man," who would swear that Becker had ordered the murder at this time.

But from that cocky crook, I learned Jack Rose was lying. No such conversation took place in Harlem. Jack Rose had hired the car with money from Tammany Hall. And another gambler, Harry Vallon, had done the deed. He had fired twice at Rosenthal's face with one of the gunmen's weapons. Two of those poor depraved boys didn't fire at all. Gyp the Blood fired, but after Rosenthal fell. Their bullets hit the hotel wall.

As well as owing Jack Rose, it was my job to defend my client. I was a criminal lawyer after all and had defended many guilty people. Besides, to speak now, would make an eternal enemy of Whitman. So I tutored Schepps and rushed him out of town. It was important to keep him from being arrested and incarcerated with the other gamblers before he made a statement. I did this, knowing Schepps was implicated in the murder and that Jack Rose had organized the whole thing.

The trial opened before Judge Goff, sitting in the Criminal Branch of the Supreme Court. In the same gloomy room, six years earlier, people had fallen under the spell of Evelyn Nesbit. This time there was no Floradora girl. The only love interest was Helen Becker, pregnant after seven years of marriage. She was a small dark woman dressed prettily in blue to whom my heart went out. I too was a married man and deeply loved my wife.

It's important to understand that there was a great antagonism between the trial judge and Becker's counsel, Lawyer MacIntyre. The stern, white-haired Judge Goff was born in Wexford. He'd been orphaned early, and like many Irish come up the hard way. As a young man, he had served on the reforming Luxow committee, and hated the police because they were so corrupt. MacIntyre had been on the other side. Although both were Irish, they were opposites: Goff was small and sarcastic; MacIntyre, large, verbose and kindly. Tammany had hired him to keep Big Tim Sullivan out of it.

The antagonism started with the rush to trial. MacIntyre rightly pushed for an adjournment in order to let the press clamour die down. But Judge Goff refused. At any rate, the press had done their damage. Becker was condemned in advance by that worst enemy of justice: public opinion. The public were clamoring for his blood like hounds for the kill.

The trial was a mockery. As well as a prejudiced judge, the witnesses were bought and paid for. One was actually brought from a jail and put up in a comfortable New York hotel. His testimony was thrown out by the appeal court.

I can still see that whiskey-faced yankee, Whitman, ranting and raving against the policeman. I can see Helen Becker, pale and dignified, hidden behind a screen for fear that she would gain the jury's sympathy, who were mainly middle-class men. On the day Rose came on the stand, there wasn't a breath of air. It was hellishly hot for October and the court was crowded with people who had queued since four in the morning. But Judge Goff ordered the noisy electric fans to be turned off, so that the witnesses could be heard. Also the blinds drawn and windows closed. After all, we had come to an execution and the stage had to be properly set.

The defence was weak, but it was impossible to undo

the impression Rose made. He came on the stand, immaculately groomed in a dark blue suit, his egghead slightly powdered. As I had instructed, he presented himself as cool, and Becker as hysterical. He spoke all day in a low chilling voice, telling his story in enormous detail. "Nothing for that man," he claimed Becker had ordered, "but to cut his throat, dynamite him, or anything." Rose was still going at nine that night, but Judge Goff, who didn't seem to have any natural functions, refused to adjourn. The little man was reputed to have an ulcer and live on cookies and milk spiked with whiskey. The antagonism between himself and MacIntyre now boiled over.

"I am physically exhausted," pleaded MacIntyre. "I can ask no more questions."

"If there are no more questions, the witness is dismissed." And the judge banged down his gavel.

Rose's testimony was never refuted.

The next important witness was Sam Schepps. I could see his grinning insolence was making a bad impression on the jury, so during the lunch adjournment, I whispered in his ear, "Do you want to take Becker's place?"

This changed his attitude.

On the night the jury filed in, I watched Becker carefully as they announced their verdict of guilty. It was arrived at without any physical evidence, only circumstantial: bank deposits, and much was made of Becker going to the police station in the early hours of the morning of the murder. Becker took it without flinching, looking sadly to his wife's empty seat, which was now without a screen and occupied by a sob sister journalist. I had seen many men condemned to die, but never witnessed such bravery.

I had become known as the man who persuaded Jack Rose to confess, but now left the case. I was glad to be done with Rose, and it was my hope that Lieutenant Becker would be cleared by another jury. But although he was granted a new trial and had the famous Bourke Cochran as counsel, he was not cleared. Again Whitman rounded up false witnesses. Lieutenant Becker haunts me like Banquo's ghost. He was guilty all right, but of graft, like all the police at that time, and almost every public official from the Mayor down. Not of murder. The Rosenthal case was rigged to gain political popularity for Charles Whitman. There was sympathy for a rich man like Harry Thaw, but none for a crooked policeman. Again the law had nothing to do with justice.

Through the Democratic party, I'd kept in touch with Bill Bryan, so now, at his request, I threw myself into Woodrow Wilson's presidential camgaign. I strongly supported Wilson's policies, and have always thought him the best American president until Roosevelt. My reward for my efforts was an appointment as Minister in Santo Domingo. I cannot go into the chicaneries of that uncivilized country. If only they played more baseball, they might have given up their national hobby of revolution – ball players are better peace keepers than marines.

The work was heavy, the heat hellish. The fevers and bugs, I will not mention. But there were no priests for my wife to confess to. No Mass on Christmas day. I suppose it was pleasant, driving with my wife in the cool of the evening. There was beautiful tropical vegetation: orchids and frangipani trees. But on the whole it was not a place to sell one's soul for. My descendants will hear of the Farrell Inquiry, where I was accused of

*supporting a corrupt dictator. But in this I was merely
following instructions. Has the White House not always
supported dictators?*

*I was also accused of representing the interests of
Tammany bankers, by transferring funds. This is true,
but everywhere I saw the most terrible poverty. Unlike
the Republicans, we Democrats were mainly bred in
poverty ourselves and believed in releasing money to
improve the conditions of the poor, rather than letting it
rot in banks. I gained nothing myself. I was also
accused of helping my cousin gain building contracts.
To this I answer: What sort of man does not return a
favor?*

*The report demanded my resignation. My wife was
heartily sick of America and had returned to Ireland. So
I resigned and followed her, and we had our happiest
years there. Oh, we had our disagreements like everyone
else. But the secret of a successful marriage is to master
the art of losing an argument and we never let the sun
go down on a quarrel. My life ended when she got sick
and died along with our beloved elder son. Both were
victims of the deadly fevers which swept Europe after the
war. In 1922 I brought my three surviving children
back to New York and reluctantly resumed my law
practice. I thought I had finished with characters like
Jack Rose, but now found myself defending them again,
only two-bit ones. My hands would never be clean. At
the time of the Great Depression, I could not pay my
office rent, so put my children in the car and drove to
Florida where we have since lived.*

*These are my public sins. My private ones, I leave to
my Maker. Death holds no terror for me: I long for it. If I
have learned anything from over seventy years of life, it
is this: You don't have to wait for the next life to be*

punished for doing wrong. You are punished right here.
I had helped to deprive Helen Becker of her husband
and child. For this I lost my own wife and child. It was
an eye for an eye, a tooth for a tooth.

I am now going fast down hill, so entrust this
document to my niece, Elizabeth O'Connor, hoping she
will do the right thing with it. Nothing will bring back
Lieutenant Becker now, or undo the past, but I cannot
face my Maker without confessing my part in a great
injustice. For now . . .

The next page was missing.

Now there could be no doubt – Becker was innocent.
The flesh and blood Marcus wasn't pompous, but a person
who'd done one wrong thing, which ruined his life. Or he
thought it had. But why had Elizabeth done nothing with the
document? While she was sunning herself in the Caribbean,
Becker was rotting in Sing-Sing. Why had she later hidden
the truth?

If I confronted her, I'd have to admit theft.

Well, at least, I'd found out that Marcus was neither good
nor bad. But a mixture like everyone else.

He said William Jennings Bryan would be remembered
by history. But people today only remember the movie
about the Scopes trial, with Spencer Tracy playing Clarence
Darrow. If the legend is better, print the legend.

"Tickets please!" The conductor wobbled down the
carriage.

"Is there a bar?" I asked.

He tore off my ticket stub and placed it above me. "At
the end of the train, Ma'am."

I didn't go.

Instead I leafed through Xeroxes, looking for something
on the Caribbean. The Dominican Republic had the first

university in the new world. Now it was the third world. America had never understood its huge problems. Espanola was the Ireland of the Caribbean – poor and divided. I'd always dismissed the charges against Marcus, because my mother had. She said he was sacked because he was anti-British and refused to allow their ships to refuel during the first war, and this had irritated Wilson.

There was an article about the revolution he quelled, depicting him as a hero sent by Wilson to "extinguish the conflagration."

> *The cause of the revolution is little understood here, but is supposed to be due to the ambition of a leader to get into power by force of arms after having been defeated by constitutional methods. It is understood that Minister Quilligan O'Neill will throw the influence of the United States to the support of the President, who was elected last Spring by one of the fairest general elections ever held in the republic.*

That had a *déjà vu* ring to it. Were the Americans getting it wrong then too? Their bungling's still endless – Vietnam, Nicaragua, etc. In one of Oonagh's stories a Dominican servant had once been appointed to assassinate Marcus, but had shot himself instead.

"Next stop, Wilmington, Delaware!" the passing conductor shouted.

Outside was a hideous sprawl. It was like some sort of moonscape.

I read an article about a blockade. It must have been dangerous for my grandmother and child-uncle.

Then John McCormack's voice sang behind me:

My wild Irish rose,
The sweetest flower that grows . . .

Marcus swayed down the train. He was now dressed in diplomatic garb, wide trousers and a tilted top hat.

In all the wide world
There's none can compare,
With my wild, Irish rose . . .

Frozen, I hid behind my Xeroxes. I couldn't even move, never mind kill him. Were Bald Jack *et al* behind him? He'd warned me about them.

Also he carried a stick of French bread. "Ah, there you are!" He was breathless. "Looked for you everywhere! Gotya some bread."

I'd meant to buy bread for Molly in a Georgetown bakery. "I don't want it."

"OK!" He stuffed the bread into his top pocket and sat down stiffly. "Whatcha reading?"

"A story about the revolution. Oonagh said you were almost assassinated."

He roared laughing. "The poor bum lost his nerve."

"It sounds like today."

He snapped his braces. "They were savages down there."

There was a silence.

I broke it. "Look, what do you want?"

He gave me a watery look over his wire glassses. "You forgot the bread. And I want to clear up a few points – "

I went back to the cuttings.

"You're my biographer!"

I leafed through the Xeroxes. Why couldn't he leave me alone?

Marcus was silent, as if patiently waiting for something. Cigar ash had spilled down the front of his suit.

"You brought your family to the Caribbean?"

"Yes, Nora worried about Danny getting fevers. We had our own doctor. Silly . . . considering – "

"Danny's death must've – "

He held up an arm, as if warding off a blow. "Stop . . ."

"It must've been hard, bringing up children alone."

He relaxed again, puffing on his cigar. "That was all in front of me. Did my son, Mark, ever straighten out?"

"He died in a veterans' hospital."

He sighed. "And I got him a job as senate page."

"You don't seem to care about him now."

"Sure, I do." Marcus flicked his cigar butt and sat beside me. As he did the bread dropped to the floor, but he picked it up and thrust it back in his pocket. He peered over my shoulder. "Whatcha reading now?"

I hated people doing this, but didn't say. "The 1913 papers are full of Home Rule and women's suffrage."

Marcus pulled his moustache. "The British were tyrants."

"So are men," I snapped.

He held up his stick bullyingly. "You're not one of those suffragettes?" He thumped the stick on the train floor. "They aren't ladies!"

"Did Nora ever vote?"

"Your grandmother was a lady."

"She smoked in public."

His eyes crossed in exasperation. "She never raised her voice."

"Victorians didn't."

He clutched the stick between his legs. "She was – " He broke off, looking into space. Then frowned, his eyebrows meeting bushily. "Everyone should be married. Are you married?"

I couldn't go into that.

He thumped the floor again. "Never mind those suffragettes. You're researching me!"

I flicked to another story. "You defended Thaw?"

He looked interested. "Got him off on a crime of passion. I was in great demand. I won the Townsend medal in Yale."

I went on reading.

"You don't seem impressed?"

I didn't answer. All her life Oonagh had praised him – till that last time.

Then he was singing in a lovely tenor voice *"The place is little changed, Nora. The day as bright as then . . . "*

"You knew William Jennings Bryan?"

"He owed me."

"He was the man with the golden voice?"

"No, that was me." He filled the train with cigar smoke.

"This is a no-smoking compartment," I said.

He waved his hand dismissively.

"It says you transferred funds."

Marcus stared through mushrooms of smoke. "Where?"

He leaned over, as I pointed to the article.

Marcus put a hand to his heart. "I served my country."

I guffawed. "According to Dr Johnson, patriotism's the last refuge of a scoundrel."

Outraged, Marcus stood up and limpingly paced the train. "Listen, Wilson sent me down there to sort those people out. They resented it and framed me. So don't believe a word of that. Here, give me those!"

He grabbed the Xeroxes, but I held on.

"Next stop, Philadelphia!" The porter swayed down the train. "Philadelphia, 30th Street Station!"

CHAPTER TWENTY

* * *

I CAME BACK TO ANOTHER ROW WITH COUSIN BUD.

He was sitting in the apartment in his underwear, as I unlocked the door. Hell, he was meant to be gone. We'd talked about it calmly, there was no question of him having to go until he was ready, but he had been with me for over two months. He had to think of his future. Yes, he'd assured me, he had a job in Atlantic City as a card dealer and would be gone when I got back. We'd actually said goodbye.

I pretended to be cheerful. "Did the job fall through?"

No answer.

I dumped my stuff and went into the kitchen. Was he angry again, because I was late? Since our last row, he'd taken up cooking in a big way, baking apple tarts as well as endless rocklike oatmeal cookies.

I kept my voice light. "What happened about the job?"

He swigged coke.

Something was definitely wrong.

I came into the living area. "What is it?"

"The cat's run over."

"Gosh, I'm sorry."

"Yuh let it out."

"I did not! It gets out if the window's open."

He still sat, gloomily shaking his head. "I buried it in the garden. I put a cross up and treated the wood. It'll last."

"That's good of you. Did you clear it with the office?"

"What?"

"Digging up the garden?"

"Naw."

"It might've been a good idea." I made for the bathroom. Now what would the landlord say? Luckily I didn't know them.

He jumped up. "Don't know why they think you could take care of a cat."

I'd had enough. "Oh, shut up, Bud."

Then he rounded on me. "First you're an adulteress, now you're into kinky sex!"

I reeled. Why had I taken in this maniac? A maniac who never dressed. But I had to keep calm. He hadn't had an easy life. "I don't know what you're talking about, Bud."

Triumphantly he held up a video. "Explain this!"

"Eh – what is it?"

"It's a porn video!" he hissed. "Your beau, Chuckie, left it here!"

"So what?"

He was pale now. "I hate kinky sex!"

"Now you listen to me! If it was a crime to watch porn videos, there'd be a lot of criminals."

"You might get hurt. If I'm caught protecting you, I might . . . "

"What?

"Oh . . . break parole."

Parole? He hadn't said anything about being in jail again. "I can take care of myself."

"No, you can't!"

He looked ridiculous in his underwear. "If you want to play the Victorian patriarch, you should at least get dressed!"

He looked hurt. "I am dressed!"

"I'm sick of this, Bud. I want you to leave my apartment."

He flung down the tape and stormed into his bedroom.

I went into mine. There, I had said it – the one thing I didn't want to say. Of course, I had a miserable night. I was worn out but still couldn't sleep. But at least I had no visitations.

In the morning Bud was gone. He left a note, thanking me and saying he'd call before I left for Ireland. I was relieved, but sorry. Now he'd remember me badly, despite all my best efforts. He'd think I'd rejected him, along with everyone else in his life. I was failing at everything, Fergal, Molly and Theodora, and now Bud.

I played a scene or two of the video and immediately zapped it off. I'd never seen a porn movie, so was surprised that it was exactly Teri Scales's fantasy. A man in Zorro clothes breaks into a woman's apartment and holds her captive until she agrees to parade topless.

Was Molly right, after all? Was Chuck violent? But what was so wrong with having a porn video? Surely everyone had a dark side to their sexuality? According to Freud, we were all at odds with ourselves. Jung believed in a shadow self. But if Chuck was into violence, what did it say about me? He was assertive sexually, and didn't take no for an answer. But there was nothing violent about our love-making. It was just hard to keep up with him.

I lunched with Molly the next day. These days she never talked about Chuck. As we ate in the lovely old kitchen we nervously avoided the topic, talking about almost everything else.

"How's the biography going?" she asked at one point.

"Oh, I've dug up some stuff. My Washington cousin had a journal. But I'm thinking of abandoning the project."

"You're getting back to fiction?"

"Yeah. The grandfather's interesting OK, but to the family."

Later, over coffee, she asked cautiously about my hallucinations.

I was tired of secrecy. "It happened on the train from

Washington. It happens anywhere." I held up my cup, smiling. "I've discovered coffee helps."

"It sounds like narcolepsy."

"Narcoleptics fall – I don't."

She looked at me worriedly. "Maybe you should see someone."

I was nervous. "You think I'm crazy?"

"I didn't say that! You're a writer – a highly intuitive person. You're going through a – crisis." She spoke slowly, cautiously. "A midlife crisis, which has triggered the condition."

It was a relief to talk.

"It's probably very treatable." She hesitated. "Eh – have you touched base with Fergal?"

It was the same old thing, but this time I didn't flare up. "No. I'm afraid to. He knows about Chuck."

"How?"

"He phoned and heard him in the background."

Molly was puzzled. "But he knows it's an *affair*?"

"I wrote and told him."

Molly didn't answer. I knew what she thought by the look on her face. Nothing would ever make her dislike Fergal, or like Chuck.

But those who had judged Chuck guilty were soon proved wrong. A few days later the committee cleared him of all Teri's charges. He was exonerated, while she was impugned. I was relieved for him, but not surprised. It was a victory in prudish times. Chuck was on a high, and that night we went out to celebrate.

Afterwards he came back to the apartment for drinks.

As I poured brandy, he looked at my research notes on the dining-room table. He picked up Marcus's journal. "What's this?"

"My grandfather wrote a sort of last testament. He mentions his legal career – "

"Bald Jack?"

I nodded.

"You should sell it to a library."

"Maybe I will. He's interesting on Evelyn Nesbit."

"That little bitch!"

I was surprised at his tone. "Was she a bitch?"

"Doctorow mythologizes her, but the reality was otherwise."

"What became of her?"

Chuck knew a lot about her. "She lived till 1967 – in California."

"Did Thaw really flog her?"

Chuck snorted. "You bet. She deserved it too!"

"Oh, Chuck, come on."

He quickly changed the subject. "Bet you're glad to be rid of your lodger?"

"He got a job in Atlantic City." I didn't say anything about our row. "He grew on me. He phoned last night. He's coming back to see me."

Chuck nursed his brandy glass, smiling at the chess board. "If I didn't watch every move, he'd wipe me out."

"He was the same with Fergal. It's an obsession with him."

Chuck sprawled back on the sofa, laughing. "A strange character."

"The world's full of 'em." Then I asked casually, "Did they ever find Teri's intruder?"

He gulped his brandy. "I told you she invented the whole damn thing."

I said nothing.

"They questioned a few *Playboy* subscribers at the newstand." He laughed lightly. "They even came to me."

"It's a crime to buy *Playboy*?"

"They thought the suspect – if he exists – was a boobs man."

"Oh . . ." Chuck was a boobs man.

Then I gave him the video, nervously watching for a reaction. "I think you left this."

"Oh, thanks." He tossed it into his tennis bag without any hint of embarrassment or guilt. "Wondered where I'd left it."

I must've been staring, because he said, "What is it?"

"Nothing."

He grinned sheepishly. "Ah, you played it."

"Eh – yes. It's not very edifying."

He squared his jaw. "No, it sure ain't. It was part of my campaign to discredit Miss Muffet."

I breathed more easily. "Teri? How?"

"You noticed it's exactly her fantasy?"

I nodded. "The man in Zorro clothes."

"Video Americain have an adult section at the back. If I could prove she checked this out and invented the story, they wouldn't believe the sexual harassment shit."

"Did she check it out?"

"Couldn't find out. Video store records aren't available."

It was a reasonable explanation.

As I told Molly, I was giving up the idea of a biography. Marcus's role in the Rosenthal case had been important but peripheral. I had phoned Cyrus Van Dam, telling him I was sending him a journal for an opinion, but asking him not to mention it to Elizabeth as the topic upset her.

"I understand, my dear," he said tactfully.

Then he wrote back three pages of explanation, repeating what he'd said at Elizabeth's party, as to why the journal was hearsay and inadmissible evidence. "There'd be no way of rebutting your grandfather, as he's dead . . . I don't think you should lose confidence in the law, my dear. Most people are guilty as accused . . . "

God. How many innocent people were in jail today?

And the Becker case stank. Yet Governor Whitman refused Helen Becker's pleas for mercy.

"In the presence of my God, I proclaim my absolute innocence of this foul crime . . ." were Becker's last words. After the botched execution, over ten thousand people attended his funeral. The police confiscated Helen's plaque calling Charles Whitman a murderer. He never became President, but ended up as a drunkard, spending his old age in a New York hotel. Jack Rose got himself a wig and became a preacher, and then made movies on the evils of gambling. He lived to old age, dying in the mid-1940s. The other gamblers lived out their lives. Helen Becker finally retired as a respected principal of a New York grade school. "I shall never rest until I have exposed the methods used to convict my husband," she wrote. "He was just an ordinary human being and that is why I loved him so."

The law was meant to be a process from which justice came. But so often it didn't.

I saw a lot of my neighbour, Frances. I'd never met anyone who got such pleasure out of simple things -- Roy Rogers for breakfast, Howard Johnson's for dinner. I'd often gone there with her and Bud. And he'd made himself useful by driving her to the hospital for treatment, which was way out on some impossible highway. Bud was gone now, but Frances still dropped in most evenings for an aperitif, singing gaily, "Do you like iced tea, do you like lemonade?"

"Where's your cousin?" she asked one day.

I told her he had to go.

She looked sad. "I like men. I like 'em young."

Did Bud qualify? I wondered again about her life. Had she had many affairs? Although now her purple shorts had become jeans, she still wore her backwards baseball cap. And she always brought little Frances, sometimes in a stroller, or sometimes cradled against her shoulder.

One day we were sitting on the balcony when she picked up the doll and cooed over it. "Is the sun in your eyes, hon? No, but you want a Kleenex? Mom's getting one."

Then, without asking me, she rummaged in my nearby handbag. It was a harmless eccentricity. She'd been through it before, also all my drawers and had tried things on from the wardrobe.

"The Kleenex are in the bathroom," I said, when she didn't find one. "Will I get you some?"

"That's OK, hon." Jauntily she carried Little Frances to the bathroom, coming out in a few minutes with a bottle of *Ma Griffe* perfume in one hand and Little Frances in the other. "My, but you're a classy lady."

"Why don't you keep it?"

She put her baby in the stroller, unscrewed the bottle and sniffed. "Hmm. No, hon, it's too good."

"But I never use it."

"You don't?"

"No. Keep it."

She dabbed herself, entranced. Then tenderly she dabbed Little Frances. "See what Auntie has given us?" Then suddenly, her eyes filled up with tears.

I was alarmed. "What's wrong?"

"You know what, hon?"

"What?"

"I've never had one of those."

"One of what?"

"One of those!"

"But what?" Did she want something else in the bathroom?

"Those or-or-orgasms."

I was taken aback. "Well, sex isn't everything."

"But it is. That's why I'm here. Old, lonely and divorced." She went on sobbing. "I couldn't fake it. I'm a good person."

I held her sobbing shoulders. "Of course you are."

It was all Bud's fault. He had talked non-stop about sex. But then, I was pretty obsessed myself.

CHAPTER TWENTY-ONE

***

THE SEMESTER WAS WINDING DOWN. THERE WAS ONLY ONE MORE week of classes. Then a reading week. Then exams. But I still kept office hours twice weekly, and students occasionally came in to discuss paper topics or their stories. Now that people were busy writing or preparing for exams, I didn't have too many takers. But one day Teri Scales appeared at my door.

"Hello, Teri. Come in."

She hovered uncertainly. For a change her stringy hair was washed under the hat, and she wore an attractive peasant skirt instead of the usual dirty Bermudas or baggy men's jeans.

"Could we talk, Professor O'Brien?"

"Certainly, take a seat." Although uneasy, I was determined not to let Chuck's problems interfere with class business. No matter how neurotic, she was the only undisputed A. "How can I help?"

She sat in the armchair, glowering and biting her lower lip. She had a habit of chewing her lips. And despite the effort at grooming, was drawn and distracted. Her pimply skin was pale, and her eyes red-rimmed behind the slipping glasses.

She pushed them up now, staring silently.

What did she want?

"What is it, Teri?"

"I've sure enjoyed your class, Professor O'Brien."

This was a surprise. "Well, thank you."

Then another silence.

"Your approach is – different."

What was coming?

"Eh, thanks."

"Refreshing."

Was she being sarcastic? After all, she was disturbed. I cleared my throat nervously. "You realise I'm a writer, not an academic. Writers are hacks."

She grimaced. "Everyone else here is so mind-bogglingly tedious."

"Surely, not everyone?"

She nodded. "They're all pathetic theorists."

"Well, perhaps I'm more of a common reader."

Something sinister was coming. Nervously I fumbled with some papers on my desk. Then remembered she was writing on Edna O'Brien. "Eh, how's your paper going?"

She shoved her glasses up again, staring.

"You're having difficulties?"

Her lip curled in scorn. "I *don't* have difficulties with papers."

"No, of course not. Your mid-term was excellent. There's something else on your mind?"

"I *saw* you with Professor Matthews."

I made myself smile. "You probably did."

"In the Crabshack. Last night." Her tone was accusing.

"Yes, we often dine together." I kept my voice light, trying to tread carefully.

"You heard what happened to me?" Her mood had shifted to anger.

"I did hear a vague rumour, Teri. Something about a break-in."

"It's not a *vague rumour*!" She looked outraged. "I was assaulted in my own bedroom."

"But the police found no evidence?"

"It was *him*!"

"Who?"

"Matthews!"

I caught my breath. "Professor Matthews?"

"Yeah, that snake."

I struggled for composure. "Let me get this straight. Professor Matthews broke into your apartment in the middle of the night – "

Her face crumpled as tears came.

" – and threatened you?"

"He did more than threaten me!" She was sobbing hysterically now. The girl was obviously ill.

"But, Teri," I said gently. "Isn't that a bit paranoid?"

She stood up suddenly, whipped up her skirt and turned her behind to me.

"You think this is paranoia?"

There was a small but deep round mark on her large thigh.

"See it?"

I nodded, stunned.

She pulled her skirt right up. There was another burn near her white pants. "See the other mark?"

"I do indeed."

"The bastard stubbed his cigarette on me." The girl sat down again.

I put an arm on her shoulder.

She pulled away abruptly. "I don't like to be touched!"

"Sorry."

"The police think I burnt myself."

I took a deep breath.

"He did it because I hate cigarettes."

I was too shocked to speak. Chuck got angry if people objected to smoking. But it was because he felt harassed and also guilty. Most smokers did. But he'd never do this.

"Could I burn myself?"

She was from a dysfunctional family. Her father was sexually deviant. Dr Finnegan had explained her self-destructive personality type.

"Could I?" she yelled.

"Teri . . ." I tried to collect myself.

"Well, could I?" She was now an angry red.

"Calm down, and tell me why Professor Matthews would do something like this?"

"I told you – he's a snake!"

I sighed.

"I blew the whistle on his sexism."

"Yes, I know all about that. But why would he make things worse?"

She lapsed back to sullenness. "He thinks he can wear fancy dress and no one will recogise him. He was wearing a mask like Zorro, a sort of scarf with holes. And a black hat."

"It sounds a bit wild." Should I reason with her or not? "But it doesn't make sense."

"No, cos he's a weirdo."

"But, Teri," I said. "Why would he? He was already in enough trouble."

She was sobbing hysterically again. "But can't you see? No one ever believes the woman."

That was true.

"He made sure no one would believe me."

He had admitted to me that he wanted to discredit her. "Look, if it was dark, how can you be so certain it was him?"

She gave me a despairing look. "I guess you don't know then?"

"Know what?"

"We were lovers."

I was stunned again. "You . . . and Professor Matthews?"

"Sure, all last semester. But he dumped me for you."

I felt weak. Why hadn't Chuck told me?

"He can't treat people like they never existed!"

The mad look in her eye was back. She was dangerous all right, and had probably made the sexism charges to repay Chuck for dropping her. But this was more serious. If it was true about their affair, why hadn't he told me?

"I suppose he gave you all that shit about his wife being dull? A southern belle who took to the bottle?"

The mire was getting deeper and deeper.

"Know why she took to the bottle?" She was shouting again.

I held up my hand. "Please, Teri."

"Because he abused her!"

"I don't want to continue this, Teri."

"You better! You'll be next!"

I was breathless. "Please, Teri. Stop it!"

"No!"

"I'd like you to go now."

"Go?"

"Yes!"

She stood up, outraged. "Well, I warned you!"

And she slammed out the door.

I was shattered and sat on in my office, wondering whether or not to confront Chuck. That afternoon I walked into the wrong classroom and talked for about ten minutes, until someone said it was a class in Elizabethan Poetry.

I found my right class, but Teri wasn't there. It was just as well. Her depiction of Chuck as a psychopathic torturer was deranged. He'd already gone through enough because of her stupid accusations. But why had he never mentioned their affair? This niggled me. Finally, after agonizing all night, I rang him the next morning.

We met for lunch at the student cafeteria. Mostly the faculty went to a staff dining-room, so it was private. When I arrived, the huge room still hadn't filled up. I got coffee and a doughnut at the self-service counter and sat at an empty booth, inwardly rehearsing what I would say. The cafeteria was dominated by a giant TV – the biggest I'd ever seen. There was an awful games show on. Every few minutes, the players screamed hysterically and lights lit as they scored. It was soul-deadening. Why have this in a college? Finally I dragged my gaze away, focusing on the people around me.

Then I saw them – four, dark-suited, Fedora-hatted boys two tables away. The same boys who had followed me in New York, all in their early twenties and brown-skinned, and, except for their neat, sombre clothes, just like the boys on campus. One caught my eye and smiled sweetly. As he took off his hat, a lock of black, greasy hair fell over his eyes. He flicked it back, revealing a scar over one eyebrow – Gyp. Then the others were Lefty Louie, Dago Frank and Whitey Lewis. The last two needed a shave.

"Come on out, Annie!" a voice yelled from somewhere.

I pretended not to hear.

Through the long glass wall, I saw the campus. A figure was hurrying through the drizzle under the bare trees. He wore a black hat and a belted raincoat. The raincoat puzzled me. I'd seen it somewhere before. But the head was down, so I didn't immediately recognise the wearer. Then he came into the room and stood at the door, looking around.

It was Bald Jack. His rubbery face was emotionless, but he was coming for me. Oh, hell . . . I'd reason with the boys. Tell them that they'd been set up for Rosenthal's murder. It wouldn't help to kill me too. Besides I had evidence which might help their case.

I smiled, but they moved to a nearer booth.

I tried to stand, but couldn't.

Lefty Louie held up a gun, his right wrist tattooed.

They'd shoot me here in broad daylight, like they had Herman Rosenthal.

"Dirty squealer," the same voice jeered.

Who was it?

The boys now moved to the next table, the four of them squeezing in.

I was still stuck to my chair.

By now Bald Jack had reached them and signalled with a rough jerk of his head. "Come on, you rat guerillas!"

They looked sheepishly at me.

"We gotta croak her now!" Jack rasped.

"Will I plug her, Gyp?" Lefty yelled.

"No, let's get outa here." Gyp ran and the others followed.

So Bald Jack turned on me. "OK, you dirty rat squealer!"

I cowered, as he made for me. His hands were in his pockets. In a minute he'd pull a gun on me. It was the end.

"Please!" I begged.

Then I saw Marcus. It was the old Marcus, limping in through the door on his stick. "Duck, Anne!"

"What?"

"Get onto the floor."

I put my head under the table.

Then a familiar voice asked, "What is it, Anne? Dropped something?"

I rubbed my eyes. Chuck now stood in front of me in a belted raincoat and large black hat.

I stared at the hat. "Eh, I didn't see you come in."

He sat down. "But you were looking right at me."

"I was?"

He nodded.

My dreams were back with a vengeance. "I didn't know you had a black hat."

He took it off, laughing easily. "What about it?"

Teri had described it exactly. "Nothing. Eh – Fergal has one the same."

"Oh." He ran his fingers through his hair. "It keeps the rain off. Well, what's up?"

I had lost my courage. Maybe it was the hat. "Nothing. I just – eh – wanted to see you. It's been a while."

He frowned. "Sorry, I've been busy."

Chuck went for food, getting me another doughnut. I breathed deeply to calm myself down. I wanted to ask him about Teri's accusations, but couldn't. I rationalised, telling myself that the hat was only circumstantial evidence. And if Chuck hadn't said anything about their affair, why should he? The past wasn't my business. Teri was brainy and would go on to further laurels. Even if she stood on her head, she couldn't avoid going to the top. But she'd always be unlovable. A troublemaker who upset others with her poisoned pen. Chuck hadn't done anything wrong. College professors often had affairs with students, and, despite political correctness, so long as it wasn't an undergraduate, it was still considered private. People like Molly and Theodora would frown on such behaviour, but they could hardly condemn Chuck for something so usual.

When we went back to the apartment, I managed to say it. "Teri came to see me."

He sat up, paling under his tan. "When?"

I avoided his eyes. "Yesterday. She had marks on her – cigarette burns."

He swigged back brandy. "Self-inflicted."

I couldn't repeat Teri's accusation. "Apparently, that's what the police said."

He looked irascible. "I told you she's nuts!"

"She told me about her affair – "

He sighed heavily. "Look, a girl like that – "

" – with you."

"What?" The wrinkle between his eyebrows appeared. "What did she say?"

"That you two had an affair."

Presently he shrugged. "I wouldn't call it an *affair*. I was hard up one night. Well, a couple of nights. It was sex, but not for grades. I gave her an A because she deserved it."

"Did the committee know?"

"Sure, they did. But I showed them my grade book." He spoke earnestly now. "I was warned to stay away from students. But it takes two to tango. Then when you came, the little blackmailer tried to ruin me." He lowered his voice. "But she was just a bit too clever."

"She says you dumped her."

"Look, she was a mistake." He ran his hands through his hair and looked at me pleadingly. "She was talking about marriage, that sort of thing. She even rang my wife. When that didn't work, she thought up the sexual harassment shit."

His explanation was reasonable and I couldn't see him stubbing his cigarette on anyone's backside, never mind dressing up to do it. Teri's accusations were outlandish. "You wouldn't marry again?"

He laughed shortly.

I stared into my wine.

"Would you?" he asked.

"What?"

"Marry again?"

With all the problems in the present, I honestly hadn't thought about it. "Oh, I don't know. The right man perhaps."

He nodded thoughtfully. "I might marry a younger woman."

That was a splash of cold water.

"For more children. I've lost Billy," he went on. "Zelda's done her bit there."

I was unable to say anything.

Chuck looked at me worriedly. "Have I said anything wrong?"

Tears came. I couldn't help it.

"Anne? Now what have I done?" He fidgeted agitatedly with the stem of his glass. "But you're going back to Ireland?"

I was an adult. I knew it was an affair, yet I was hurt. In my vanity, I hadn't quite realized that I too was very much a person of the moment. I wiped my eyes, laughing. "I don't know what it is? Maybe what you said about children. I'm past all that."

It was a lie – since meeting Ogie's, I didn't regret children. But I had to say something.

He looked relieved. "They're not everything. Billy hides when I go home."

I had control of myself. "Kids go through stages. Being difficult is their way of expressing pain."

Then I told him about Ogie's darlings, and he roared laughing.

That night we tried sex but failed. It was the first time it had happened, and seemed to anger Chuck. Afterwards I lay awake till dawn, while he snored. I studied his sleeping handsome face. Why were you attracted by certain people? His irreverence was refreshing in such a stiflingly politically correct campus. He had flattered me, and I'd fallen for that. Maybe also he'd helped me shed some inhibitions. But in doing so, I'd lost my husband. I hadn't had any more letters or phone calls from Fergal who would see everything from his viewpoint. Men are like that. They can fool around, but a woman who wanders is scarlet.

So I'd no idea what the future held. I had to finish up the semester, then, who knows, I might try for a full-time post at Sweetmount and be an American at last. Work had always sustained me.

About five I got up in my dressing-gown, made coffee, and started reading for class.

An hour later the buzzer went.

Who was it?

At this hour?

I pushed the listening button. "Hello?"

"It's me, Anne," a deep Kerry accent came over the intercom.

Fergal!

Here?

I was caught dead. Now there'd be a terrific row. I had to let him in, but there was no time to get rid of Chuck.

"Fergal? Come on in." I buzzed the door open and ran to the bedroom.

"Get up!" I shook Chuck's shoulder. "Quickly!"

He opened his eyes sleepily. "What is it?"

"Fergal is here?"

"Who?"

"My husband! Here!"

"What?" He jumped out of bed, and pulled on his jeans. "I'll run down the back stairs."

"No, please stay."

"Stay?" He fumbled with his shirt buttons. "I'd better go."

"No, please. He knows all about you. And I'm tired of running."

"He knows about me?"

Then the buzzer went again and when I pushed the button, Fergal's voice came through. "Anne, how do I get in?"

"Push the door!" I buzzed him in again. "Take the lift to the second floor. I'll meet you there."

Leaving Chuck frantically dressing, I went to the lift. Fergal was generally genial, but could lose his temper. Still, he'd never laid a hand on me. But I'd never been in a melodrama like this. Tabloid headlines flashed through my mind: ERRANT WIFE ATTACKED BY FURIOUS HUSBAND. VIOLENT ROW WAKES RESIDENTS OF BELLA VISTA.

Fergal stepped out of the lift. He was tired, and laden down by duty-free bags.

I was afraid to speak.

He stared grimly. Then in a deadpan voice, did his Oliver Hardy imitation. "Another fine mess!"

Then he laughed that deep laugh I loved.

I laughed too. As always, after we were separated for a while, it was like seeing him anew. Now I was struck by his ruddy bearlikeness, his wild, wiry, grey hair. There was nothing clean cut about Fergal. He and Chuck were so different: one a neat package of a person, the other a big, mountainy man.

"Well, that's no way to greet a tired husband." He dumped his duty-free bags and held out his arms.

In disbelief, I walked into them.

He bear-hugged me, then perused my face in puzzlement. "You all right?"

I pulled back. "Of course."

He looked serious. "I had a worrying phone call."

"Molly?"

"She says you're having hallucinatons."

I picked up a duty-free bag and made for the apartment. "That's a bit dramatic. I have dreams."

He followed me, grumbling, "Still as stubborn – "

I turned round. "I'm just not sleeping."

"Then you'll see a doctor!"

"OK, OK. Please don't raise your voice." I felt faint, but got it out. "Listen, Chuck is here. He's been here all night."

Fergal raised his bushy eyebrows in mock amusement. "The boyfriend?"

I nodded.

"Well, what a coincidence!" he bellowed.

"Fergal, please – . Remember you were awfully cosy with that girl."

"What girl?"

"The tall girl. I can't remember her name."

"Doreen McCann?"

I nodded.

"I didn't fuck her, if that's what you mean."

"Well, you acted like you did."

"I was sorry for her. She's a drug addict."

I didn't believe him.

"Tell me, does the boyfriend do it better?"

"Please, I don't want a scene."

He picked up his bags and marched up the corridor. "I won't challenge him to a duel, don't worry about that."

I ran after him. "Promise you won't make a scene."

"I'll promise nothing."

I leaned weakly against the wall.

He stopped too. "Unless you promise to see a doctor."

What would a doctor say? "I'm better recently."

Fergal plonked down his cases. "I want you checked out!"

"Stop shouting!"

He looked angry now. "Why do you think I came?"

He did seem to care. But I had to shut him up now. "OK. It's a deal. If you keep calm now, I'll see a doctor."

"Promise?"

"Yes." I walked on, and he lumbered after me.

Halfway to my door, I stopped. "Whiskey's cheaper here. The duty free's a tourist trap."

"Well, I couldn't come empty-handed. I got wine for you and whiskey for the girls. How are they?"

"They're always the same – great." I was irritated with Molly for breaking my confidence, but couldn't show it. "I'm out of whiskey. I'll go out and get you some."

"Don't bother. I've quit."

I laughed. "Tell me another."

"No, I'm serious."

Was this an attempt to mend things? How would I cope with that? And how would I cope now?

But I needn't have worried.

When we got to the apartment, Chuck was gone.

Only Mr Coffee gurgled discreetly.

CHAPTER TWENTY-TWO

* * *

I WAS DISAPPOINTED CHUCK HAD FLED, BUT UNDERSTOOD.

I suppose you never know anyone. I certainly couldn't have predicted that Fergal would be so accepting. But he's generally forgiving and, I suppose, I'm not. Perhaps men get softer and women get tougher? One good thing: he didn't think I was seriously ill. But he alone understood how disturbing and exhausting my experiences were.

After he'd rested, we went out to dinner in the Crabshack, where I had gone so often with Chuck. "Waking dreams aren't that abnormal," he said.

I was doubtful.

"Ask any analyst. Your subconscious is asking you to address something," he said. "To come to terms with the past."

That's Fergal — consoling and understanding. I found myself talking in a way I hadn't for years, explaining how Marcus appeared everywhere. "My mother had an odd relationship with her father."

He shrugged. "Many women do."

Fergal was so cool, after all my agonizing.

He held his hand a foot high from the floor. "The Department of Justice has a file that high of cases. Did your mother say what happened?"

I shook my head. "She said he wasn't a 'proper father.' What could that mean?"

"Anything." He sighed. "He was too old. Too strict, too easy-going. Besides, it's in the past, Anne. It didn't do Oedipus any good to find out the truth."

"No."

"Your sleep patterns aren't helping. You may need medication?"

What was he saying?

He read my mind. "For sleep."

"Well, I'm not taking it!"

He brushed his wiry hair in exasperation. "You're a stubborn woman. Why not?"

"I don't like drugs."

"What's alcohol?"

"I see. I'm an alcoholic. I suppose Molly said that?" I could hear her.

He was patient. "Now, don't be so prickly. You just can't make blanket statements. All medication isn't bad."

"Psychiatrists *make* people ill!"

"That's a bit ignorant."

I controlled my irritation. "Remember, I've experienced them. I thought I'd explode with madness till I was thirty."

His blue eyes were kind. "But that was another life."

It was. I had met Fergal about then. He had given me a sense of myself, the confidence to write. Even if my books were rubbish, they got published and people seemed to enjoy them. We were able to live well on the money. I deliberately didn't mention that now. We didn't talk of the future at all. Maybe it's better not to? Better to live from day to day like the alcoholics? For the moment I had to finish the semester. I had to admit, it was consoling to have Fergal around now, but if we ever got back together, he'd have to start consulting me about things. But that was in the future. For now I reluctantly agreed to see a doctor.

Fergal first made an appointment with Molly's GP who said my failure to sleep "looked like depression". He was a nice affable idiot who had once given me the wrong medicine. He referred me on to a psychiatrist who said they had wonderful drugs nowadays. I told him outright that I didn't have schizophrenia. Didn't he know how gravely ill schizophrenics were? How could I carry on a job if I were so afflicted? He finally suggested the problem was a form of bi-polar illness and recommended Prozac. I refused to take it, so he gave me sleeping pills and a stimulant in the morning. He was worried by my auditory hallucinations, so first sent me for a CAT scan.

Of course, nothing showed up. So I was referred on to a neurologist.

It's meant to be a sign of age when authority figures look young. Well, this third doctor was amazingly young and amazingly frank. He made no effort to spare my feelings. My dreams could be caused by: a) sleep disorder: b) epilepsy; c) brain tumour.

In boarding school years ago, I had sleep-walked, so perhaps this was a related disorder. Fergal had insisted others had waking dreams like mine. I'd always had exotic night dreams anyway. So perhaps this was just an extension? I could never understand my dreams. We live with so much undertow, a lost Titanic of the mind.

The latest doctor doubted it was epilepsy.

And, as I'd had no personality change or headache, he also doubted a tumour but couldn't rule anything out till I had an MRI which was scheduled for the end of December. The idea of a tumour scared me as my father had died of one. So I became pessimistic about the results and started imagining funny headaches. But it's odd, when you face fear, it lessens. I began to feel detached and no longer dreaded death. I just thought: what a pity if I'm dying. My life will be cut off in middle age. I won't write any more door-stoppers, which will be just as well. And, as I won't be here, there'll be no need to worry about the future.

Fergal only stayed a week and spent most of it escorting me to doctors. Otherwise, we sort of clicked into our old life: reading, visiting Molly and Theodora, going to shows in Philadelphia. Tommy Makem was playing there, so we saw him, as Fergal loved Irish music. Also we went to several art galleries in the city.

"I won't be able to irritate you anymore," I said one evening, having burnt myself preparing dinner. Fergal wasn't a new man and, unlike Bud, left the cooking to me.

He looked up from his book. "What do you you mean?"

"If I die, I can't be a terrible cook."

"Oh, I'll be cursing you for a few years yet."

"You think so?"

He looked at me in his kind way. "'I love everything that's old: old friends, old times, old manners, old books and old wives.' As Goldsmith so aptly put it."

I laughed. "What about old wines?"

"Not any more, I can't."

It was true he hadn't drunk since he came. Fergal has an iron will, which made it awkward for me.

That night we made love for the first time in a year. Was this his way of saying all was forgiven? And had I been wrong about the affair? I didn't believe it wasn't physical. But it probably just happened. As Molly always says, Fergal's a carer and needs to mind people. I filled that role for the moment.

The last evening we went to Molly and Theodora's. It was to be a farewell dinner, as he was leaving for Dublin the next morning. There were no other guests. As usual, "the girls" were delighted with him and Molly had cooked a terrific meal. The house looked lovely. Mozart was playing as we came in, and the table was lit by candles. Americans really live life. They're so much more hospitable than the Irish, who are famed for it. Despite Molly's alliance with Fergal, her friendship gave me great joy. I'd miss her when we separated at Christmas. There'd be no one to exercise with, and I'd turn into a flabby recluse again.

I abstained from drink, noticing approving glances from Molly. Everything was going well, until we sat around the fire for coffee and talked of Fergal's world-bettering schemes.

Molly brought up the subject. "Tell me about this free school, Fergal."

"Oh, it's going well." Then he looked guiltily at me. "But Anne disapproves."

She turned on me, puzzled. "Still? But why?

"Because I'm *paying* for it."

"But you're not short of money?"

I was taken aback. "No – but – "

"Then why not give it a try?"

"Because it's crazy!" I escaped to the loo.

"People think too much of security," Theodora chipped in wisely, as I crossed the room.

Typical.

Just typical.

It was easy to talk like that when you had a pension – two pensions.

When I came out, they were still talking animatedly about spreading the light in Present Age Ireland. I listened grumpily but didn't join in. People always liked Fergal more than they liked me. Oh, I know it's childish to care, but why did it always happen?

Back at the apartment, he chided me for being difficult.

"You mean, I can't express myself?" I snapped.

"My grants have come through. I'll be able to pay you back in full."

I said nothing.

"I'm trying to do something – useful."

Of course, we had a row. On his last night. Men just don't communicate properly. They're fine so long as you agree with them and do everything they say. Why is life always one step forward, two steps back? I was awake all night, finally giving in and taking a pill, which left me drugged the next morning. The airport shuttle came and we parted formally, with no discussion about the future. Just another nagging about my tests. And an announcement that he was going to the west of Ireland for Christmas and I was welcome if I could be agreeable. Agreeable? How's that for lack of communication. I said I'd stay in New York with Ogie. Damn Molly and her idealism. No matter what Fergal did, they'd take his side. He could stand on his head, and they'd always love him. Whereas I was a pennypincher. A Scrooge, depriving the world's poor of an education.

So I was alone in the apartment again. But sleeping better, as I still wasn't drinking. There was grading to do. The writing class had a final story. The others a take-home exam and final paper. Gradually I was getting through them. Oddly, Teri Scales didn't hand hers in. Then Dr Finnegan, the college psychiatrist, rang and asked if I'd give her an incomplete – that's permission to make up the work. She was in a Philadelphia mental hospital.

I was worried by this. But told myself the girl was

seriously disturbed. Then Molly was asked to visit her by the Women's Shelter. Coincidentally, she was driving me to another hospital in the same area for my MRI, so she asked me to accompany her.

Grumpily I agreed.

Molly had caused the last row with Fergal. And, although the affair with Chuck seemed to have fizzled out, I didn't want to hear any more accusations against him. We taught on different days, so we didn't run into each other in Sweetmount. I only saw him once since that morning in my apartment, and then he had nodded curtly. He was probably afraid to phone, thinking Fergal was still around.

We drove to Philadelphia in silence. I was tired of Molly's do-gooding. This visit was a further attempt to persuade me against Chuck. But I felt vaguely guilty about Teri. I didn't believe her, but she'd come to me, and I hadn't followed it up. Oh, I wouldn't have done anything about her crazy accusation, but I could have reported that she was showing symptoms of mental illness – from that first day in my office. Somehow, I had failed her.

One hospital is like another. This was cheery enough, but overheated with that usual institutional smell, a mixture of hamburger and disinfectant. We found Teri in the cafe, huddled over a cup of coffee. She looked awful. Her hair was greasy and she'd developed worse acne and put on weight. She greeted me comatosely, without any hint of her previous rancour. She was like someone de-wasped.

"Hi, Professor O'Brien."

I nodded hello, chatting while Molly went for our coffee.

The girl's wrists were bandaged.

"I'm sorry about the paper and exam," she said pathetically.

I dragged my gaze from her wrists, hiding my shock.

"That's OK, Teri. Take your time. Sarah'll send them on to Ireland."

Her voice was drugged. "I got depressed."

"You'll be out of here soon, Teri." Molly carried the coffee over and sat down.

Teri shook her head. "No one believes me."

"I do, Teri." Molly took her hand, giving me a significant look.

I stared into my coffee. Despite Teri's lies, I couldn't help feeling for her. I had been incarcerated in a mental hospital myself. And this hospital reminded me of a place my mother had spent time in. She would go on benders and end up falling out with all her friends. Or doing something self-destructive. Had Teri been abused too? By her mad father?

We didn't stay long and, on the way out, Molly looked grim.

"She has a history of depression." I could read Molly's thoughts. She was getting mad with Chuck all over again. "Dr Finnegan told us – that night at your house."

Molly walked on, hugging herself. "Your friend didn't help her."

"You still believe her?"

She didn't reply.

She wanted me to think badly of Chuck. Well, he was a nice person, a devoted father. I'd never, never believe he'd done those horrible things. He'd been cleared, and Teri was a well-known liar. It was like the Becker case. A person was being convicted by the thinking of the times – Becker was done in by the movement for police reform. And Chuck by political correctness, the new puritanism which had swept over America. It was ridiculous. He couldn't have broken into her apartment. True, he had a black hat, but that was only circumstantial evidence. I'd recently seen *three* just like it in town.

Molly waited while I had the MRI.

It was frightening.

I refused to be injected with a dye, which would help the doctors but which had harmful effects on a small percentage of people. I mean, why die of dye? This puzzled them, but they agreed and strapped me into a coffin-like box. I came out in a sweat. But a girl was lovely to me, saying she'd be right there. Then she gave me headphones, asking me what kind of music I wanted. In loneliness and panic, I requested John McCormack, actually hoping for the first time that it would stir up Marcus who hadn't appeared for some weeks now. He'd keep me company. Anything would be better than this coffin. But I had to make do with Mozart.

When I went back to the psychiatrist, he beamed idiotically. "Well, the MRI found nothing."

I was relieved. "I've been reading up on Jung. He belived in angels."

He shook his head kindly. "Ah, no. He's completely dated. No, your brain chemistry is upset. The neurologist says, and I agree, that you have a sleep disorder. Your hallucinations are hypnogogic."

"Hypno what?"

"Hypnogogic. That's before REM sleep. Also hypnopomic – before waking."

They'd say anything. I was haunted, that's all. "Is there a cure?"

"You're my first," was all he said, not really answering me. "There are eighty-four sleep disorders in the International Classification of Sleep Disorders, mostly very rare. Yours is linked to creativity. They believe Blake had Hypnogogia. Also Van Gogh. Although he had temporal lobe epilepsy as well."

I felt weary. "Do I have that?"

"I think you're depressed."

"I gathered that."

He ignored this. "We'll have to control that. You mentioned a panic attack?"

I nodded wearily. "In a taxi. I couldn't breathe. Then imagined someone was following me."

He nodded sagely. "A misperception. Depressed people get suspicious."

"Look, I'm not that depressed."

"But you often work all night?"

"Yes . . ."

"You're manic then."

"Manic?"

"Yes, bi-polar."

It was back to the same old mumbo jumbo of psychiatry. He was very black and white, depression is all chemical. Everything's chemical. Even our dreams involve the release of a chemical, and our conscious states are controlled by other chemicals. REM sleep is necessary for sanity. It normally comes after several hours and toward the morning, which is why we sometimes remember dreams. But I fell into it immediately and all the time, because I was sleep deprived, due to depression. People who meditate, Buddhists for instance, experience similar things. But they reached the state on purpose.

At least I wasn't the only one, and my illness wasn't terminal. But there are so many things you don't know about, like green potatoes being deadly poison. Or raw kidney beans killing people. Oh, they're no comparison to hallucinations. It's just that things exist that you've never heard of, until they happen to you. Then you're more sympathetic, more understanding. It's not them and us. It's just people, suffering.

I was taking the pills, so was sleeping better and free of Marcus. Or maybe I just knew more about him and didn't need to dream. My ghost had been exorcised. It wasn't only houses that were haunted. People could be too.

A few students hadn't yet handed in their papers. But there were other things to see to.

I had written to the landlords about the cat. Now the apartment had to be cleaned. There wasn't much to do, as I'd hardly used the oven, but I wanted to leave everything perfect. Frances came over to help, but spent her time poking round as usual, while I worked. She was like a kid with her purple baseball cap back-to-front, playing and talking to herself and Little Frances. She particularly liked bathing the doll in the bathroom sink and trying out the cosmetics there. I had some expensive Lancôme duty-free face cream from the flight over. It probably isn't any better than the cheap stuff, but everything else gives me a rash. Well, Frances liked putting this on herself and Little Frances. It was a harmless extravagance and in a sense justified the expense. I wanted Frances to be happy.

After a while, she came out to the kitchen where I had my head in the fridge.

"Can we dress up?" she asked.

"No, Frances."

"Did you trick or treat at Hallowe'en?"

"No, but we did as children."

"But you went to a masked ball," she insisted.

I laughed. "No, Frances."

"But you have a mask."

I whipped round. "I do?"

"Sure. Here it is." She gave me a black cloth mask with holes for eyes – a Zorro mask.

I knew immediately what it was. "Frances, where did you get this?"

283

She pointed to the bathroom. "In there."

I was trembling. "Show me."

In the bathroom, she pointed to Chuck's black washbag, unzipping it to reveal a hidden compartment. Teri had described the mask exactly. It was evidence, direct physical evidence. Chuck was caught dead.

"What is it, hon?"

"Nothing."

"But you're pale as a ghost. And shaking."

I went back to my cleaning, working mechanically. It was all I could do. Frances went down to Roy Rogers for her evening meal. Afterwards she usually walked Little Frances in the garden, singing her to sleep. I was grateful to be alone.

Chuck was a liar. I saw him for the first time as he was, a weak bore full of pretensions – someone who got kicks out of hurting girls. If Frances hadn't found the mask, he'd have got away with it. He'd live on the fat of the land. He'd turn out more dull, unreadable articles and go on getting his secretary to check his spellings. He would marry again and maybe bring up another family and play tennis into old age. He might still do all those things, except not in Sweetmount. Now he'd be ruined. Even America wasn't that big.

Teri had been sadistically burnt by a man who had shared my bed for nearly four months. What did that say about me? I couldn't stop seeing her bandaged wrists.

I rang Chuck immediately and asked him round.

"Now?" he quizzed. "What's so urgent?"

"I have to see you, Chuck. It won't wait."

"Oh . . . I see." He laughed lewdly. "The husband's gone?"

"Yes."

It sounded like an urgent need for sex, but I didn't care.

The thirty minutes it took him to arrive seemed more like thirty hours. I waited numbly, silently rehearsing what I'd say.

He came in, joking and looking around suspiciously. "Made a quick exit the last time. He's definitely gone?"

I nodded, and he put his arms around me. "I've missed you."

He had showered and smelt of soap.

As I pulled back, the wrinkle between his eyebrows appeared. "What is it?"

I put the mask on the hall table.

He looked at it. Then pocketed it, registering nothing. "Wondered where that got to."

"Frances found it in your washbag."

"I guess everything comes out in the wash."

I couldn't look at him.

Then he laughed. "Well, you have to admit the little bitch deserved it?"

I was still too stunned to speak. Why hadn't it registered that he despised women – his comments about Teri at the party, even his remarks about Evelyn Nesbit.

"Anne? Please, look at me!"

I studied the floor.

"I suppose you'll turn me in?"

"I've no choice."

Then he panicked. "But that little bitch deserved it! You know that! Anne, look at me!"

"I know she's in a mental hospital."

"Best place for her!"

"You've destroyed her, Chuck."

He laughed hysterically. "She tried to destroy me. And now you're joining the pack. You women are all the damn same." He paused, laughing again. "But they'll never believe you!"

Frances was singing out in the garden. *"'Hush, little baby, don't you cry . . . '"*

Chuck was suddenly triumphant, patting his pocket. "I have the evidence."

"And I have the witness," I said coldly. "Frances."

Her voice floated up again. *"'Momma's gonna sing you a lullaby . . . '"*

"That loony?" Chuck flung off his jacket. He was grinning. "The Prisoner of Bella Vista. And you're the lady who sees things!"

I felt my tic starting. "Please go, Chuck."

"That's a new one!" He threw his jacket on the sofa and turned up his sleeves, flexing his strong wrists. "Why didn't you turn me in that day in the Scrounge? You knew then."

"I couldn't believe it! I still don't!"

Then he slapped my face.

"You believe it now?"

I reeled in shock. "Chuck!"

He flexed his wrists again, his eyes panicky. "It's a taste of what you'll get, if you turn me in."

It seemed to be happening to someone else. I heard myself say quietly, "I *am* turning you in."

Tears came as he hit me again.

I held my stinging face. Chuck had lost all control. "Stop it, please!"

"Did your husband kick the shit out of you? I would've!" This time he grabbed my hair and pulled me across the room. Then I saw his erection. Unzipping his trousers, he pushed me backward.

"Chuck?" How had he turned into this maniac?

He gritted his teeth. "Get your ass into the bedroom."

"Stop it!"

"Husband comes, and you dump me. Now get into the bedroom and take off your clothes."

I had to keep calm. Talk him out of it. "You're making a big mistake, Chuck."

He pulled his belt from his pants and started hitting me around the body. "No, I'm not. You're all shit, and y'all want it!"

I ran to the balcony, calling into the garden. "Frances!"

But her singing had faded into the distance. And there was no one else out there. I turned, bumping into Chuck, who grabbed me, and frog-marched me to the bedroom, kicking me, and hitting me viciously with his belt.

"You're all the damn same."

I struggled. "You won't get away with this!"

"You'll tell your dyke pals?" He laughed madly again. "Who tried to poison me with their food."

Somehow I got free and made again for the balcony door. "Frances!"

But the singing had stopped.

"Frances!"

Chuck grabbed my hair again, throwing me down. We struggled, rolling on the floor. He was on top of me, when the apartment buzzer went.

He hesitated. "That's your loony pal?"

It went again.

He was distracted, so I pushed him off me.

I made for the buzzer, but Chuck got there first.

He pushed me back, laughing. "You're out to all!"

All was lost. "You won't get away with this, Chuck."

"Oh, no?" He pushed me back down on the floor. "Take off your damn clothes!"

Time had stopped. Molly's warnings echoed in my ears. Bud's grim prediction: yuh screw, yuh get screwed.

"Take 'em off!"

He hit me again.

I gasped for breath.

"Take off your damn clothes!"

As I wouldn't, he kept slapping me senseless, as he pinioned me down.

Then there were voices.

Frances's: "She'll get a lovely surprise."

And a man's: "Yeah. She was a doll to me."

The apartment door opened.

It was Cousin Bud and Frances. She had Little Frances in her arms and the apartment key in her free hand. He a bunch of flowers and a Chinese takeaway. He wore the beautiful fringed jacket, high boots, and wide stetson hat. Then Marcus appeared behind him, an old man, waving a stick. "Croak that thug!"

So he was back. But only briefly.

"Coz?" Bud stood for a second, taking everything in – us on the floor, my dishevelled state, Chuck's pants half down.

"Croak him!" a voice yelled.

Chuck struggled to his feet, pulling his pants up. "Ah, it's the convict cousin."

I remembered Bud's gun.

What if he shot Chuck?

"You sonofabitch!" he roared, throwing the flowers and the Chinese takeaway at Frances. Then flinging his stetson across the room, he dived for Chuck, stopping his escape. They struggled for a minute, then fell to the floor. Chuck was slighter, and soon overcome.

"OK, cool it!" He held up his hands.

"Take that, you cheat!" Bud kicked him in the balls. "And that!"

As Chuck writhed in agony, Bud twisted his arm behind his back. "Frances, call the cops!"

I struggled to my feet. "But your parole?"

"Fuck my parole! You OK, Coz?"

I nodded in reply.

He looked grim. "Told yuh I'd be back."

Maybe the closer you get to someone, the crazier they are. The police came and took Chuck away. He was charged with attempted rape and released on bail. Everything blurs in my memory. But I know Bud rang Molly who came over. I remember her saying, "Oh, my God!" Hugging me, then driving me to the Emergency Centre.

I had a broken rib. My face was badly swollen and one eye blackened.

And I was in shock.

I'd been so wrong.

Bud couldn't stay, and I was afraid to be alone. So Molly and Theodora took me in. They couldn't have been pleased, but didn't recriminate, or crow about their warnings. I'd made a terrible mistake but they were kind and nonjudgemental – both of them. Of course, I had all the usual reactions: that it was my fault, that I deserved it.

Molly counselled me. "That's pretty typical. Rape victims always feel that."

I was still dazed. "He just went berserk."

"Most rapists are known to the victim. And most threaten serious violence. Date rape isn't usually a matter of going too far because of misreading signals." Then she added grimly, "At least, this time he won't get away with it."

There was some satisfaction in that. I never wanted to see Chuck again. But I owed it to others to testify. He would be sacked from Sweetmount, but he still had to be stopped. His behaviour was a pattern. He'd go on doing it. I begged Molly not to tell Fergal. She agreed on the condition that I went home for Christmas and came back in the New Year to testify.

But my trust had gone.

I felt stupid and was anti-man generally. Which was unfair to Fergal. Because if I loved anyone, I loved him. But men were too dominating. And were wrecking my life, even from beyond the grave. I longed for some simpler, uncomplicated life. Maybe to be unmarried.

Molly was philosophical. One evening she said, "These things have a way of working themselves out. I'm going to a meeting tomorrow, want to come?"

The Quaker Meeting House was a large white barn-like building, out in the Pennsylvania countryside. It was a most beautiful drive through a hilly wooded area much like County Wicklow. When we arrived, the Friends were already assembled, and sitting facing each other in a square semi-circle. There was no pulpit and no service. A log fire was roaring at one end. Visitors were asked to introduce themselves, so I stood up, saying I came from Dublin. Then Molly and I just sat, staring into space or else with eyes closed. At least it was peaceful.

After a while a woman spoke about acceptance, and things not turning out the way you'd planned. Then after another silence, a man spoke about abandoning the search for meaning in all western literature and obeying the law of God – which was to love.

Lastly someone quoted Francis Thompson.

Oh, world invisible, we view thee.

Oh, world unknowable, we know thee.

At sixteen, he was my favourite poet. I had left that self so far behind. Was it a message for me now? Or was I being idiotic? For the last four months I had lived in an invisible world, that is, one invisible to others. To me its existence was more reasonable than brain chemistry. I had experienced the past, but couldn't solve its problems. You couldn't undo things, or bring back the dead. From now on, I resolved to live like Keats in "doubts and mysteries, not vainly seeking after fact and reason."

On the way back, as we approached the town, Molly stopped for a traffic light. "Have you called Fergal?"

I sighed. "No. He's probably still mad."

"People get over things. You two had a very strong relationship."

"Yes, but not any more. He does things without consulting me."

"Like what?"

"Oh . . . he cut down a tree." It was nit-picking, but you latch onto details.

Molly looked exasperated. "Is that all?"

"It was the nicest tree in the garden."

"Oh, God!"

"There are other things." I didn't want to go into the money again. Besides I felt mean about that now. Life was a gambler's throw. Marcus had taught me that.

"Do you ever express your feelings? Tell him what's bugging you?"

"He walks into another room."

She sighed knowingly. "Men are like that."

We drove on for a while in silence. Then she said, "Women repress anger, get depressed. Then go into overkill about something like a tree."

"I'm always competing with younger women."

"Fergal has younger women?" She looked at me in disbelief. "Who are they?"

"Oh, students. There's one in particular."

"And you think it's an affair?"

"He has this lame-duck complex."

"He wanted children?"

"Very badly, I think. I was always work-obsessed."

"Maybe the lame-ducks are substitutes."

It was pop psychology, but true. I knew it was true. But could I go back? Still Molly's words brought things home to me. I did repress anger. I repressed it with my mother for fear of offending her. It was the reason I stayed living with her until the age of thirty-one. And now I was afraid to discuss things with my husband. I needed his approval too much. I couldn't bear to be unloved, so had found a substitute in Chuck. For that I was punished. Were all women punished? I thought differently now about Molly's shelter. About all the women, all over the world, who were abused on a daily basis.

Teri's bandaged wrists still upset me. The police had taken a statement from her also, because of the mask, and she was pressing charges too. I wanted to see her, but couldn't bring myself to go back to that hospital. So I rang and told her what happened – I owed her that.

"Thank you, Professor," was all she said.

"I'll be coming back to testify. Perhaps we could meet then."

"OK. Professor . . . ?"

"What?"

"Know what's the strongest muscle in your body?"

"No."

"Your jaw!"

"Oh . . . "

"I'm studying self-defence. And, Professor . . . "

"Yes, Teri."

"Your class was great!"

"Thanks, Teri."

That cheered me up.

Somehow I finished up at Sweetmount, getting all my

grades in. My rib became less painful, but my eye was still black. Christmas loomed. Frances disappeared from Bella Vista to stay with her daughter. I promised to keep in touch. Cousin Bud had to stay on in Atlantic City. I rang him several times to say goodbye, but he was never in. I was sure I'd see him again. He'd turn up in Ireland in about ten years, demanding to play chess with Fergal. And Fergal would take him in. He's like that.

When Molly and Theodora went to California for Christmas, I packed for Dublin. But I still couldn't ring Fergal. I was too ashamed.

On the way home I stayed overnight at Ogie's. I wanted to see her again and drop off Christmas presents. I told her my black eye was from a minor car accident, and she didn't question me. It seemed an eternity since that first visit when Marcus had been so terrifying. I was taking uppers during the day now, so didn't expect him again.

There was something different about the New York apartment. Then I noticed: the ivy was gone.

Ogie shrugged. "Yeah, they just came and ripped it off."

"Makes the place brighter."

While she cooked, I was entertained by the children. They were mellower now and chatted openly. Especially Jessica, who had just turned twelve. She was doing a school project on her family, and dragged me out to Ogie's photograph gallery. I identified some of the faces from the past, telling anything I knew about them. When we came to Nora, my grandmother, I couldn't help noticing how much Jessica resembled her. Jessica had the same black hair and slightly tipped nose and protruding teeth. The child's were now confined by a brace.

She stopped at Marcus. "Mom said he was famous."

"He was a bit."

"What'd he do?"

I hesitated. "He helped people in trouble."

She wrinkled her nose at the moustached smiling face. "Did he ever do bad things?"

"We all do bad things, Jessica. Now, be honest, are you good all the time?"

"Well, not all the time." She giggled. "But why was he famous?"

"He survived, Jessica."

"You're writing a book about *that*?"

"That's a lot. But I decided against a book."

"But why?"

"Because . . . he doesn't need one. He's in our dreams."

After dinner Hans took the children to Mass. That intrigued me, but Ogie said that, although Jewish, he had promised that the chidren would be brought up Catholic. So he still went, although Ogie had abandoned the church.

We lingered over coffee. I gave Ogie back all her Xeroxes. Also a copy of Marcus's journal. I didn't admit to stealing it.

She examined it carefully. "What's it about?"

"His early life and legal career. He was good on marriage."

She grimaced. "Oh?"

I laughed. "The secret of a happy one is to master the art of losing an argument."

"I'll have to work on that!" Ogie looked up. "Did Elizabeth mention mother's china?"

"No. I had enough trouble getting the journal."

She frowned. "After all that, you're not even writin' the book?"

I shook my head. "I can't find out enough."

As Ogie clutched her trophies, her chin jutted obstinately. "You'll change your mind."

I went out to Kennedy the next day. As usual, there was time before the flight, so I sat in the bar, sipping orange soda. Airports make me metaphysical. Why did things happen the way they did? Are the Greeks right about character being fate? Or do the Chinese have the answer? Western ideas of time are entirely culture bound, I'd recently read. The Chinese don't see the future as being spatially located somewhere out in front. Past, present and future are all one, not three separate states. You're born with a blueprint of the future. It was revealed gradually in dreams. Here I was going back to Fergal. Would it work out?

I was reading a biography of President Wilson. Marcus's customs scandal was mentioned. He was investigated for ordering the transfer of funds from one bank to another. He was cleared by the enquiry, but asked to resign because a letter from him, insulting the Dominicans, came to public light. He called them "heathens, corrupt," and suggested that they could be dissuaded from their "hobby of revolution" if they had a proper baseball team. The book described the incident as a major embarrassment to Wilson – an "opera bouffe."

All nationalities milled round me and, after awhile, I gave up reading and watched them. How many times had I sat in this airport? The feeling of being between two continents was so familiar to me. Animals had migration trails, so why not humans?

Perhaps Ogie was right. I would write about Marcus – but another historical novel, not a biography. An Irish American lawyer-politician in Wilson's cabinet gives up everything to fight for Irish freedom in the 1916 Rising. I took out my notebook and started making notes for a plot.

A grandfather is pretty far back, so why was I so fixated? It was to do with my mother – I blamed myself for not understanding her better, for not being kinder. It killed me that she had died before the money came from my books. But I'd never really know why she had disliked Marcus. Perhaps he'd just been irritating, as Elizabeth said. But my mother's accusation had been grave. She had brought his body home to be buried with his wife in Dublin's Glasnevin cemetery. You never knew anyone, the living, never mind the dead. "There is an unchanging silent life within everyman that none knows but himself . . . " My grandfather's unchanging silent life was his memory of his wife. And if he loved my mother too much, it was because they were alike.

Anyway it was all over. All paid for.

A woman shoved a leaflet at me.

I groped for my glasses, as she held up a dollar keyring.

I AM A DEAF MUTE. THE COST OF MY KEYRING IS $1. THANK YOU

I gave her a dollar.

Then found myself staring at the bar.

An old man stood with his back to me. He was wearing a white suit . . . Marcus? It was his build. The same straw hat plonked over white hair. And he was staring at change in his hand.

I walked over and was lifting my hand to his shoulder, when he swung round.

It was a dark-skinned Indian gentleman.

I dropped my arm. "Sorry – I thought you were someone else."

The old man lifted his hat, his dark eyes glittering. "Madam."

I was free at last.

Our flight was called and I boarded calmly, glad to see the familiar green uniform of the Aer Lingus hostesses. This time there were no ex-schoolfriends to give me free drinks and ask after my books. Just as well, as I wasn't drinking. The plane filled up, but the seat beside me remained empty. Without young Corkmen, I'd get some sleep. We got clearance quickly and taxied to a runway. As we took off, my stomach squeezed nervously. I closed my eyes. Would we stay up? I was jetting back to the future. What would happen next? If Fergal and I were to have any life together, I had to conquer fear. I'd learn to drive again for one thing. Then I wouldn't have to take taxis.

The seat-belt sign went off and drinks were announced. The lights of New York danced below. Soon we'd head up the coast of North America. Then out to sea and home.

I closed my eyes, trying to sleep.

Then John McCormack sang:

"Keep the home fires burning.
"While your hearts are yearning!"

And a familiar voice startled me. "Ah, there you are!"

Marcus swayed down the aisle. He was younger than the first time I saw him, and dressed in a high white collar and straw hat. This time there was a shamrock in his lapel.

He plonked stiffly down beside me. "Good! We're going home. Now, I never told you about my arrest in 1916 . . ."

As I stared, his moustache started growing into handlebars.

He pulled at them in alarm. "Now, what's happening!"

"I'm giving you a walrus moustache!"

"You can't do that!"

"Yes, I can!"

He fled back up the aisle.